Tillman

SEMIOTEXT(E) NATIVE AGENTS SERIES

Published by Semiotext(e)
PO BOX 629. South Pasadena, CA 91031
www.semiotexte.com

Cover Art: Louise Lawler, *She Wasn't Always a Statue (A)*, 1996–97, black and white photograph, 17 3/4 x 18 1/2 inches.
Courtesy the artist and Metro Pictures, New York.

Back Cover Photography: Craig Mod
Design by Hedi El Kholti

ISBN: 978-1-58435-190-0
Distributed by The MIT Press, Cambridge, Mass. and London, England
Printed in the United States of America

THE COMPLETE MADAME REALISM

AND OTHER STORIES

LYNNE TILLMAN

Introduction by M. G. Lord

Afterword by Andrew Durbin

<e>

CONTENTS

For Craig Owens
1950–1990
With everlasting love

Introduction by M. G. Lord

THE UNCONSCIOUS NEVER TAKES A VACATION

A little over ten years ago, the *New York Times* asked me to review Lynne Tillman's *This is Not It*, a collection of fictive responses to works of contemporary art. Reproductions of the art that inspired her stories were included in the book.

In Tillman's new collection, *The Complete Madame Realism and Other Stories*, some of those fictive responses—as well as many stories that are new to me—have been cut loose from the art that may have sparked them. Untethered, the stories gain power. They converse with one another. They don't *just* stand alone; they dance, they somersault, they dodge bullets, they take to the road, they peer at forbidden objects, they lurk, they skulk, they rabble-rouse, they soar. They allow the reader to explore Tillman's complex intelligence, and the obsessions, preoccupations, and recurring themes that make her work both deeply satisfying and compulsively readable.

Written over three decades, the stories are as much about social history as they are about art and the history of art. I did not see "Treasure Houses of Great Britain, Five Hundred Years of Private Patronage and Art Collecting," when it was shown at the National Gallery in Washington in 1985. But thanks to Tillman's character, Madame Realism, I didn't have to. In a gimlet-eyed tour of the exhibition titled "Dynasty Reruns," Madame Realism says and thinks all the seditious things that any viewer, aghast at the show's elitist presumptions, would say and think. Tillman uses the show to critique the rift between rich and poor that opened during Ronald Reagan's presidency and evolved into a chasm over the last 30 years. She meditates on the invisibility of the poor.

Madame Realism doesn't adhere to the audio tour—narrated with predictable unctuousness by J. Carter Brown, director of the National Gallery. She reminds the reader that Brown's version—funded, like much of the show itself, by the British Government and the Ford Motor Company—reveals only the perspective of those in power. Instead, she hunts for a different perspective and finds it--in a painting titled *The Tichborne Dole*. The image, painted in 1670 by Gillis van Tillborch, explains the origin of the word "dole"; it shows Sir Henry Tichborne and his family distributing bread to the poor, a tradition "that continues to this day, even though the dole itself is under attack from Thatcher."

"This painting may have been made to demonstrate the worthiness of that wealthy family," Madame Realism observes, "but at least the poor are shown to exist...which is more than can be said for Reagan's picture of America."

Many essays written in the past have great resonance today. In "The Museum of Hyphenated Americans," Madame Realism mounts a trenchant critique of the "Via Dolorosa" followed by immigrants to the United States—a subject that could not be more topical as Donald Trump and other political candidates debate building a wall along the Mexican border and barring Muslims from America. The essay was triggered by a visit to the $157-million renovation of the Ellis Island Museum, which opened in 1990. Madame Realism quickly cuts through the museum's glossy sentimentality and homes in on an ugly aspect: forced migration—slavery—which affected both Africans and, to a surprising degree, Europeans. Between 1700 and 1810, she notes, "an estimated 6,000,000 Africans were enslaved and transported to cultivate cash crops." In roughly the same period, 75 percent of white migrants were indentured servants.

Some migrants faced another debilitating fate: denial of admission to the country for medical reasons. The anguish of those turned away has been scrubbed from the new facility. But it lives in Madame Realism's memory. She describes a visit to the Ellis Island visitors' center in 1979, when it, like much of the cash-strapped city of New York, was in bad shape: "Its walls were cracked, the paint peeling. Some of the benches upon which immigrants had sat were still there, reminiscent of a set from Ionesco's *The Chairs*. The space was both surreal and gothic. Madame Realism could easily imagine the ghosts floating above, hovering near the dirty tile ceiling; and in the eerie silence, she wanted to hear fabled ancestors speak to one another." But what most haunted her was the medical examination room: "It was filthy. Evil-looking instruments, covered in dust, lay on wooden tables. A horror chamber."

What I love about Madame Realism is that she isn't Tillman, the author, by another name. As a fictional character, she plays by different rules, which can be the rules of magical realism. She does things that a mere author can't—morph, for instance, into a living exhibition catalogue. *Inhabiting* a catalogue allows Tillman to meditate on what it means to be a published, illustrated text—to be, for example, both ephemeral and enduring: "Many would throw her out. Some would save her." As a catalogue, she yearns for shabbiness. To be "well thumbed" is to be "well regarded." Blessedly, Madame Realism does not remain a catalogue forever. But she is forever changed by the metamorphosis. She understands that her identity—like the identity of an exhibition catalogue—can be affected by the perceptions of others. In the sort of pithy and profound sentence one finds often in Tillman's prose, Madame Realism reflects: "To some extent, a work or text relied on the intelligence, the kindness, of strangers."

Madame Realism is acerbic, ironic, often just plain funny. I laughed out loud at her depiction of a tour guide at the Freud Museum in London. The poor fellow "pronounces Freud's name as if there were a 'w' after the 'F,' sounding very much like Barbara Walters." When he tells the visitors "what Fwoid ate for lunch," she bolts from the group and explores on her own.

Fond as I am of Madame Realism, I don't want to give short shrift to the other two sections of Tillman's collection, "The Complete Paige Turner Stories" and "The Translation Artist and Other Stories." Unlike Madame Realism, Paige Turner is not an entity through whose eyes the reader sees the world more clearly. Turner is as lost—if not more lost—than the reader, and Tillman doesn't necessarily clarify things for her: "I call her Little Miss Understood. Naming is everything. Sticks and stones will break your bones and names will always hurt you. Names will make you cry. A comic and ominous taunt to Little Miss Understood sitting at her Underwood."

Paige Turner is, however, at the center of "Thrilled to Death," a tour-de-force of cinematic narration that brings together a disparate group of danger-seekers at a carnival, where an act of gun violence occurs. Turner does not appear until the fourth paragraph of the story. The first three paragraphs introduce other characters, who may or may not be connected to Turner. Tillman's narration disorients the reader; she subverts the conventions of the crazy gunman narrative that has become a staple of network shows like "NCIS" and "CSI." Even as Turner senses danger, she realizes that she is not part of a by-the-numbers thriller: "No one has planned it all, it's not plotted, it's not a plot." But Turner cannot escape her destiny: "She thinks, I'm such a cheap date, maybe I'll have a cheap date with fate."

Although Tillman has placed "Stories Tell Stories," a recent work about a Joan Jonas' film, in the third and final section of this collection, it might be a good essay for a reader unfamiliar with Tillman to read first. It obliquely introduces Tillman's concerns—and, in certain instances, her fictive methodology. The story talks about the "Kuleshov Effect," named for Soviet filmmaker Lev Kuleshov, who demonstrated that viewers gain greater meaning from the contrast between two shots in a film sequence than from one shot alone. "Stories Tell Stories" addresses the way people want to impose a narrative on random images. "Human beings are like interpreting machines," Tillman writes. "Whether one wants to be against interpretation or for it, meanings occur, haphazard, benign or malignant, often unconsciously: only consciousness of one's responses affords any freedom from them."

"Still Moving" challenges the reader to interpret it. Like the demanding juxtapositions of film shots that Tillman explores in "Stories Tell Stories," the seemingly disparate snapshots of American life in "Still Moving" present the reader with visual scenes that the reader can connect into a story.

Making connections is part of the pleasure of reading Tillman. Even in her Madame Realism stories, which are narrated in a more linear fashion, Tillman expects the reader to follow

Madame Realism's train of thought, which can border on stream of consciousness. But Tillman arranges her paragraphs deliberately. More than mere chronology informs their placement. Nothing feels random or slapdash in this or her work, which means that the arrangement—the ordering—of stories also matters in *The Complete Madame Realism and other Stories.* Stories don't just *tell* stories; they build upon stories.

At the beginning of "Madame Realism in Freud's Dreamland," Madame Realism discusses her allergy to collecting. She discards a seashell she has picked up on a beach. She refuses to collect; she doesn't have room for stuff. Yet *The Complete Madame Realism and Other Stories* is a collection—and, like all collections, it raises certain questions: What does it mean to collect? "Collecting always points to what is missing and thus has not been collected, or can't be found," Madame Realism thinks. Must collecting "always represent the absence of something and the impossibility of entirely fulfilling one's desire"?

These questions haunt Madame Realism as she examines the prints, books and art in a traveling exhibit of objects collected by Sigmund Freud on display at the SUNY Binghamton Art Museum. The show's subtitle, "Fragments from a Buried Past," strikes her as apt: "Ideas of death hovered like a storm cloud: Freud's death in exile in London in 1939, his father's death, deaths of friends of hers."

She scrutinizes the objects to get a sense of what they might have meant to the psychoanalyst when he was alive, lingering on "Freud's treasured statue of Athena, a work Marie Bonaparte saved from the Nazis. Athena's breastplate is adorned by the decapitated head of Medusa, who represents, Freud wrote, castration." After looking away, she focuses again on the statue of

Athena and pictures Freud staring at it: "This Athena is missing her spear. She saw him worried about women."

Both during and after her visit to the exhibition, Madame Realism makes connections. The objects and their history stay with her; she doesn't stop thinking about them—or about death and loss—when she goes home.

Tillman's stories often have a similar effect on the reader. Their images and ideas remain. I look with more respect at dog-eared catalogues now, having witnessed Madame Realism's temporary metamorphosis into one. More bizarrely, I have dreamed about Ellis Island as it was in 1979—never mind that I was never actually there. I only know it through Tillman's description.

Tillman's best stories have stayed with me in a way I cannot entirely explain. So I will defer to Madame Realism, who has a pertinent aphorism for just about every phenomenon: "The unconscious never takes a vacation."

ONE

THE COMPLETE MADAME REALISM STORIES

MADAME REALISM

Madame Realism read that Paul Eluard had written: No one has divined the dramatic origin of teeth. She pictured her dentist, a serious man who insisted gravely that he alone had saved her mouth.

The television was on. It had been on for hours. Years. It was there. TV on demand, a great freedom. Hadn't Burroughs said there was more freedom today than ever before. Wasn't that like saying things were more like today than they've ever been.

Madame Realism heard the announcer, who didn't know he was on the air, say: Hello, victim. Then ten seconds of nothing, a commercial, the news, and *The Mary Tyler Moore Show.*

She inhaled her cigarette fiercely, blowing the smoke out hard. The television interrupts itself: A man wearing diapers is running around parks, scaring little children. The media call him Diaperman.

The smoke and her breath made a whooshing sound that she liked, so she did it again and again. When people phoned she blew right into the receiver, so that she sounded like she was panting.

Smokers, she read in a business report, are less productive than nonsmokers, because they spend some of their work time staring into space as they inhale and exhale. She could have been biding her time or protecting it. All ideas are married.

He thought she breathed out so deeply to let people know she was there. Her face reminded him, he said, of a Japanese movie. She didn't feel like talking, the telephone demanded like an infant not yet weaned. Anything can be a transitional object. No one spoke of limits, they spoke of boundaries. And my boundaries shift, she thought, like ones do after a war when countries lose or gain depending upon having won or lost. Power has always determined right.

Overheard: A young mother is teaching her son to share his toys, the toys he really cares about. There are some things you can call your own, he will learn. Boundaries are achieved through battle.

Madame Realism was not interested in display. Men fighting in bars, their nostrils flaring and faces getting red, their noses filling with mucous and it dripping out as they fought over a pack of cigarettes, an insult, a woman. But who could understand men, or more, what they really wanted.

Dali's conception of sexual freedom, for instance, written in 1930. A man presenting his penis "erect, complete, and magnificent plunged a girl into a tremendous and delicious confusion, but without the slightest protest.... It is," he writes, "one of the purest and most disinterested acts a man is capable of performing in our age of corruption and moral degradation."

She wondered if Diaperman felt that way. Just that day a beggar had walked past her. When he got close enough to smell him, she read what was written on his button. It said BE APPROPRIATE. We are like current events to each other. One doesn't have to know people well to be appropriate.

Madame Realism is at a dinner party surrounded by people, all of whom she knows, slightly. At the head of the table is a silent woman who eats rather slowly. She chooses a piece of silverware as if it were a weapon. But she does not attack her food.

One of the men is depressed; two of his former lovers are also at the dinner. He thinks he's Kierkegaard. One of his former lovers gives him attention, the other looks at him ironically, giving him trouble. A pall hangs over the table thick like stale bread. The silent woman thinks about death, the expected. Ghosts are dining with us.

A young man, full of the literature that romanticizes his compulsion, drinks himself into stupid liberation. He has not yet discovered that the source of supposed fictions is the desire never to feel guilty.

The depressed man thinks about himself, and one of the women at the table he hasn't had. This saddens him even more.

At the same time it excites him. Something to do—to live for—at the table. Wasn't desire for him at the heart of all his, well, creativity?

He becomes lively and sardonic. Madame Realism watches his movements, listens to what he isn't saying, and waits. As he gets the other's attention, he appears to grow larger. His headache vanishes with her interest. He will realize that he hadn't had a headache at all. Indifferent to everyone but his object of the moment, upon whom he thrives from titillation, he blooms. Madame Realism sees him as a plant, a wilting plant that is being watered.

The television glowed, effused at her. Talk shows especially encapsulated America, puritan America. One has to be seen to be doing good. One has to be seen to be good. When he said a Japanese movie, she hadn't responded. Screens upon screens and within them. A face is like a screen when you think about the other, when you think about projection. A mirror is a screen and each time she looked into it, there was another screen test. How did she look today? What did she think today? Isn't it funny how something can have meaning and no meaning at the same time.

Madame Realism read from *The New York Times*: "The Soviet Ambassador to Portugal had formally apologized for a statement issued by his embassy that called Mario Soares, the Socialist leader, a lunatic in need of prolonged psychiatric treatment. The embassy said the sentence should have read 'these kinds of lies can only come from persons with a sick imagination, and these lies need prolonged analysis and adequate treatment.'" Clever people plot their lives with strategies not unlike those used by governments. We all do business. And our lies are in need of prolonged analysis and adequate treatment.

When the sun was out, it made patterns on the floor, caused by the bars on her windows. She liked the bars. She had designed them. Madame Realism sometimes liked things of her own design. Nature was not important to her; the sun made shadows that could be looked at and about which she could write. After all, doesn't she exist, like a shadow, in the interstices of argument.

Her nose bled for a minute or two. Having needs, being contained in a body, grounded her in the natural. But even her period appeared with regularity much like a statement from the bank. Madame Realism lit another cigarette and breathed in so deeply, her nose bled again.

I must get this fixed, she thought, as if her nostrils had brakes. There is no way to compare anything. We must analyze our lives. There isn't even an absolute zero. What would be a perfect sentence?

A turn to another channel. The night was cold, but not because the moon wasn't out. The night was cold. She pulled her blanket around her. It's cold but it's not as cold as simple misunderstanding that turns out to run deep. And it's not as cold as certain facts; She didn't love him, or he her; hearts that have been used badly. Experience teaches not to trust experience. We're forced to be empiricists in bars.

She looked into the mirror. Were she to report that it was cracked, one might conjure it, or be depressed by a weak metaphor. The mirror is not cracked. And stories do not occur outside thought. Stories, in fact, are contained within thought. It's only a story really should read, it's a way to think.

Madame Realism turned over and stroked her cat, who refused to be held longer than thirty seconds. That was a record. She turned over and slept on her face. She wondered what it would do to her face but she slept that way anyway, just as she let her body go and didn't exercise, knowing what she was doing was not in her interest. She wasn't interested. It had come to that. She turned off the television.

MADAME REALISM ASKS:

WHAT'S NATURAL ABOUT PAINTING

Madame Realism, like everyone else, had a mother, and her mother had bought and hung two prints by old masters in their home. One, by Van Gogh—a bearded man sucking on a pipe. One, by Renoir—a red-headed girl playing with a golden ball or apple. Since there were redheads in her family, Madame Realism assumed that the girl was a relative, just as she assumed the bearded man was one of her grandfathers, both of whom had died before she was born. As a child Madame Realism thought that all pictures in her home had to do with her family. Later she came to understand things differently.

With some reluctance Madame Realism went to a museum in Boston to look at paintings by Renoir. By now she felt a kind of despair when in an institution expressly to look at and judge something which she could no longer feel or experience as she once had. Boston itself was a site of contradiction and ongoing temporary resolution. She knew, for instance, that in Boston the arts were led by the Brahmins, the Irish dominated its political machine, and the Black population was fighting hard to be allowed anything at all. But in an institution such as a great museum, where lines of people form democratically to look at art, such problems are the background upon which that art is hung.

Madame Realism was moved along by the crowd, and in another way she was moved by the crowd. "Sinatra is 70 this year," she heard one woman say to another as they baked at a picture on the wall. There's nothing of Sinatra in this picture, Madame Realism thought. Not the skinny New Jersey guy who made it big and for a brief moment was married to Ava Gardner, also thin, then. On the other hand (one has so many hands these days), he did rise like cream to the top, not unlike Renoir, whose father was a tailor. The crowd swelled, especially at the paintings whose labels had white dots on them, as they had been chosen by the museum for special auditory instruction through machines. Madame Realism loitered in the clumps and listened as much as she looked.

In front of a nude, one young woman asked another: "Do you think that's how fat women really were?" Automatically, Madame Realism moved her hand to her hip. She strained to hear the answer, but the crowd advanced, and she completed it as she thought it would be. Women were allowed to be fatter, it was the style. You'd be considered more desirable, voluptuous. There's more of you to love. Diets hadn't been invented. Madame Realism felt self-conscious standing alone, if only for a moment, in front of that nude, her hand resting on her own 19th-century hip. And she thought again of Frank Sinatra and supposed, whatever other troubles he'd had, he'd never had a weight problem. Quite the reverse, she thought, giving the phrase her version of an English barrister's accent.

She didn't like these paintings. They were almost ridiculous when they weren't bordering on the grotesque, and then they became interesting to her. What had happened to this guy on his rise to the top? Was he so uncomfortable that what he painted reflected his discomfort by a kind of ugliness? The women were all flesh, especially breasts, and the faces of men, women and children were notably vacant. Madame Realism imagined a VACANCY sign hanging in front of *Sketches of Heads*, like a cheap hotel's advertisement that rooms were available.

In the middle of her own mixed metaphor, which unaccountably made her think of *The Divine Comedy*, Madame Realism followed a museum instructor, whose students were trailing her with the determination of ducklings after their mother. The woman was saying something about me differences between the 18th and 19th centuries, but became confused as to whether the 18th century meant the 1800s, or the 19th century the 1800s. Madame Realism's heart went out to her on account of this temporary, ordinary lapse, and she wondered how this might affect the students' imprinting. The instructor recovered quickly and said, "You have to look for the structure. The painting, remember, is flat." It wasn't hard to remember that these paintings were flat she thought, and stood in front of a painting of onions. Renoir's onions are flat, she said to herself. His onions. It's funny that in the language of painting what someone paints becomes his or, sometimes, hers. His nudes. His people. Madame Realism recalled a still life of peaches by Renoir that she'd seen in the Jeu de Paume. Years ago she stood in front of the painting and thought they were perfect, just like peaches. The peaches of Europe, her grandmother was recorded as having said, how I miss them. And there they were. In a bowl. His peaches. Nature at its best. Not vacant like those happy faces. His happy faces.

Two women were deep in conversation, and Madame Realism eavesdropped with abandon. The first woman was saying, "He had an apartment near his dealer's, and his wife didn't know about it, and he had to distort her face so that she wouldn't know who the model was. So he made the faces like penises and vaginas." "The *faces*?" the second woman asked. "Yes," said the first, "like the nose coming out? That's a penis." They were talking about Picasso, Madame Realism figured out, because whatever else you might say about Renoir, his noses didn't look like penises. Although, upon viewing a late painting of nudes, she wanted to rush over to those women and tell them that a Renoir elbow looked like a breast. Or like a peach. Peaches and breasts. Peaches are much more like flesh than apples, or for that matter, onions. A bowl of breasts—a still life. She looked again at the masklike faces of children, the hidden faces of men dancing with women whose faces and bodies were on display. If masks, what were they hiding? she asked herself, moving closer to the painting as if that would reveal something. Instead, she saw brushstrokes. Disappointed, she walked on and thought about D.H. Lawrence and how the flesh and its passions refuse education and class, are, in a sense, used to defy them. She wanted to look at these paintings with something like sympathy rather than indifference. But somehow this evocation of the simple life and its joys, the contented family, the gardens of Eden, did not produce in her pleasure, but she did become aware of how hungry she was. Madame Realism was not one to discount this effect, and couldn't wait to sit down and eat. But there was more to see.

Facing *Sleeping Girl with a Cat* Madame Realism heard two young women agree that the cat looked just like theirs; it was so real, down to the pads on its paws. But, said one, "Doesn't that girl look uncomfortable?" Madame Ralism agreed, silently. The sleeping girl had been positioned so that the light would hit her bare shoulders and partially exposed chest. This was supposed to be a natural position, though any transvestite could tell you that naturalness wasn't easy to achieve. Although, according to one of the writers in the exhibition's catalogue, Renoir had "an instinct" for it. Naturalness, that is, not transvestism. Shaking her head from side to side, Madame Realism followed the crowd to *Gabrielle with jewelry*. Women are home to him, she thought, big comfortable houses. And if representation has to do with re-presenting something, what is it we repeat over and over but our sense of home, which may become a very abstract thing indeed. She imagined another sign. It read: Representation—A Home Away from Home.

Wanting very much to leave and eat, to go home, tired of the insistent flow in front of paintings, of which she was very much a part, Madame Realism was entrapped by another conversation, carried on by two men and a woman. The first man to speak was waving his arms, rather excitedly, saying, "The washerwomen were square. He was painting things as if they were rigid, fixed in a space that wouldn't move." The woman responded, "You can see why his paintings would appeal to the common man and woman. His people are just so unselfconscious." The first man countered, "But his talent was remarkable." The second man asked, "In his notes and letters, is there a more cerebral quality?" The first man answered, "No, and he wasn't a happy person." The woman exclaimed, "But his paintings have such joy." Both men said "vitality" in unison. "It's often true," said the first man. "He was a very cranky guy from a poor family. The sensuality in all his paintings… Just wishful thinking." The woman said, "He was like Mozart, a basic talent, but without intellect." The first man threw his arms out again and implored, "But he was a natural flowing talent. It just flowed out." The seoond man said, "Genius." At genius, Madame Realism walked out of the exhibition to the souvenir shop. He sounds more like a fountain than a painter, or more like an animal who holds a paintbrush. If, according to that same writer in the catalogue, Renoir's brush "was part of him," then maybe he didn't even have to hold it. Madame Realism bought five postcards and thought the paintings looked better in reproduction than as originals, just as a friend of hers told her they would. Maybe that's why he's so popular, she thought.

Back home, Madame Realism surrounded herself with the familiar: her cat, cheese, beer, the television. She turned it on, a public service broadcast which just happened to be about investing in art. She sat up in bed, dislodging her sleeping cat from her lap, and moved closer to the set. The host asked the art-as-investment expert: "The oldest cliché in your business is, 'I don't know anything about art, but I know what I like.' You've suggested that that attitude is a sure loser for an investor in art." "Exactly," answered the expert. "The word is appreciation. I don't care what you like, if you don't learn how to appreciate art, you'll never become a collector." The host smiled and said, "If you don't appreciate art, it won't appreciate for you." "Exactly," said the expert.

Madame Realism switched to another channel and turned the sound off. Her cat returned to her lap and she fixed the reading lamp as best she could. Often it burned into the top of her head and gave her headaches. Robert Scull had just died, an art collector of some notoriety. When asked, it was reported in his obituary, if "he bought art for investment and social climbing, Mr. Scull responded, 'It's all true. I'd rather use art to climb than anything else.'" Madame Realism put the paper down and the day's words and phrases bounced in front of her eyes. She turned off the light, got comfortable and fell into a deep natural sleep, undisturbed even by the screams in the street.

DYNASTY RERUNS

The banner for the show stretched across the width of the National Gallery's East Building. TREASURE HOUSES OF GREAT BRITAIN, FIVE HUNDRED YEARS OF PRIVATE PATRONAGE AND ART COLLECTING. The letters were gold on a royal blue background, edged with a majestic red. Madame Realism hoped the show would have rooms with dioramas like those at the Museum of Natural History—with stuffed lords and ladies at tea or in conversation or at dinner, all behind glass, all perfectly appointed. Because "houses" was in the title, she was looking for rooms as they might have been lived in. When she thought about the past she always wanted to know, But how did they live and what did they talk about?

Madame Realism entered the slide show that introduced the exhibition. A taped English voice narrated the images of beautiful countryside and enormous houses. Why aren't these called palaces or even mansions, she wondered. The Englishman's voice explained: "British Houses are as much a part of the landscape as the oaks and acorns"; the people in these houses, "vessels of civilization," developed a "civilized outlook, which helped to produce parliamentary democracy, as well as the ideals that helped shape Western civilization." The term "civilized outlook" set Madame Realism's teeth on edge. Houses natural like the scenery? The divine right of houses? She doubted that something could be both natural and civilized at the same time.

Accompanied by the disembodied voice of J. Carter Brown, the director of the National Gallery, on the audioguide, Madame Realism entered the first rooms, which were called "From the Castle to the Country House." Carter Brown told her that the country houses began in 1485, with the accession of the first Tudor to the throne. With relative calm in England and Wales, the castle becomes house because it no longer needs defense—high walls and moats. Madame Realism thought there was always some need for defense, and moats and high walls were perfect metaphors for human ones. Listening to Carter Brown's narration, she felt she was back in grade school. His voice, friendly and authoritative, recited dates and facts that jerked classroom memories. Back then she'd absorbed things wholesale, the way kids do, but now she was able to remind herself that there isn't one history, there are at least two. The official version and the unofficial, whose dates were not taught in grade school—the history of those without access to power. There was no doubt which version this would be, inaugurated as it was by Charles and Di, and funded in part by the British government and the Ford Motor Co.

Madame Realism stared hard at the portrait attributed to Rowland Lockey of Elizabeth Hardwick, Countess of Shrewsbury (ca. 1600). Bess of Hardwick had four husbands, outlived them all and inherited everything, making her the richest woman in England, next to Elizabeth the Queen. Bess's almost heartshaped hair frames a resolute face that is cut off from its body by a high white collar. That old devil issue, the mind/body split, popped into her mind but did it apply to Bess? This portrait was not meant to imply personality or psychology, but, like the other portraits in these rooms, to be emblematic of position and power. Everyone was holding scepters, wearing important jewels, or being represented in allegories that assure their right of succession and that of their dynasties. Even so, Madame Realism wondered if Old Bess was bawdy like the Wife of Bath, what with four husbands—more husbands even than Alexis on TV's *Dynasty*—and were she and the Queen friends? In *Elizabeth I: The Rainbow Portrait* (ca. 1600), attributed to Marcus Gheeraerts the younger, the Queen wears a cloak and dress that have eyes and ears embroidered all over them. J. Carter Brown informs Madame Realism, and others standing with her in front of the painting, that this means Elizabeth had many informers in her employ, maintaining power through a spy system in which she also used her servants. Again Madame Realism thought about *Dynasty*, and imagined that Elizabeth I might have been like paranoid Alexis and Bess of Hardwick like trusting Krystle. Guiltily she looked around her and wondered if anyone else was making such plebeian comparisons.

"There are many symbols everywhere," Madame Realism heard one woman say to another. "Everything means something else." They were standing in the Jacobean Long Gallery, modeled after the picture gallery in the background of Daniel Mytens's portrait of the Countess of Arundel, Alatheia Talbot. Madame Realism and others are directed by the audioguide to pretend they are in the Countess's house, to stroll down the hall and gaze at the paintings. On cue she and several others move in unison. Madame Realism halted in front of the painting of *Barbara,*

Lady Sydney, With Six Children, again by Gheeraerts the younger (1596). How had Lady Sydney survived six children births? Mother and children look identical, as if stamped rather than painted. Clearly dynasty isn't concerned with individuals, only continuity. So it's faceless. Maybe that was what was so funny about *Dynasty*. Sons and daughters disappear, are thought dead, then reappear with entirely different faces that should be unrecognizable but aren't. Of course the series has to continue, even when principal actors leave for other jobs. The series must continue, she thought, looking around her. And then she heard a man say to his companion, "They don't have beauty. It's the one thing the British don't have." What about, she wanted to argue, Vivien Leigh, Vanessa Redgrave, Annie Lennox, Bob Hoskins. She suspected that the man, awed by how much these people did have, may have been comforting himself with the idea that no one has it all.

Madame Realism would never have been invited, in that time, to stroll down the Countess's picture gallery. The British don't fool themselves about all being one happy classless family. She appreciated *The Tichborne Dole* by Gillis van Tillborch (1670), one of the few paintings on view that depicts workers or the poor, and which explained to her the origin of the term "the dole." The painting shows Sir Henry Tichborne and his family about to distribute bread to the poor of the village. It's a tradition, she reads in the catalogue, that exists in Tichborne to this day, even though the dole itself is under attack from Thatcher. This painting may have been made to demonstrate the worthiness of that wealthy family, but at least the poor are shown to exist, she thought to herself, which is more than can be said for Reagan's picture of America.

J. Carter Brown was talking to her over the audioguide, his voice reassuring and almost familiar. The reign of the Tudors passed to the Stuarts in 1603, and everyone kept collecting and patronizing. Upheavals in other countries, such as French Huguenot craftsmen getting kicked out of France, added to British treasure troves. The British made a killing on social upheavals, and, Madame Realism learned, they became rich tourists, taking what came to be known as the Grand Tour, the title of the exhibition's next rooms. "The Grand Tour" is dated as beginning in 1714, when Richard Boyle, 3rd Earl of Burlington, made his first jaunt abroad, returning to Chiswick and building a villa there after designs by Palladio. What the British brought back—according to Carter Brown, "the fruits of these tours"—were "souvenirs." A villa in Chiswick, paintings by Canaletto, all these Roman sculptures and busts—souvenirs? Two Venetian Lattimo Plates (1741) did look like contemporary tourist views of Venice on dinner plates. Horace Walpole carried back twenty-four of them in his luggage; she wondered whether he and his family had ever eaten off them.

There were paintings of English gents posing among Roman ruins—Narcissistic Neoclassicism. *William Gordon* by Pompeo Batoni (1766) is wearing a kilt, with a view of the Colosseum in the background and a statue of Roma on a pedestal sharing the foreground—the spotlight—with him. Colonel Gordon's kilt was draped like a toga, reminding her of a letter to the *Times* she'd read when she was in London one summer. A mao wrote the editor suggesting that, because it was so beastly hot, men wear togas rather than suits, ties and bowlers. To maintain class distinctions, different kinds and colors of stripes could be sewn on the hems of the togas, and, of course, men could still carry umbrellas. Lots of Englishmen walking around the City in togas carrying umbrellas would turn the English summer into a Monty Python skit. Madame Realism laughed out loud, attracting some attention.

A china serving dish shaped like a boar's head made her chortle quietly; porcelain figurines of prominent 18th-century actors were objects any fan could relate to. In gift shops across the U.S. today there'd be something similar—a little figurine of John Forsythe, maybe. Embarrassed to find *Dynasty* so much on her mind—she might explain to scoffers and nonviewers that she watched only the reruns, as if that made her less adolescent than the rest of the nation who were watching it on prime time—she heard a man say to his young daughter, "That's where we got off our gondola to go to our hotel." They were in front of a view of commerce in the Campo Santa Maria Formosa in Venice by Canaletto, one of the souvenirs J. Carter Brown had mentioned earlier. As accurate as any tourist snapshot.

Madame Realism entered the room called "Chinoiserie and Porcelain" and walked immediately to the state bed. It had elaborately embroidered Chinese silk curtains and looked pretty narrow for a bed of state, but then how many heads of state were expected to lie in it at one time anyway? State bed or sex and politics. Musing about 18th-century sex lives of the rich and famous, she wished that Carter Brown would get even more familiar. But instead he directed her to the tiaras and crowns, which rested on shelves in a glass cabinet, so gaudy they looked fake. One woman nudged another and said conspiratorially, "That's why the people rebelled." Madame Realism wanted to tell this woman and her friend, if they didn't already know, about Guy Fawkes Day, when the English celebrate an abortive attempt to ovenhrow King James I. Were they the only people in the world to celebrate a failed revolution?

The exhibition's brochure claimed that the love of landscape was "essentially English," but to Madame Realism the way the English took the piss out of each other was even more essential. But wait, she said to herself, what did they mean by essential? Natural? By now she was in a room called "The Sporting Life," surrounded by paintings of animals, primarily horses, like those done by George Stubbs. There were gentlemen in red hunting jackets, men on horseback in black jackets, and men surrounded by live dogs and dead game. Britain's contemporary Animal Liberation Front might have something to say about the English love of landscape, populated as it is by dead prey hung next to portraits of dogs who were much loved by their owners.

Sentiment was very definitely in the air, what with these sweet animal portraits and the works in the last, "Pre-Raphaelite and Romantic" room. *Love Among the Ruins* by Burne-Jones (1894) was just the kind of painting she might have had a print of on her wall, when she was a teenager, as consolation for yet another broken heart. Now Madame Realism wished she could steal the title, just as Burne-Jones had stolen it from Browning. She liked the title much better than the picture; it was tougher than the wistful backward-looking image. But was that really true? she asked herself, wondering why this kind of adolescent sentiment didn't appeal to her anymore and *Dynasty*'s did.

Parody, she told herself, and walked into the last room, called "Epilogue," which was devoted to family photo albums of some late 19th- and early 20th-century collectors and patrons. By comparison with the rest of the exhibition, "Epilogue" was homey and dimly lit, small in scale in both size of room and in what was on display. Madame Realism thought it odd that an exhibition devoted to the display of wealth and power should end on so mundane a note, though it did allow the spectator a moment to reorient, as in a decompression chamber, for reentry into ordinary life.

Spotlights shone on the albums and photographic portraits. The differences between the paintings and these photographs were overwhelming. Family photo albums compared with paintings meant to last forever. Casual pictures in black and white and posed portraits in magnificent color. The lords and ladies "captured" at unguarded moments, letting us know that, in the end, we're all "just folks." Especially in these dimly lit rooms.

A small plain book caught Madame Realism's eye. It was, the caption read, a scrapbook of photographs of the servants of a particular household, taken by the lady of the house. Madame Realism wanted to see these photographs, but she couldn't because the book was barely open. These were the invisible people, part of unofficial history, who built the country houses and packed up the souvenirs so that they wouldn't get broken on the trip home. Carter Brown directed everyone's attention to the doll's house replica of an English country house, attributed to Thomas Chippendale (ca. 1745). It was behind glass at the end of the room, but this wasn't the diorama she had hoped for. There was a very long line, and Madame Realism stood on it for a while, only to leave the crowd and return to the small, plain book with its glimpse into.... The repressed, she said to herself. It's like the return of the repressed. She wondered what Carter Brown looked like... Vincent Price?

When Madame Realism got outside, it was snowing. The White House was surprisingly and deceptively invisible. The young black taxidriver, wearing a Coptic cross earring, explained that D.C. had been designed by mystics and visionaries, and that through their writings he knew that the end of the world was at hand. "God makes no accidents," he warned.

Back home, Madame Realism lay in bed, thinking about the exhibition and reading Virginia Woolf's *Orlando*, to satisfy her desire to know how people lived and what they talked about in the treasure houses of Britain. There's a wonderful scene in which Elizabethan poet Nick Greene has dinner at Orlando's country house, and though the poet mocks his host and his efforts at poetry, still Orlando "paid the pension quarterly" to Greene. Woolf is taking the piss out of patrons, while the exhibition had pumped them up. Nothing is sacred in *Orlando*. Madame Realism reached the page where Orlando changes from a man into a woman. She put the book on her lap. Was she expected to be grateful to or respectful of the aristocracy for having first created and then preserved Western civilization? The show's banner could have read: WESTERN CIVILIZATION BROUGHT TO YOU BY.... It was too tall an order, and besides, respect was something Madame Realism didn't like to be asked to give. Just too much to swallow, she said to her cat, who had sat himself down on the sex-change page. Closing her eyes, she had a hypnogogic vision: If Steven, the son on *Dynasty* who goes from gay to straight to gay, were to come back as a woman, would he be a gay or a straight woman? Madame Realism fell asleep smiling.

MADAME REALISM'S IMITATION OF LIFE

A cigarette hung from Madame Realism's lips, invitation to disaster, for with it there she noticed that few people came over to talk to her. Sometimes, Madame Realism felt as if she just didn't exist. Maybe it was her imagination, but she put the cigarette out anyway, using the museum's floor because there were no ashtrays. Under the weight of this relatively new stigma, she hummed aloud, "Another opening, another show," and walked past everyone she knew, without looking at the art, heading for the ladies room. How easy it is to become a social outcast, she reflected, which made her want another cigarette as she approached a door with a sign on it. Like many of the bathroom signs around the city, this one proved difficult to read, and as Madame Realism felt that all signs were signs of the time, she wished she could have instantly known whether it was unisex or not, and was relieved to find inside small stuffed chairs and large full-length mirrors, a stage set from some previous time. This must be parody, she thought, sitting on the toilet, notebook in hand, and entered this in a large scrawl: IS PARODY A CONDITION OF AMBIVALENCE, WHERE DISDAIN AND NOSTALGIA MIX? AND JUST MIGHT BE THAT CRAZY THING CALLED LOVE? DON'T FORGET TO WRITE ABOUT THE TIME I WENT INTO A BATHROOM AND IT TURNED OUT TO BE SOMEONE'S

ARTWORK. ARTIST CAME RUNNING WHEN I FLUSHED TOILET. Madame Realism flushed the toilet and put her notebook away.

Standing in front of a full-length mirror, she was startled to see herself once again. It was always weird to see what she was inside of, her conduit, so to speak. Certainly Madame Realism tried to control her image and hoped to register as someone with a sense of style, even if the style was hers alone. Madame Realism feared seeming *au courant* in a desperate and hungry way, yet wanted to be of her time, not to deny its marks on her, something not true of persons called mentally ill, their faces and bodies stamped with their troubles, their clothes thrown together, signifying distress. One does not want to seem disturbed even in disturbing times. But who can really control how other people see you? Madame Realism grabbed her notebook: GUY AT PARTY SAID HE HAD FOUR FAKE TEETH IN FRONT. DOES THAT TURN YOU OFF? HE ASKED. OFF WHAT? I ANSWERED.

Two women rushed the mirror and smiled at Madame Realism whose reverie was interrupted as she quickly hid her notebook. "Are you really Madame Realism?" one asked. "Not really," she answered, continuing to smile. "Why, do I look like her?" All three women looked at themselves and each other in the mirror, and Madame Realism made a face she never made unless she was looking at herself in a mirror. Apart from the opposite image problem, Madame Realism silently noted the left side/right side dilemma that everyone had. All their faces lacked symmetry and it evidenced life's contradictoriness, even its betrayals. Hadn't a friend with a baby recently told her that infants lie, or dissemble, almost from birth, pretending to be in pain when they simply want attention. Lying, Madame Realism's friend said, is obviously necessary for survival.

One of the women said, "This isn't a good mirror," and Madame Realism relaxed a little, the idea of a perfect mirror terrifying anyway, and besides she didn't like the way she looked just then. Still, she thought, if there is no inner life or self, and I'm not being conduited, this physical presence, this facade, might be all one really did have. This raised the image stakes immeasurably, making the peculiarity of her image to herself even more burdensome. On the other hand, it could be consoling to know that that empty feeling is not just a feeling. After Madame Realism left the room, one woman said, "I think that is Madame Realism, but do you think a fictional statement can ever be true?"

Shaking her head from side to side, Madame Realism returned to the large space, so open that its transient inhabitants could lose themselves for a moment or two and lie like babies. As if they'd never be found out. The test of a good friendship is the ability to keep secrets, she thought, and avoided walking near someone who might tell her one. In this room full of fellow co-conspirators—conspiracy is merely breathing together—suddenly Madame Realism wanted to flee.

Perhaps she'd been in town too long. Never wanting to outlive her welcome, Madame Realism every once in a while disappeared, without telling anyone, and returned some months later, reassured. For as much as she needed to leave, she needed to return. One produced the other, in a sense.

There are ways to leave without leaving, suggested a friend. A cultural sleight of hand might be to dress as a man, to become Sir Realism, for instance. Madame Realism told him she could never be Sir Realism, but that one time she attempted to dress as a man, for a costume party, and had bought a tuxedo and everything that went with it. But with the outfit on and her hair slicked back with gel the consistency of aspic, she'd transformed herself into just the kind of man she couldn't stand. Or that she'd never be attracted to.

That she could become that which repelled her shocked her in a way only falling in love over and over again usually did. "I was," she told her friend, "like a quotation from a work or book I hated." Disguise in this instance uncovered more than it covered. "What'd you end up wearing?" the friend asked. Madame Realism said she put on a long black velvet skirt, a black and white checked jacket from the Thirties, and tied a loose, floppy bow around the neck of the tuxedo shirt. She pretended to be a French or English governess from the Thirties. Everyone else was either in bondage outfits or in nineteenth-century gowns. She talked with a book editor whose face was entirely covered by a leather mask, except for his lips. She said she had a great time. Madame Realism's face clouded over. Maybe, she thought, I didn't look like a French governess from the Thirties.

The phrase "life drawing" popped into her mind, almost like a cartoon, and Madame Realism complained to her friend that she had always been bad at it. Her people had been too big for the drawing paper, essential parts like heads or legs left off. "Larger than life were they?" her friend teased. "Yes, like a movie," she smiled. From art imitating life, to life imitating art, and here they were at art imitating art and life imitating life. But instead of Frankensteins and golems running around town, versions of Diane Keaton as Annie Hall. Or that man Madame Realism had seen near the Algonquin, dressed just like James Joyce as recorded by a famous photograph of the author taken in the Twenties. Imitation of life or art or both? Madame Realism sighed audibly. Perhaps imitation is the insincerest form of flattery.

Nothing ever worked the way it was supposed to, everything having unintended effects, and all you could do was get used to it. Like getting used to living in a world of knock-offs, she mused, and said goodbye to her friend, leaving the opening without ever having looked at what was on the walls. If asked she could say she had been temporarily blinded, and truly, as she walked along Broadway, staring in windows but not seeing anything, it was as if her provisional lie might be true. MADAME REALISM REVEALED AS A HOAX, she wrote in her notebook. Just a matter of survival, she reassured herself.

Madame Realism's lie would be insignificant compared with Wendy Ann Devin's. For one brief moment, Wendy Ann Devin had been news in the *New York Times*. "SOVIET GIRL" AN AMERICAN HOAX, the headline read. A certain Valeria Skvortsov, 14, a Soviet hockey player from Kiev, is really Wendy Ann Devin, 21, of Braintree, Massachusetts. Wendy Naleria convinced residents of Brainerd, Minnesota, and other communities, that she was a well-known Soviet hockey player, whose father was a Soviet pilot. He had left her in the States, she said, to fend for herself. Wendy's real father turns out to be a Braintree, Massachusetts cop, said Sergeant Ball, the detective assigned to the case. Sergeant Ball explains, "Apparendy, she's got an obsession with hockey," a quote that ends the story. Wendy had posed as at least five different Soviet hockey stars and had even crossed over to Canada where she got herself a Soviet visa, and in doing so nearly was deported from the U.S. Wendy Ann Devin, where are you now? And, who are you now? Madame Realism wondered. No charges had been filed against her, but she was urged to seek psychiatric help.

And what does her disguise reveal? To have portrayed herself as an abandoned and homeless Soviet girl? Perhaps a longing to un-state herself, maybe like the yearnings of would-be transsexuals who find themselves submerged in the wrong body. In Wendy Ann's case, the wrong body politic. Could this be the unconscious' attack on nationalism, that which binds body and psyche to place of birth? A *New York Post* story might have read, WENDY BETRAYS HER BIRTHRIGHT. NOT SINCE ESAU SOLD HIS BIRTHRIGHT TO JACOB....

Madame Realism walked home, lost in thought, interrupted only by people asking for money. She gave a quarter to the last one, a young man whose eyes met hers for a brief moment. She turned to watch him ask others, noticing how they, like she, avoided "the homeless" in similar ways. Anything she thought about people who had no homes sounded as canned as a studio audience's laugh track or a recorded announcement over a P.A. The word homeless itself naming, categorizing, and dismissing in one blow. And so unrepresentable were these people, that when Pat Harper impersonated one on TV, to get "their" story across, it became the story of the newscaster who cried on television. PAT HARPER CRIES, Madame Realism wrote in her notebook, followed by: IS THE UNREPRESENTED LIFE WORTH LIVING? And, NO TAXATION WITHOUT REPRESENTATION.

Inside her home, the one she could afford to leave and return to voluntarily, every once in a while, she felt the evening unravel like a badly knit sweater. And soon it would be all gone, like Wendy Ann Devin, who had disappeared into thin air, along with the homeless and the people at the opening. Thin air. Madame Realism walked over to her window and looked up at the dark sky, the kind that in the country would be full of stars. But here just a few were visible, positioned economically, almost like asterisks or reminders. Madame Realism left the next day.

ON THE ROAD

WITH MADAME REALISM

PALAIS MENDOUB

TANGIER, MOROCCO: It's the Feast of Isaac, and much of Tangier is shut down and will be for the next three days. Second only to Ramadan in holiness for Muslims, the feast celebrates Isaac's not being killed by Abraham. Sheep are sacrificed in his honor and their bleating resounds throughout the city. For the Moroccans, the cost of one sheep (about $90) is burdensome; I'm told that families save all year round to buy one. The acrid smell of burning sheep heads and sheep fur wafts through the Casbah. Thin rivers of blood mark the narrow streets. Men gather around wood fires, built in oil drums, turning over charred sheep heads to make a special dish to eat the next day.

The next day I ask my one-day guide to drive me to the Caves of Hercules, but find myself first at the Palais Mendoub. "The Palais," as it's referred to by all Tangier, is one of Malcolm Forbes' many residences. It houses the American multimillionaire's toy soldier collection, and there are about 70,000 toy soldiers in it. Because it's the Feast of Isaac most of the Palais is closed and I get to see just a fraction of what's on display. Given the context of the Feast, one can't help thinking things like "lambs to the slaughter" when gazing at the tiny model men, "toy armies," set up in miniaturized reenactments of great battles. One is an exact replica, the caption says, of the 16th-century Battle of the Three Kings, "in which Moroccan forces routed a European army." The Forbeses have gone to some trouble to represent their host country advantageously; the museum was even officially opened by Moroccan Crown Prince Sidi Mohammed in August 1978. Present-day Morocco is not known for its progress toward democracy, I think, picturing the Crown Prince and the multi-millionaire toasting the toy soldiers. Politics certainly cannot be disregarded when viewing a museum dedicated to the valorization of war, no matter how nonsectarian and representative it claims to be.

The scaling down of war itself is disturbing: the spectator looms over thousands of little men. The soldiers are "just pawns in the game," a saying made literal by these displays. The desire to collect these little men seems to be made up of many parts: mastery not only over the collection's field of choice (to have the best objects or the most complete set), but also, on an unconscious level, over the armies of one's childhood, which live in the imagination forever.

I try to imagine one battlefield in motion, as in those movies where a ship-in-stormy-waters scene is shot in a bathtub. I love taking baths and like the opportunity, whenever it presents itself, to imagine one. Behind the Palais lies the Atlantic Ocean, a majestic backyard, or bathtub, for that matter, which, along with the Palais itself, overshadows the little men and scenes of great struggle "writ small." Reconstructed by the Belgian architect Robert Gerofi, the Palais is the scene of many grand parties, and I realize that the terrace has been used in at least one movie I saw, where swingers cavorted jet-set style.

I always like the idea of travel but I don't actually like jetting from place to place. I don't really mind being a tourist—it exaggerates the sense of life I generally have, like going to the movies, being in part a spectator. To find myself wandering around streets I don't know or streets I do know and call "home" is not so different, I've discovered. Products follow me wherever I go. Familiar brands breed a false sense of security. As for false senses of security, today's *Herald Tribune* reports that Cyrus Reza Pahlavi, the son of the late Shah of Iran, "announced a campaign from Paris to overthrow the Khomeini regime and to restore a constitutional monarchy." Bani-Sadr, in exile in a Paris suburb, says: "I dont think he knows what he's talking about."

FREUD MUSEUM

LONDON: The newly opened Freud Museum, at 20 Maresfield Gardens, where Freud lived last, has the real, the authentic couch. Anna Freud refused to allow the Viennese to keep it, symbolic retribution for that country's treatment of the very old and ill Freud who had to flee Austria, lucky to get out. His study has been kept as it was, Greek and Roman antiquities on the desk, on shelves, in glass and mahogany cabinets. Oriental rugs cover the floor and the fabled couch, making the couch seem like an extension of what's beneath it, which isn't a bad metaphor for psychoanalysis. (This reminds me of a movie made by Jung's students—whenever they wanted to show the unconscious at work, people got into elevators and went down.) The room is rich in deep reds and browns, and produces in me the feeling I had when read aloud to from the

Arabian Nights. It also made me wonder if Freud ever got that Scheherazade feeling about his patients, all those individual repositories of culture and society he listened to so unceasingly. The study's a conducive, even seductive setting in which to hear the red (shameful) and brown (dark) narratives of his analysands. With all the statuary around, you sense the "family" surrounding Freud—representations of mothers, fathers, daughters and sons; they were props perhaps, or the cast of his constant theater.

The tour guide moves us to the dining room. Unfortunately he pronounces Freud's name as if there were a "w" after the "F," sounding very much like Barbara Walters. He tells a little group of us what Fwoid ate for lunch—soup, a bit of meat, a vegetable. I'm not interested in his eating habits, nor is my friend, so we leave the tour and wander through the rest of the house, unescorted and untutored. We remark on how Sean Connery's office in *Marnie* obviously refers to Freud's.

METROPOLITAN MUSEUM OF ART

NEW YORK: Those indignant people who wrote to *Art in America* are right. I'm not a professional museum-goer. I do go to museums and galleries, but I'm especially drawn to out-of-the-way places, like houses of famous dead people, where society preserves what it deems instructive and valuable. When I visited the Metropolitan Museum of Art, from the moment I mounted those monumental stairs, an immense exhaustion overcame me. I tried to ask directions at the information desk, but the noise from the crowd of museum-goers was deafening, an acoustical nightmare, like being in a large swimming pool. With map in hand, I followed the crowds to "Suleyman the Magnificent," the "Hudson River School," "Image of the Mind" and, by accident, medieval art; a couple of Vermeers; the Greeks; a Noguchi, and a Japanese woman demonstrating the art of Bower arrangement.

The Met's brochures and signs accompanying the Suleyman exhibition contain the same written material, so that if one wanted to memorize the information it would be easy, as in grade school where the teacher is supposed to follow the textbook and reproduce it in class. Faced with the unfamiliar, we the public have been trained to rely on museums, like schools, to serve up art and culture like pieces of pie: little wedges of esthetics, criticism, politics and history. Sultan Suleyman the Magnificent (1520–66) was "renowned as a legislator, statesman, poet and generous patron of the arts. Like all Ottoman emperors, he was taught a practical trade." In his case, it was goldsmithing, and therefore he supported jewelers most enthusiastically, which accounts, in part, for the jewel-encrusted Korans, boxes and scabbards on display. Oohs and aahs from the crowd around me are well-deserved. "I can't see very well," one woman says to another. We're walking around in a dimly lit set of rooms, underlit to protect the beautiful scrolls and gold-embroidered fabrics from fading. I'm reminded of being in a hamman, or Turkish bath, which is always cloudy with steam, but unlike one you might go into in Istanbul, there's art surrounding you, not naked bodies. I'm also reminded that when naked East met naked West, the amount of body hair Western women had shocked the Turkish women, who giggled in embarrassment for us.

In the semidarkness I transform the gallery/hamman into an exotic movie theater that doesn't turn its lights completely off. Reagan and Meese flicker on the screen wearing turbans and carrying elaborate scimitars. Suleyman could be a hero to them, he doubled the Ottoman Empire during his reign. To my amateur eye, even the lettering on the pages from rare books is a mysterious sign of a complex society I know little about, and at moments like these I take heart in Yogi Berra's dictum: "Sometimes you can see a lot just by looking." Suleyman's portable throne, made of walnut and inlaid with ivory, ebony and mother of pearl, was carried to battles where it was set up in the royal tent. It always accompanied him. The throne looks uncomfortable, an appropriate seat from which to direct a war, I suppose, and the way I see Suleyman sitting on it is straight out of the movies. Yul Brynner.

THE UNKNOWN MUSEUM

SAN FRANCISCO: I'm very comfortable just sitting around hotel lobbies or reading in a friend's room. People say, "You might as well be home," and without friends I might never venture out, even though I think of myself as a person with curiosity. Once I'm someplace new, however, I do get interested. My friends, also transients, have rented a car for a day trip up the coast to the Unknown Museum in Mill Valley. I used to get carsick but now I can travel for hours as long as I'm in the backseat. Occasionally the driver, who lives in London, wonders whether she's on the right side of the road, and only this mars ever so slightly a perfect kind of day. Blue sky, sun shining, fluffy white clouds.

The Unknown Museum, a house of popular culture, is situated in a suburb alongside other similar houses that are used residentially. It's artist Mickey McGowan's creation, and he's around the place, a kind of host to a kind of house. The house of memories, it might be called, with bathroom scales leading out of the kitchen, past the refrigerator, to the backyard: a very American memory lane. McGowan has collected American ephemera from the past 40 or 50 years and arranged it so that each room maintains its original function. The arrangements fill the rooms as much with metaphors as memory and objects—a lost and found, or pound, for so-called trivia. The girl's room: a life-size model bride lying flat on her face on a rug of uncooked rice. The boy's room: war games, toy soldiers, chemistry sets, test tubes. In the living room, where a book rack is filled with lurid '40s and '50s paperbacks, there's a TV which is used as a display case for atomic energy info from the '50s. A stack of lunch boxes, from every children's TV show you could think of, comprises a column in the kitchen. A model Mom lies on the bed in the master bedroom, her hair in curlers, a hair dryer with plastic bouffant hood close by. There's Barbie. There are the Flintstones.

McGowan's arrangements are deliberate, and sometimes I resented it, the artfulness; it interfered with an unmediated look into the past made up of toys, games, gadgets, and objects that usually get thrown away. On the other hand, there is no such thing as an unmediated past, and that someone has retrieved so much of what's considered junk, but which later generations will in part characterize this culture by, is valuable. A layer of civilization from an archeologist's point of view, something I consider reassuring. Seeing all this stuff around seemed natural, a landscape I understood, an environment conjured by and contained within its cultural products. And the silliest piece means something simply because one remembers it, has lived with it, and has associations to it. My madeleine for the day turned out to be a Roy Rogers lunch box. Happy trails to you, too.

What you don't see you begin to bring back, remembering a toy that isn't there, which then makes you realize how much lies just below the surface of consciousness, recalled by a pink plastic toy handbag or those wacky pet rocks. Also, I think later, riding in the back of the car, if this is a museum for the commodity, and if our social relations exist in each object, then what's unknown here must be, apart from what one forgets, the labor behind each commodity. This work is always forgotten, making this into a museum, maybe the first, but probably not the last, that pays tribute to the fetishism of the commodity.

THE LUTHER BURBANK HOUSE AND GARDEN

SANTA ROSA, CALIFORNIA: There's as much off the road as on it. One engages expectation and perception just as readily in spaces designated for art as in those that aren't. It's a thin line between art and popular culture, and one can jaywalk easily if all objects are not thought of as inherently valuable. The Luther Burbank house and garden, a museum of sorts, has been preserved as it was when he lived there, and it's the major tourist attraction in the area. His name is, if not a household word, familiar, and saying it over and over, I get a picture of someone like Frederic March in a white coat, playing a hearty country doctor. Burbank's name is vaguely associated in my mind with fruit. But this, I find out, doesn't even glimpse the man. Not that anything could, I suppose. From the East originally, he made his fame and fortune in the West. An anarchist, a self-taught botanist, a free thinker in all sorts of ways (his wife, 40 years younger, never remarried, because, to paraphrase her words, no man could ever equal him), a celebrity in his time, Burbank's great achievements include inventing the russet potato, splicing 526 different kinds of apples onto one tree and developing a daisy that didn't smell. In his preserved backyard there is a large patch of these daisies and I bend to sniff some. It's hard not to be impressed with a mind that's challenged to deodorize nature—though other forms of tampering with nature are perhaps more impressive—as well as one that can also think of a way to make a living from it. An eminently practical approach to life spliced itself onto the visionary and turned Burbank into the gardener of the world, as he was once called, rather than, say, an artist. An artist satisfies herself or himself with a more circumscribed piece of the world, the world of representations, whereas Burbank's vision is directed toward what we call the real world. Looked at through this frame, if the garden is his canvas, is he the van Gogh of the Real? Driving away from Burbank's house with my friends, we discuss the fact that this man of seed and his adoring wife had no children. This has all sorts of implications. I mail a packet of souvenir flower seeds to my mother, who used to have a garden and will probably have her own memories of Luther Burbank.

MONTICELLO

CHARLOTTESVILLE, VA.: Some people go north in the fall to watch the leaves turn; I go south to watch them cling. Hearty breakfasts of grits and biscuits, and a motel that looks pretty much the way it did when it was built in the 1950s, set you up for a trip into the past. But unlike *Back to the Future* and *Peggy Sue Got Married*, which are like anthems to that recent past, restored houses or villages are more like theme parks, where America's history is an everyday celebration. Jefferson's Monticello, especially in the Constitution's bicentennial year, is the pièce de résistance of American historical kitsch. The house reminds me of a savings bank I once bought in Texas which was in the form of the Bible. Here, long lines of people pay their way into something sacred. At five bucks a head, Monticello must be a profitmaking institution, which might have pleased its industrious designer and resident.

I linger in front of the graves of Jefferson, his mother, and the Levy family that bought Monticello from Jefferson and saved it for posterity. Although, I'm told by insiders, because the Levys were Jewish, this fact has been obscured over the years. To me, this fact seems to symbolize the cracks and contradictions in the democracy that the enlightened and brilliant slaveholder Jefferson helped build and which might also be contained within his own character. Jefferson, like Burbank, was an inventor, a gadgeteer. His pantograph machine makes a copy of whatever's being written, a kind of arm attached to the writer's pen that moves along with it. He also made labor-saving devices, like a dumbwaiter, and designed a bed in a wall that he could get out of from either side, depending upon whether he wanted to go to his office or not. As I don't go into the house, I see all these objects through the windows, as well as my own reflection staring back at me.

Sitting on the lawn, next to what was once Jefferson's working farm, I gaze out at the view, the Virginia Piedmont farmlands to the east, the Blue Ridge Mountains to the west. The pamphlet, given free by the historical society that runs Monticello, makes no mention of the Levys or of the black mistress and children

Jefferson is supposed to have had. I walk back to the slave quarters, and discover that in Charlottesville they're called servants' quarters. A sanitized version of the past, then, not so different from period movies, and as mighty a fantasy as any that Edgar Allan Poe might have written.

Poe attended the University of Virginia, Mr. Jefferson's university as it's called here, and late at night, having drunk quite a lot of champagne, I tiptoe onto campus, to the eerie and beautiful quad where his room has been maintained as it was when he was a student. It's hard not to compare the myths about these two famous men: one, the brilliant writer who died in a gutter; the other, the "great man," who almost singlehandedly gave us democracy. What's left to support their images are tracts and stories, as much open to interpretation today as they were originally. But today little ambiguity remains—these histories are packaged for public consumption and memory as inert rooms and houses. Which reminds me of a recent piece in the *New York Times*. Under the headline "A Patriotic Halloween," it reported that parents in Louisville, Colorado, were worried about the "dark side" of Halloween and were banning traditional Halloween activities and making the day a celebration of the 200th anniversary of the Constitution. This neatly merges one idea of Poe and Jefferson, I think to myself.

WAR AND MEMORY

WASHINGTON, D.C.: I marched, walked really, in the Gay Rights Parade, reported the day after by the *Washington Post* as nearly as large as the March on the Pentagon in 1969 (600,000), and by the *New York Times* as numbering about 200,000. History in the making. A lot of jubilation and every imaginable kind of organization from almost every state. Parents' groups. ACT-UP. Psychologists. Conservationists. Feminists. Gay liberation groups from everywhere. There was a great moment when in front of the White House men in leather, from the Eulenspiegel Society, saluted a policeman in leather who stood by on horseback. He returned the salute and smiled.

The next day my friend and I run from one exhibition to another, seeing the capital in the way it seems to have been designed, as a town of holding bins for information (and the ever-present disinformation). At WPA (Washington Project for the Arts) is an exhibition called "War and Memory: In the Aftermath of Vietnam." It seems fitting to be here after having marched the day before, when one had the sense of having participated in something that will also become part of living memory, if one lives long enough. The show is organized by many groups, a "multidisciplinary program of visual art, installations, photography, film, video, literature, theater, music and discussion."

Several of the photographic works (Wendy Watriss, Sal Lopes and Lloyd Wolf) "document" the Vietnam Memorial, the Wall. Shots of people touching the engraved names, single flowers and wreaths, men hugging each other, children, women and men crying. Images like these have been reproduced so often in the last few years they are already part of the national family album, like the photograph of the riderless horse in JFK's funeral procession. There's one installation (Richard Posner) about having been a conscientious objector during the war and another (Richard Turner) that fabricates a cemetery/hotel lobby in Saigon, which necessarily refers to the war's "other" side. A kind of altar, Nancy Floyd's memorial installation to her brother,

James, consists of his "effects," dog tag, letters home from Nam, pictures, the remnants of a lost life. The show is sobering, and the exhilaration of yesterday's march disappears.

Affecting as some of the work is, the absence of political analysis of the war the U.S. lost is more disturbing. How to distinguish Vietnam from any other war? Nothing much was made of the opportunity to work with the changing representations of the war in the past twenty, nearly thirty years. From vicious, deranged killer, as in *Taxi Driver*, the Vietnam vet has been transformed into heroic and misunderstood victim, as in, for example, *Platoon*. Which means Vietnam isn't contained within that past moment, with its present "effects" being the attendant sadness and loss that wars inevitably bring. Competing representations—of the vet then and now, for example—deserve analysis precisely because the interpretation of the war's meaning has real effects today. Are U.S. political aims so different today, one might reasonably ask oneself? I try to imagine a toy soldier display of a battle in Vietnam. On exhibit at the Palais Mendoub. I feel as if I am thinking the unthinkable. But instead of thinking about Herman Kahn, I'm thinking about a multimillionaire with a toy soldier collection. Depressing as that is.

We continue our march around Washington and head for the Hirshhorn Museum, to a retrospective of the English painter Lucian Freud. His depressing paintings stare back at me, a distorting mirror, and shake me into a different mood. I wonder what Sigmund Freud would make of his grandson's work, portraits of tortured women and men. To me, they look like concentration camp victims, victims of the same Naziism that forced the elder Freud to flee Vienna, and something he might have imagined in his most pessimistic moments, but didn't live to see.

MUSEUM OF NATURAL HISTORY

NEW YORK: I hadn't been in the Museum of Natural History for years and years, respecting it as if it were a preserve for children. Kids are supposed to love dinosaurs. I can't remember if I did or not. I do remember digging for China in our backyard. But I'm fascinated by notions of the prehistoric. Whether it's Mel Brooks and Carl Reiner's "Two Thousand Year Old Man" or dioramas showing the Neanderthal Man in his, or her, natural habitat. An exhibition entitled "Dinosaurs Past and Present" immediately attracted me, as I wondered what a "present dinosaur" would be. But the present dinosaurs turned out to be drawings of dinosaurs by various artists. The exhibition was supposed to show how that kind of art depends upon scientific discoveries. A drawing by Charles Knight in 1901 of a Stegosaurus, a caption says, was greatly improved upon, in terms of authenticity, by Stephen Czerkas in 1961. Dino artist Knight drew his Stegosaurus for 50 years, which is a most unfamiliar kind of obsession. Another dino artist, Ron Seguin, the caption says, became a taxidermist because of his love of animals. This made me consider embalmers in a different light.

As I strolled through the Halls of Man I pondered a statement about dino artist Robert Bakker: it said that when he saw Rudolph Zallinger's famous "Age of Reptiles" mural at Yale, he knew instantly that his destiny was with dinosaurs. I rushed back to find the Zallinger mural and luckily there was a copy on display. I stood in front of it, hoping for one brief moment to feel what Bakker did. I'm looking at it: it's a fairy-tale landscape of prehistoric animals. Beautiful vibrant colors. But all I can think of is Victor Mature in that film *One Million B.C.* Except that was in black and white. But it was my most vivid introduction to dinosaurs. And to Victor Mature. As I walk to the subway I'm struck again by other people's epiphanies. I've read about them over the years in biographies of artists and writers. These people know and see clearly, and their lives are set out in front of them in one brilliant flash of insight. Will that ever happen to me, I ask myself, searching for a subway token.

THE FORBES MUSEUM

NEW YORK: The Forbes Museum on lower Fifth Avenue is another of Malcolm Forbes' residences, as well as the place where *Forbes* magazine is produced, and it occupies ground that once was home to New York's oldest families. "Old money": these are the people who made their fortunes before the Industrial Revolution, the people Edith Wharton descended from and about whom she wrote so brilliantly and disturbingly. The Forbes family is new money, as are most of the rich in this country, and two co-existent exhibitions at the Forbes Museum are oddly telling in relation to the family, their money, position, and ambitions.

In the presidential election year, the family is "sharing with the public," as the elder Forbes puts it, their collection of presidential autographs, photographs, posters, and memorabilia of all kinds and from both parties. Titled "And If Elected: Two Hundred Years of Presidential Elections: An Exhibition for the 1988 Election Year," the exhibition is filled to bursting with historic documents and trivia. On display is Malcolm Forbes' ex-wife Roberta's dress, a white cotton number from the '50s with red IKEs printed all over it. There are political posters of FDR, JFK, Teddy Roosevelt; drawings and doodles from Eisenhower and JFK; rare presidential letters; campaign buttons bearing names famous and forgotten, the also-rans. Here and there the Forbes family is represented: pictures of them with political figures; letters to Malcolm from presidents. One of Malcolm's own campaign posters—he ran for governor in New Jersey, and lost—hangs on a wall near ones for Teddy Roosevelt and FDR (a picture of a rose with the word "velt" beneath it). The ghost of Edith Wharton haunts me as I wander through these rooms: with her on my shoulder I see new money laying claim to America's past, placing itself in history, and in this instance attempting to shape it, not only through ownership but through representation and presentation.

In the smallest room are the collection's "most unique and important Presidential acquisitions." There's also a TV monitor with a tape of Malcolm Forbes being interviewed by his youngest son, Timothy, publisher of *American Heritage*—the magazine that the Forbeses bought not so long ago (and under whose auspices this exhibition is mounted). These acquisitions include Matthew Brady's photograph of Abraham Lincoln and his ten-year-old son Tad, taken shortly before Lincoln was assassinated, and a rare first edition of Thomas Jefferson's only book, *Notes on the State of Virginia*. Next to President Truman's famous letter attacking Paul Hume, the music critic who attacked the musicianship of his daughter, Margaret, sits the diary kept by a crew member of the *Enola Gay*. The *Enola Gay* was the plane that carried the men who dropped the bomb on Hiroshima on August 6, 1945. The positioning is curious, and just as I'm staring at the *Enola Gay* logbook, I hear Malcolm Forbes on the videotape say that he thinks of this diary as "human documentation." Human documentation of an event inhuman in its effects placed next to Truman's all-too-human letter defending his daughter. Side by side we share these pieces of evidence—awesome and awful presidential power and a president's personal tantrum.

It's often said that position is everything in life. In an exhibition position is, if not everything, almost everything; objects very obviously "mean" in relation to what's around them, how they're arranged. Is this positioning a bad joke on the part of the curators? Or a bit of irony? Talk about irony—I discover that the plane was named after pilot Paul Tibbet's mother, "the former Enola Gay Haggard."

Haggard mother indeed, I think as I cross over the hall to a show called "Chairman's Choice: A Miscellany of American Paintings," a personal selection made by Malcolm Forbes from the family's art collection. On TV and to the press, the senior Forbes disarms with his eagerness to talk turkey—money—at the drop of a hat. He's happy and unselfconscious. True to form, he's written a statement introducing his choices and placed it at the entryway to the show. "Art is a many splendored thing.... Vigorous differences and preferences make for horse races and stock market gyrations. They account for the total gamut that art collections run.... When I was young...my father used to say to me, 'Son, I have enough money for three square meals a day for the rest of my life. The money you want to spend in large measure is your own.' What's on these walls is one fellow's joy. And we'll enjoy them even more if you do too." There aren't many collectors who'd so gaily and boldly conflate their aesthetic choices with money.

The painting of a dollar sign that Andy Warhol presented to Malcolm on one of his birthdays (is Warhol telling us that money is not "no object"?), which eventually was used as a cover for Forbes, hangs diagonally across from one of Gilbert Stuart's portraits of George Washington. Stuart did 22. This one, the placard under it reads, is the image of Washington that appears on the dollar bill. Going clockwise around the gallery, one finds landscapes, like Thomas Hart Benton's *Chilmark Hay* (1951), as well as abstracts, like Stuart Davis' *Anchors* (1930). Bringing Edith Wharton back to mind again is *The Silvery City*, by Guy Wiggins (1925). It's a view of the First Presbyterian Church on Fifth Avenue with the Forbes Building in the background. It's snowing, a White Christmas kind of scene. The painting allows the curators the opportunity to tell us something about the building we're standing in: it's designed by Carrere and Hastings, the same architects who built the Empire State Building, the Frick Museum and the New York Public Library.

A lackluster Hopper called *Hotel Window* (1956)—a woman in a red hat and dress looking out a window—introduces work of a sexual nature. Paul Cadmus' sexy *Sailors and Floosies* (1938) is surrounded by a number of nudes, including *Nude on a Sofa* by Howard Chandler Christy (1933) and Walter Stuempfig's *Voltaire and Apollo* (1948), in which a young boy sleeps in a chair while an older man watches, himself just a reflection in a mirror. Nearly at the entryway, which is now the exit, is a 1982 Andrew Wyeth called *Roll Call* in which the flag waves again—after all that bawdy stuff—and a drummer boy beats his drum. Until I looked at the date, I thought it was one hundred years old.

Walking around the room again, I'm stopped by the Warhol dollar sign which is placed above a painting by James Bama titled *A Sioux Indian* (1977). The S-like figure on the Indian's Superman shirt parallels the dollar sign itself. To what end, I ask myself, wondering about the curators and the exigencies of hanging work of such diversity. I begin to imagine a writers' conference for the David Letterman show (on which Malcolm has appeared), where a cutesey skit might be thought up to fill time when a better one just didn't work. On the other hand, with money and power, with position, with a mythical Superman behind them, the American Indians might not today be suffering a startling number of suicides on reservations. Or there might not even be reservations. But this is probably not what the curators intended. What's intended is a celebration of a private collection of American art and a celebration of America.

I walk past the First Presbyterian Church thinking about the two exhibitions and I'm struck by the idea that if you can't get elected to public office, as the Kennedys have, you can buy art and get on the boards of worthy cultural institutions. Alexis de Tocqueville predicted just such behavior from America's wealthy dynastic families in search of tradition. He didn't predict the lengths to which Joe Kennedy Sr. went, and a letter on display in the presidential collection is immediately committed to memory. Joe Senior told his son John, "Don't buy one vote more than is necessary... I'll be damned if I'm going to pay for a landslide."

By the time I get to Eighth Street, I'm wondering if I should go shopping, although I usually hate to. Unless I know exactly what I want, the abundance of things confuses me. I don't think I could be a collector, not in any systematic way, although I find it hard to throw things out. Especially since I'm convinced that every little scrap of paper has meaning. Perhaps Malcolm Forbes makes his choices with a great deal of anxiety. Although with the amount of money he has, when he can buy whatever he wants, what does choice mean? It's depressing to think that either choices mean nothing or one doesn't have any choices at all. I can't face shopping, with all its false promises. I head home mulling over campaign promises and campaign purses. How much does a landslide cost? I take out change for the bus and think of Warhol's dollar bill painting. It reminds me of what a friend once said, years ago, to a guy who dismissed Warhol's Campbell Soup Can painting as stupid. He said, "What you expect to see there is just as stupid."

MADAME REALISM:

A FAIRY TALE

"It makes letters! It makes words!" Bruno whispered, as he clung, half-frightened, to Sylvie. "Only I ca'n't make them out! Read them, Sylvie!"

"I'll try," Sylvie gravely replied. "Wait a minute—if only I could see that word—"

"I should be very ill!" a discordant voice yelled in our ears. "Were I to swallow this," he said, "I should be very ill!"

—Lewis Carroll, *Sylvie And Bruno*

In the winter the days end suddenly and with such ferocious indifference that Madame Realism felt at a loss. Day after short day she was caught short, surprised. I'm still capable of surprise, she told herself. When it's dark, one expects surprises, Madame Realism reflected as she looked out the window. Anyone could imagine anything. The evening sky covered the ordinary street. Upon a night screen we can project wildly but usually we don't, she reassured herself, most of the time people fill in the spaces, with the familiar. Madame Realism closed the curtains and wondered if she had disappeared. Even if she were visible, and viewable, she wouldn't necessarily be any better known. Recognized perhaps, but not known. Madame Realism didn't subscribe to the wisdom that what you see is what you get.

That night, after watching television and reading Lewis Carroll's *Sylvie and Bruno,* Madame Realism couldn't fall asleep. She tossed and turned, much like a ship at sea during a storm, much like a well-used phrase. Finally, exhausted, she fell into a deep, undisturbed sleep. She dreamed that she entered a museum which was a labyrinth. She didn't know what to look for or where to look. She stumbled about, searching for clues. A friend guided her through a cavernous space and pointed out a word or letter from an alphabet Madame Realism didn't know. These shapes appeared on walls and suggested answers. At the end of the dream—do dreams have ends?—Gertrude Stein's deathbed retort to the friend who had asked her, "What is the answer?" flashed on an unfinished wall: "What is the question?"

The next morning Madame Realism awakened slowly, perplexed by the question as an answer. Taken comprehensively, Stein's deathbed statement could require that each day become an investigation, if not an invention. What a struggle, Madame Realism thought, to invent each day. She tried to lift the blankets off her and swing her legs over the side of the bed as she did every morning. But she couldn't move. She could barely open her eyes. It was as if a veil had been placed over them.

"Gradually, however, the conviction came upon me that I could, by a certain concentration of thought, think the veil away...."

After a while Madame Realism was able to pry her eyelids open. And instantly she apprehended a change in herself. It was nothing short of fantastic. Madame Realism was enfolded between stiff cardboard covers, on creamy white paper, stuffed with references and descriptions, and illustrated with photographs, charts and drawings. There were numbers and letters next to some of her paragraphs which referred to artwork that might hang on walls or sit inside plastic boxes on platforms. Madame Realism had turned into a catalogue.

It was frightening and oddly pleasurable. Uncanny. Uncategorizable. But Madame Realism was at home with ambivalence. Her metamorphosis, not that dissimilar from Gregor Samsa's into a cockroach, could be liberating, she told herself as she smoothed her pages and admired her typeface. (She had once been a menu but not for long. The restaurant had closed. It was possible that now she might accompany a permanent installation. She didn't know.)

Ordinarily Madame Realism existed as, or in, a story or essay. No matter, she soothed herself by thinking—I am always fiction. And now, she remarked aloud, reviewing herself, I do not have to pretend to be a tabula rasa, to pretend that I don't have a past, that I don't have a history. She turned herself to another page, imagining that she was "taking a page from this book." She reconsidered: I am a page from this book. As she studied herself Madame Realism mused, I am a compendium, a list, a detailed enumeration, a register. I can provide a provenance. Haughtily and awkwardly she whirled about and sang: I am a woman with a past, a danger to the community.

"How convenient it would be," Lady Muriel laughingly remarked, "if cups of tea had no weight at all! Then perhaps ladies would sometimes be permitted to carry them for short distances."

Perhaps I'm dreaming, Madame Realism told herself, maybe I haven't actually awakened. Didn't the *Tibetan Book of the Dead* insist that one could not know one was alive? Consequently one might be dead. As if an idea had blown in from the chilly outdoors and seized her, Madame Realism seized upon the notion that she might have become the catalogue to the exhibition she hadn't found in her dream. Her immaterial dream world might have a life of its own. And Madame Realism could merely be the key to it. (She struggled between proposing herself as its analogue or homologue.) It made a strange kind of sense, that she was a catalogue to herself more than to anything else, and to her unconscious rather than the other way around. What she perceived and apprehended was necessarily and always in some way constitutive of herself. This wasn't exactly reassuring. But Madame Realism expected to view herself with alarm. She suspected some would grow complacent in her place.

In this new guise, Madame Realism could be a Beatrice or Virgil to any Dante in need of Faith or Reason. She was meant to enlighten and educate. She could be taken off the shelf, opened up, browsed through and absorbed; she could become well thumbed and might even become well regarded. Madame Realism pushed aside some of her words, set in Times Roman, to enter in spidery marks traces of her enduring skepticism. How seriously should she be taken? It was hard to think, as she had already been thought.

"That's just what Sylvie says," Bruno rejoined. "She says I wo'n't learn my lessons. And I tells her, over and over, I ca'n't learn 'em. And what do you think she says? She says 'It isn't ca'n't, it's wo'n't!'"

Focus, Madame Realism demanded of herself, concentrate. She couldn't find her reading glasses. Sometimes she misplaced things just to be able to find them again. She spent a certain amount of time every day searching for what she knew was there. Yet relief always arrived at the end of her search—her glasses, book, bag were precisely where she had left them. Still it bored her, going over and over the same territory. Perhaps I am looking for something else, she theorized, and by misplacing things I am actually displacing things, displacing what I think I know, the familiar. The way art does. She wrote invisibly in her margin: If art has a purpose, is it to point to the absence of invention?

But now she was a museum catalogue and the very territory she went over and over was her. In this form she would always be. "something that couldn't find its glasses." To others this would be a necessary part of Madame Realism's constitution. Where was her ambiguity to reside? Between her lines, or in her margins, which some might not even notice? To some, margins were nothing more than a frame for the center.

"One needn't be a Doctor," I said, "to take an interest in medical books. There's another class of readers, who are yet more deeply interested—" "You mean the Patients?" she interrupted.

She couldn't get her own measure; it was a matter of scale. from one point of view, she was small. From another, she was big. I am insignificant as well as important. Like Saint Peter, she was the rock upon which the Church was built, she was also ephemera. Many would throw her out. Some would save her. She could no longer adequately describe herself. She had been put in her place and had been transformed into a place. As a reference she was undeniably self-referential.

Madame Realism was puzzled (probably she was a puzzle). As she fretted, she knew her pages would become frayed. That, too, she feared, would be part of her forever. But she didn't know. There were so many things she didn't know and which remained incomprehensible to her. Even as a guide to herself, if that's what she was, she couldn't offer certainty. She could only suspend comprehension long enough to allow questions to rise to the surface, like cream on milk. For instance, was she a source or a resource?

At this Madame Realism's paragraphs shifted. Precis, dates, places and names jiggled about as if an acrobat were upsetting and resetting her type and throwing it into the air. Her pages fell out of order, and like Humpty Dumpty she didn't know whether she'd ever get back together again. It dawned on Madame Realism—in fact it was impressed on her that explanations were as complex as what they were meant to explain. Elementary, my dear Madame Realism, she exclaimed, laughing. She became optimistic. She could overflow with questions. She could be difficult. She could be not easy to follow. She could appear to be transparent and turn out to be opaque. She could even admit her influences—Lewis Carroll, for one. No one would doubt she was a construction. The exhibition in her dream—the art—could be herself. Wasn't she sometimes given to exhibitionism?

"So, either I've been dreaming about Sylvie," I said to myself, "and this is the reality. Or else I've really been with Sylvie, and this is a dream! Is Life itself a dream, I wonder?"

Dreams are wishes, dreams are wishes. This must be a wish, Madame Realism realized as she woke again. Was this the beginning of a new day, one she had to invent? I must want to be an ordinary catalogue. Part of me must have desires in that direction. I want to be cited, to be secure, helpful and clear. Yet I also don't want to be, since I am a continuation of many ideas including, what is the question? who asks? where is it? who decides? am I it? Madame Realism leaped out of bed.

Though alone in her apartment, with just the sound of steam rising through the pipes and radiators, Madame Realism glanced over her shoulder. Would History, or Fate, be standing there, ready to shake her to her very foundations? She felt weighed down by the past and the present. Madame Realism wished she could rise above her concerns, but more and more she knew she was her concerns. She didn't want to be buried beneath her own inchoate and unachievable hopes, like the desire for immortality. It was probably there, though, embarrassed and absurd, mocked and made irrelevant by death.

No longer a catalogue, if she had ever been one, Madame Realism walked to the window and opened the curtain. The sun was shining. She really wasn't sure what she was anymore. She hoped others would have a few ideas. To some extent, a work or text relied on the intelligence, the kindness, of strangers. Madame Realism smiled to herself and stared out the window. She was transfixed by the street's plenty, its wonderful ordinariness. "Ah, well!" the Gardener said with a kind of groan. "Things change so, here. Whenever I look again it's sure to be something else."

MADAME REALISM
IN FREUD'S DREAMLAND

After walking on the boardwalk at Coney Island, Madame Realism looked for shells on the beach. A medium-sized pale-orange shell seemed just right, and she clutched it happily in her hand. I could, she thought, start collecting these. They cost nothing and can be found on any beach. The search might take me around the world should I become avid. Of course, she worried, traveling costs a lot of money.

I don't have room to collect, Madame Realism decided, then dropped the orange shell onto the sand. Lying there, it seemed poignant, already forgotten. She turned to look at the beach-goers. In the background loomed the skeletonlike roller coaster. It was no longer in operation. Madame Realism remembered reading that Coney Island was the only place in the U.S. that interested Freud.

Freud must have visited Coney in its glory, about the time he delivered his lectures at Clark University, in 1909. Coney Island was then a model city of artificial miracles, of human experimentation. Luna Park, constructed in 1903, was meant to be like the surface of the moon and really out of this world. It held amusements such as the Circus, the German Village, the Great Train Robbery and the Tango (one rode in cars that moved as if they were tangoing). The park was a fantasy land, with minarets, towers and domes that by 1907 numbered 1,326.

Madame Realism thought it was probably Dreamland that most fascinated Freud. In Dreamland, one could visit the Canals of Venice, Fight the Flames, enter a japanese Teahouse, walk on the Steel Pier (which jutted half a mile into the Atlantic) and dance in the World's Largest Ballroom (25,000 square feet). There was also Lilliputia, the Midget City, where 300 midgets lived on display, as a "permanent experimental community," with their own parliament, beach, fire department, and unconventional behavior—80 percent of their children were born out of wedlock. Dreamland also offered the Incubator Building, where most of the premature babies of greater New York were brought and nursed, part of the spectacle of human life and scientific progress. In May 1911, Dreamland perished in flames in just three hours—it later became a parking lot. In 1914, Luna Park met a similar fiery death. Steeplechase Park remained, and in 1919 the Palace of Joy was built, but the miracle that was Coney Island seems to have lasted a short time.

Monuments to voyeurism and exhibitionism, Coney's houses of mirth, mayhem and curiosity may have been homes away from home for Freud, who could have produced magnificent associations from rides and spectacles, to obsessions and sessions, to neurotic displays and case histories. Or he may have viewed Coney Island as the place where his theories were enacted in theaters of pleasure and danger, instincts and their vicissitudes. Today Coney is a shell of its former self, Madame Realism thought, a hollow reminder of that glorious past. It could even be construed as a "found" exhibition. Buildings in various stages of dilapidation are festooned with faded signs announcing good times and cheap thrills which one can no longer have. At least not here, she thought. Coney Island was not salvaged and collected. Looking around, Madame Realism didn't conjure notions of pleasure but ones of death and loss, of what gets remembered and what gets thrown away.

THE CONEY ISLAND OF HIS MIND

Freud began to collect art and antiquities in December of 1896, two months after the death of his father. So, Madame Realism reflected, here are objects to replace the lost object. As she walked about the exhibition, in the SUNY Binghamton Art Museum, of a selection from Freud's collection, ideas of death hovered like a storm cloud: Freud's death in exile in London in 1939, his father's death, deaths of friends of hers. It was a strange feeling, an uncanny one, which the exhibition's title, "The Sigmund Freud Antiquities: Fragments from a Buried Past," did not dispel. In pristine glass cases or on white walls, nearly 100 objects were on display. These fragments from a buried past consisted mainly of small pieces of statuary, but also photographs, prints and books. What is buried is usually dead, Madame Realism knew, though one might fear being buried alive—one's body as well as one's work—and Freud the man was gone as were the civilizations he admired. Death and loss in the abstract, as well as Freud's response to his father's death, seemed to be a way to think about his collection and even collecting itself.

Madame Realism was drawn first to the objects Freud kept on his desk. She wished his desk were also in the room. On it, and in the room where he analyzed patients and meditated upon the causes of their problems, was a statue of Asklepios, the classical God of medicine mentioned in *The Interpretation of Dreams*. Freud must have found parallels to his theories in Asklepios' practice—a patient would visit Asklepios and be asked to go to sleep in order to "dream of remedies for his illness." Freud also kept on his desk a 19th-century Chinese table screen, of filigreed wood and jade, that was meant to aid scholarly contemplation. At the very center of these objects, in front of the screen, was Freud's treasured statue of Athena, a work Marie Bonaparte saved from the Nazis. Athena's breastplate is adorned by the decapitated head of Medusa, who represents, Freud wrote, castration. Freud's miniature Athena, goddess of wisdom and war, was a Roman copy from the 1st or 2nd century AD, after a Greek original of the 5th century BC.

Near Athena sat the statues of Osiris and Isis, looking resolute and sullen, Madame Realism decided. Osiris was the king murdered by his brother, who cut him into 14 parts and scattered him, or them. Isis, Osiris' wife and queen, collected the parts and reanimated them. Here the myth of Isis and Osiris could stand for not only the passion of the family, in this instance a bitter family romance, but also the collector and psychoanalyst Freud. He sought to put together the pieces of his patients' pasts. The objects that he collected, which existed in other contexts, might be reanimated, given new life in his home. Madame Realism looked over at Athena again and imagined Freud staring at her, too—this Athena is missing her spear. She saw him worrying about women.

Madame Realism was surprised that there were no representations of Oedipus and the Sphinx among his desk objects. There was something poignant to Madame Realism about Freud's writing to Wilhelm Fliess, his early collaborator, "I have found, in my own case too, being in love with my mother and jealous of my father, and I now consider it a universal event in early childhood." The punishment for this love was the threat of castration, so this spearless Athena, a castration surrogate, would certainly suffice, Madame Realism told herself.

Then she spied a Sphinx amulet on another table. Egyptian, late period, 716–332 BC, it was a very small piece—a lion's body with a human head. Close by, a larger statuette, a more womanly Sphinx, with wings and breasts (Greek, South Italian, late 5th-early 4th C. BC), preened mysteriously. In the Greek legend the Sphinx destroyed those who could not answer its riddle: "What walks on all fours in the morning, two in the afternoon, and three in the evening?" Oedipus answered correctly: "Man."

Madame Realism studied the Sphinx closely. Its composite body was like pieces of a puzzle that fit together but in an odd way—joined and disjointed, cohering but lacking coherence. It seemed appropriate that the Sphinx was sometimes female, sometimes male, and part animal or bird. Or both. Madame Realism realized its strange parts, though meshed, subtly forced a recognition of difference. In this peculiar creature or monster, there could only be an illusion of unity, since the Sphinx itself suggested the differences that are usually obscured. The sum of its parts is not a whole, Madame Realism thought. Even the question the Sphinx put to Oedipus was in parts, and so, Madame Realism speculated, the content of its question was like the Sphinx's body. And probably the answer—"Man"—must also be conceived of not as a unity but as representing parts: "Man"—fragmented, composed of differences, a collection. Is "Man" an answer or a question? Madame Realism fancied that she smiled inwardly, though she wondered whether a smile could be inside her body.

SUBSTITUTES FOR THE DEAD

What then caught her eye was a mummy's bandage. The piece of cloth was delicate and imprinted with pictures, hieroglyphics, which made it look like a strip of fragile, old 35mm film. A movie to enfold and protect the dead, Madame Realism mused, wondering if Freud liked movies. The pictures were vignettes from the *Book of the Dead*, and Freud's English edition of it, published in 1901 in London, was exhibited near the bandage. The *Book* contains spells and stories that the deceased were to take with them to the other world, to ease their way into the afterlife. Cold comfort, Madame Realism thought, which again brought to mind Coney Island, with its odd comforts. She wondered about Freud and what gave him solace.

When Madame Realism moved to another part of the room, small figures of Eros appeared before her eyes. They provided comic relief. She gazed at the winged and bow-and-arrowless cupids. Freud had at least six in his collection. Eros for him, she recited to herself, was the life instinct; Thanatos, the death instinct. There was no statue of Thanatos on display, but death seemed to dominate the exhibition. The "Mask from a Coffin" (Egyptian New Kingdom, 19th Dynasty, 1292–1190 BC), made of wood, gessoed and painted, was meant to be affixed to the lid of a coffin; the "Head of a Woman from a Relief" (Greek, Classical period, early 4th C. BC), a lovely face sculpted in marble, was, the catalogue explained, "very likely to have come from an Athenian grave relief"; a beautifully proportioned blown-glass jar, pale green and goldish brown, still held cremated bones (Roman, ca. 50–150 AD); and Freud's several Egyptian Shabti figures, tiny statues in the form of mummies, first appeared in tombs as substitutes for the dead—later they became deputies of the dead.

Substitutes for the dead, she thought. In his essay "Fetishism," Freud defined the fetish as "a substitute for the woman's (mother's) phallus which the little boy believed in and doesn't want to forgo." He theorized that the "horror of castration sets up a sort of permanent memorial to itself by creating this substitute.... It remains a token of triumph over the threat of castration and a safeguard against it."

Is this collection, or any collection, necessarily fetishistic? Collections of tokens and memorials.... Collecting always points to what is missing and has not been collected, or can't be found. Collecting, Madame Realism considered, must always represent the absence of something and the impossibility of entirely fulfilling one's desire. It would be impossible to make a collection that would hold all of everything within a particular taxonomy. One could collect something that was limited in number, but would that ever be truly satisfying to a collector, who most likely desires to continue looking for substitutes or tokens?

THE CHAOS OF MEMORIES

Madame Realism pictured her own desk, where there was no space for objects to gaze at as aids for contemplation, and her overburdened bookshelves, and the letters she couldn't throw out. She thought about Walter Benjamin's essay "Unpacking My Library: A Talk about Book Collecting." In it he wrote that "every passion borders on the chaotic, but the collector's passion borders on the chaos of memories." She remembered that Freud had written, in *Studies in Hysteria*, that "hysterics suffered mainly from reminiscences." Madame Realism didn't think that Freud's collecting ought to be considered an hysterical symptom, even though he started to do it after the death of his father, which was a traumatic event. In Freud's case, the death was an impetus, perhaps, to his collection, which he kept sealed up in cases, containers of "the chaos of memories." Then, she continued to herself, there were his case studies, the analysands, who might have matched in his mind, if not mimicked, the statuary in those cases.

In Benjamin's case the desire to collect started when his mother gave him "two albums with stick-in pictures which [she] pasted in as a child and which I inherited.... Actually inheritance is the soundest way of acquiring a collection." What Freud inherited from his father was the family Bible, which was also on display. The Philippson Bible, in German and Hebrew, was an unusual one for a jewish family to own, as it contained proscribed graven images—it is illustrated with Egyptian myths. The young Sigmund saw this Bible first when he was seven. Madame Realism imagined the child Freud as he studied the exotic pictures. She thought he must have been profoundly influenced—and moved—by them and the lost world they conveyed. Glancing up from the Bible, Madame Realism felt the Egyptian figures in the room nodding their agreement. She looked around the room again. It struck her that the majority of Freud's collection was fashioned and had existed in a world before Christ. The nonreligious Jew, Freud, who suffered like others of his faith from Christian antisemitism, had collected about him a pre-Christian world; it enveloped him in his library and office. Freud had, in a way, even invented a past or tradition for himself, one very different from that of his father and mother.

But, Madame Realism reminded herself, one does not want to make too much of biography. Identity is such a fragile thing, biography must necessarily be somewhat flimsy. One could think of certain facts, like the death of Freud's father and the impetus to collect, or Freud's Judaism, as fragments—the kind of fragments Freud himself collected of earlier civilizations. Within each fragment perhaps Freud saw ghosts, intimations of the past, as one does when thinking about specific facts and events in a person's life, imagining them in relation to the whole of that life. Freud compared the work of the psychoanalyst with that of the archeologist. In *Studies in Hysteria*, he wrote about the procedure of analysis as "one of clearing away psychogenetic material layer by layer, and we like to compare it with the technique of excavating a buried city." Freud wanted to dig up the past, to unbury torments, exhibit them and make them disappear or lose their power.

Madame Realism pondered another of Freud's figures of Isis (Egyptian, late period, 664–525 BC). Seated, made of bronze, she is suckling her child, Horus. They are stiff, severe figures, though, on closer inspection, Madame Realism saw that Isis touches her son's head with one hand and holds her breast with the other. The Egyptian dyad seemed not that dissimilar from Sienese depictions of the Madonna and Child from the Early Renaissance. With Isis holding her son Horus on her lap, the story had another character and chapter added to it. Following the death of Osiris—he was "restored" in the underworld after Isis collected his parts—Isis took refuge in the marshes, where she gave birth to their child and reared him in secret. A single mother, Madame Realism laughed to herself, using a locution that Freud wouldn't have known. She turned to a statue of the goddess Artemis, huntress and patroness of wild creatures (Greek, from the Hellenistic period, 2nd century BC). Freud's Artemis is made of terracotta; she's in hunting gear and shown in movement. Like his favorite Athena, Artemis represents an embodiment of the masculine in the feminine; one is goddess of war, as well as wisdom, the other is goddess of the hunt. Strong, beautiful, mythical women, neither of whom were mothers. Perhaps they hadn't wanted children.

THE UNCONSCIOUS NEVER TAKES A VACATION

What had Freud wanted, Madame Realism wondered, when he went out to collect? Collecting seems such a conscious activity, she thought, though the unconscious, which Freud discovered and named, is always lurking. In "Notes Upon a Case of Obsessional Neurosis," he wrote that "the unconscious is relatively unchangeable." A hard-boiled Madame Realism wrote in her notebook, "The unconscious never takes a vacation." She envisioned Freud, in his overcoat and hat, leaving his house at 19 Bergasse for a small vacation from work and walking less than a mile to Robert Lustig's shop Antike Kunst. This is where, the exhibition catalogue told her, Freud bought several hundred antiquities between the 1920s and '30s. With what excitement and sense of expectation did he approach this familiar store, passing so many familiar sights? He might find a new piece, something wonderful to add to his collection. He might embellish his collection—the catalogue says he liked to rearrange it—with something that represented the unchanging conflicts human beings faced.

In the gallery with his collection, Madame Realism found herself surrounded by Freud's "chaos of memories." The memories felt palpable, tangible, even burdensome. Each statue, book and vase was dizzying; so many stories and interpretations were congealed in a single object. The exhibition seemed to be a collection, or anthology, of stories; it was almost a tribute to narrative. Suddenly Madame Realism appreciated how keenly Freud loved narrative. Perhaps he was even in thrall to it. A friend told her that Freud didn't like to listen to music. That kind of abstraction didn't captivate him.

Like a novelist who amasses incidents and characters, through his collection Freud "wrote" a world around himself. His "writing" consisted of figures and pictures and bits of cloth that had tales to tell. The objects were like hieroglyphics; one wanted to read them, to learn their messages and know their meanings. Freud himself looked to words to explain flesh, even to become flesh, as they did, in a way, in the hysterics he analyzed. Perhaps without words and the stories words created, Freud felt a little lost. And then, Madame Realism thought, he looked for objects that were made of words. But did the objects represent the lost mother or father? Or do lost objects in the unconscious become like the Sphinx, neither this nor that, but collections of disparate parts?

Isis collected Osiris after his death, the Sphinx collects in its monstrous body fragmented "Man," and Freud collected objects from lost worlds and narratives from patients whose worlds were lost to them in the unconscious. Because it was Freud who collected the things in this exhibition, Madame Realism could produce vivid images, more associations than if she were visiting the Metropolitan Museum of Art and looking at its collection. It was as if Freud, who was a father to fantasy, had himself become a source for fantasy. Why would one be interested in his collection—he didn't collect "the best pieces"—if one were not ready to fantasize about him? Didn't this exhibition ask the spectator to enter into his mind, to partake of his fascination, his lover's discourse? The discourse was his theories, his discussions with patients, his lectures. His collection was a monument to that love, just as Coney Island was a monument to collective fantasy and desire, to voyeurism and exhibitionism.

FREUD AND MARILYN MONROE

When she got home, Madame Realism found a clipping from *People* magazine on a stack of papers. Marilyn Monroe's will was finally upheld by a New York court 75 percent would go to her acting teacher Lee Strasberg, 25 percent to her psychiatrist, Dr. Marianne Kris. Both are dead. Strasberg's widow, Anna, had been fighting the Anna Freud Centre in London, which inherited Kris' share, because Anna Strasberg said it was trying to commercialize Marilyn's name, by marketing Marilyn hairbrushes and the like. Madame Realism fantasized that Marilyn, in death, would be happy to learn that her money was supporting Freud's work. She would have loved its going to the Freud Museum at Maresfield Gardens in London, where his collection now lives. Freud spent the last year of his life there. He had fled Austria, to be in England where he could "die in freedom." Madame Realism was sure the tormented Marilyn would understand that desire completely.

THE MUSEUM OF HYPHENATED AMERICANS

> *One must beware of hindsight and stereotypes. More generally one must beware of the error that consists in judging distant epochs and places with the yardstick that prevails in the here and now, an error all the more difficult to avoid as the distance in space and time increases.*
>
> —Primo Levi, *The Drowned and the Saved*

Along with many others, Madame Realism waited for the ferry to the museum on Ellis Island. It was a New York kind of line: 12 abreast and chaotic. Would there be an anarchic rush when the boat came in? Something might happen, things could get crazy. While her own life was relatively stable—for now she had a roof over her head; she was healthy—the world in which Madame Realism lived was unpredictable and frightening. The dichotomy dismayed her.

Contradictory meanings overwhelmed the seemingly simple. A museum celebrating immigration to the U.S.—42 percent of all American citizens had a blood relative who went through Ellis Island—was, Madame Realism reflected, undeniably complex in its goals, nearly overwhelming. Immigration is, after all, central to an idea of America—melting pot, refuge, democracy—but the project of different peoples "melting" together to become one, one nation, was riven with conflict. Like a group marriage, Madame Realism thought.

While she waited, Madame Realism perused some guidebooks on the history of Ellis Island. The Ellis Island Immigrant Station was opened in 1892, the year after Congress passed the most restrictive U.S. immigration law to date, which enlarged the category of "undesirables" to polygamists, people with police records that involved "moral turpitude," and "all persons suffering from a loathsome or contagious disease." Previously, the individual states had been the arbiters of who might enter the U.S., but in 1881, the Supreme Court recommended that Congress exercise full authority over immigration. In 1882 the first federal immigration law was enacted. Since New York City was the primary port for most European shipping companies, the majority of immigrants arrived there.

It was odd, Madame Realism thought, that as soon as Ellis Island was established, the rate of immigration fell "dramatically, due to a cholera scare in 1892, a financial panic in 1893 and an economic depression of several years." World War I saw almost no immigration: after the war, the "Red Scare" produced new, more restrictive legislation. The Quota Act of 1924 limited the number of immigrants to 150,000 a year, with specific quotas for each nationality. By the 1930s, the Ellis Island Detention Center processed only "suspected enemy aliens, deportees, immigrants whose papers were not in order." Hardly used, it was closed in 1954.

The first time Madame Realism visited Ellis Island was in 1979, before its $157 million renovation. She had walked around a cavernous, almost empty and dilapidated building. Its walls were cracked, the paint peeling. Some of the benches upon which immigrants had sat were still there, reminiscent of a set from Ionesco's *The Chairs.* The space was both surreal and gothic. Madame Realism could easily imagine ghosts floating above, hovering near the dirty tile ceiling; and in the eerie silence, she wanted to hear fabled ancestors speak to one another. Instead, she heard the screeches of gulls flying over the island. The room where medical exams had been performed was particularly chilling; it was filthy. Evil-looking instruments, covered in dust, lay on wooden tables. A horror chamber, Madame Realism thought.

Like the crowd around her, the Ellis Island museum, which had opened on December 10, 1990, might hold surprises. She wondered how the building would look now and whether its ghosts would have vanished. There was something akin to palpable expectation in the air—a reporter might have proclaimed that "emotions ran high." Ellis Island might be a museum to and of emotions, a house of emotions. Nationality and birthplace—tribe and home—traditionally call up special attachments and longings. When these attachments are rudely broken, as they were—and are—for most immigrants, does the rupture become part of the memory of home, the new home as well as the old? The truism "some wounds never heal" occurred to Madame Realism. She glanced around to see if anyone looked wounded or raw.

Up ahead, a ferry pulled away from the dock, full of tourists, adventurers, family-tree researchers. Identity seekers? As she pondered her self, her elusive fictive self, and her desire to see the museum, a muscular black man sitting on a park bench leaped up and called for the line's attention. "I'm Alex," the man announced in a West Indian accent. "The next boat won't be here for 25 minutes, so relax, and we will entertain you."

An agile and strong acrobat, Alex juggled eggs and did push-ups standing on his hands. When he and his partner were about to do another feat, which he called the "Chinese connection by two black men," Madame Realism looked around again; not many faces were black or brown. African-Americans, the overwhelming majority descendants of a much earlier "migration" of Africans forced into this country and enslaved here, were barely in evidence; few waited for the boat to Ellis Island. A crack in the melting pot Madame Realism remembered that there was no museum to slavery in Washington, D.C., no national monument to mark an American tragedy that was mostly repressed. How could it be "celebrated"?

Madame Realism wondered if in 50 years there would be a museum to honor the newest immigrants. Now they fly into JFK or LAX, or drive or walk across the border from Mexico into Texas or California. If allowed. In her guidebook Madame Realism read that the McCarran-Walter Act, passed in 1952, was the primary law administered by the Immigration and Naturalization Service even today, though there had been "liberalizations." A quota system was still in effect. Back in the 1960s, for the first time, numerical limits were placed on "Western hemisphere" persons. Some recent African immigrants, who may have come in illegally—"illegals" are of course undocumented—were at the Battery selling watches out of attaché cases. Some others—Alex and his partner—were performing feats in front of her.

When the next ferry pulled in, Alex adroitly ended his performance. She wondered what his New York life was like—was it better or worse here? Was leaving home worth it? She imagined the scales of justice affixed to the top of an old courthouse. How can one weigh and measure someone else's subjective experience of home? And who can decide for another what struggle, which condition, is more painful, less hopeful?

On board the ferry, Madame Realism heard a mother tell her teenage daughter: "They were in steerage, they had to suffer to get here, and they suffered after, when they got here." It was certainly easy to get to the island now—though not easy for most people to emigrate to the U.S. still. Madame Realism decided she was not alone in making this type of comparison. After all, she said to herself as the ferry docked, the museum had to be about these kinds of comparisons and relationships. Walking down the gangplank, Madame Realism was immediately confronted by the restored building's new entrance, the already familiar version of postmodern archway. It partially obscured the original facade.

The late-19th century red-brick-and-limestone structure is "a premier example of the French Renaissance design period," one book told her. Its four spire-topped turrets looked to Madame Realism like German helmets from the Great War. It had been designed by Boring and Tilton, after the original Ellis Island building was destroyed by fire in 1897. With its red and white stripes, the building recalls first the mottled Duomo in Florence and then, because it looks carnivalesque, the amusement park at Coney Island, which was constructed around the same time. Carnivalesque brought to mind Bahktin and his work on carnival, as well as on the novel: Was the building a novel, or a container like a novel, with rooms like chapters, and immigrants the millions of characters filling its pages with many different voices, the heteroglossia that Bahktin theorized?

Madame Realism walked through the main entrance into a huge room, where she encountered the first installation "From Gateway to Museum." Large black-and-white photographs of immigrants hung above antique suitcases and steamer trunks which stretched across the floor. The display reminded her of the huge skeleton of a dinosaur in the entrance of the Museum of Natural History. The relationship seemed an imperfect equation: luggage=skeleton. The suitcases once carried the contents of human lives—clothes for bodies, objects used by bodies; the skeleton was the structure for a body, a prehistoric animal. Form and content, Madame Realism smiled to herself. But what was the content? The construction pointed to and represented the past—history—while history itself was simultaneously being constructed by it. It wasn't just that history was made at Ellis Island, Madame Realism told herself, it was that history was being made here, now.

Was one to imagine the immigrant carrying a piece of luggage through the entrance? Madame Realism felt she was being asked to identify instantly with images and objects. She became uneasy, even obstinate in the face of a particular kind of manipulation: the demand that she identify with historical figures and leap across space and time, to project oneself into a past she did not know. Which obscured the impossibility of bridging the gap between the past and the present. And it seemed to Madame Realism that trying to identify with an immigrant whose experience was a break from her or his past was doubly difficult, doubly impossible, precisely because of that break.

Crowds of eager people wandered about; there were many exhibits to see. Madame Realism experienced the disorientation she normally did when in such an institution. She wished that museums would choose just a few relics of the past, cite just a few statistics, so that one could actually take it all in. It was as if you were being served an enormous meal, in many courses, each tasty and good, so you wanted to eat everything but couldn't because there was yet another course, and how dare you leave so much on your plate?

Madame Realism found a map at the information desk and trudged up to the second floor. Beginnings are the hardest part, she told herself; once you begin things become easier. But endings are also very difficult. She wrote in her notebook: Beware of premature closure. Madame Realism was thinking ahead, hoping to remember, assemble and organize data in a particular way. Weren't museums like that? Am I the muse of my own museum? she asked herself.

On the second floor is the vast Registry Room, where the immigrants had once waited for their fates to be revealed. Refurbished, it looks more like Grand Central Station than a ghostly hall filled with spirits. According to the map, at all four corners were exhibitions, and Madame Realism walked west to "Through America's Gate." She passed through hallways which retained their original white tile walls. The tile was sometimes pockmarked and chipped or scarred. Off these hallways were various rooms, mazelike in effect, which displayed documentation of the immigrant's experience on Ellis Island and detailed what steps he or she had had to take to enter the U.S.

In the small interlocking rooms, so interwoven it was hard for Madame Realism to remember where she began or where to go next, each station of the immigrant's Via Dolorosa was presented in images, objects, and words—many words. Often they were the words of the immigrants themselves, on audiotape recordings that filled the rooms with a cacophony of differently accented voices. A novel's many voices, Madame Realism thought again. In addition to their voices was Madame Realism's—she was speaking into her tape recorder, hoping to capture, with something like immediacy, some of what she was viewing and some of what was written in the many captions. She noticed that several of the other visitors found this peculiar, even suspicious, behavior. And seeing this she felt, in her own way, suspect. But wasn't she merely trying to be her own narrator?

Madame Realism proceeded through the maze. She entered a room called "Isle of Hope/Isle of Tears" and looked at photographs of immigrants in groups, some of whom were called "the excluded" or "deportees." Madame Realism learned that if one traveled first or second class, not in steerage, one avoided Ellis Island altogether and disembarked somewhere else. With money one was considered fit to enter, physically and mentally. Madame Realism whispered: "Ellis Island had a dual reputation among immigrant groups, the anxiety over detention and inspection often caused emotional scenes; to the unfortunate two percent who were sent back, Ellis Island was a bitter Isle of Tears. Two percent translated into over 1000 exclusions a month."

One exhibit presented a heavy sheet of glass on which the words "Excluded," "Temporarily Detained," "Appeal Dismissed" and "Deported" were imprinted. A placard read: "Reasons for detention: SILPC—Special Inquiry Likely to become a Public

Charge…an immigrant had to convince a Board of Special Inquiry of his or her ability to earn a living and stay off the public dole…." To re-create "detention," a wire fence was placed in front of a life-size photograph of immigrants.

Madame Realism wandered into a room titled "The Immigrant Aid Societies," which displayed a large photograph of men being guided to the labor office of the Society for the Protection of Italian Immigrants: "Immigrants were easy prey for unscrupulous labor brokers… Aid societies tried to protect new arrivals from these predators who prowled the Battery looking for recruits…." In "Medical Care" there were certificates of birth and death and a picture of the hospital staff: "[The hospital] is at once a maternity ward and an insane asylum."

All the immigrants were given physicals; but before the medical exam proper, if the immigrant was found to be winded walking up the stairs, it signaled a problem to the health workers in attendance. These immigrants were marked with a chalk letter. Like the scarlet A emblazoned on Hester Prynne's bosom, Madame Realism thought dramatically. Except the mark went on their shoulders. And they didn't know what it meant

Madame Realism studied a picture, *Last Honors to Bunny*, which had been used as an intelligence test. A Norman Rockwell kind of image of several American children standing around a dead rabbit, *Bunny* was shown to immigrants, many of whom regularly killed and ate rabbits at home. Some projected their own experience into it and understood the image to mean that the children had killed the rabbit. But what the investigators wanted them to "understand" was that the children were giving their pet bunny a funeral. Whose intelligence was being tested?

Madame Realism put away the tape recorder and walked upstairs, to the third floor, where the exhibition rooms were off a balcony that formed the perimeter of the floor. She discovered in the space indicated on the map as "Changing Exhibits" a temporary show celebrating the workers of the INS, "The Immigration and Naturalization Service, 1891–1991—A Century of Service to a Nation of Immigrants." She took a brochure. "Immigration law and policy must change in response to changing American and world circumstances. It is a theme that will forever be a part of our history." This show was probably conceived according to the reality—not the pleasure—principle, Madame Realism mused. An unremarkable presentation of the stalwart men and women of the INS, it was definitely meant to express realpolitik. After all, the INS still determines the status of a political refugee, bestowing sanctuary or not, and decides the "acceptability" of persons with HIV infection, permitting entry or not. (Not, in the case of HIV.) And not all political unrest is equal in the eyes of U.S. foreign policy, no doubt due to those "changing American and world circumstances" the brochure had noted. The job of the INS is as much to keep people out as to let them in. Ironic, Madame Realism thought. In the midst of a permanent celebration of Ellis Island as "gateway," a fleeting celebration for the bouncers at the gateway. Madame Realism remembered John Adams' remark that "the spirit of liberty spread where it was not intended." And what, Madame Realism asked herself, did it mean to become "naturalized" anyway?

On the other side of the balcony, Madame Realism viewed a restored Ellis Island dormitory room—grim and gray, with triple-decker steel bunk beds. Then, walking east, she arrived at

"Treasures from Home." In large glass cases, according to nationality, were clothes, bedclothes, decorations, and utensils that immigrants had brought with them to America, which might once have been crammed inside those battered steamer trunks and pieces of luggage downstairs. Except, Madame Realism reconsidered, everything was in extremely good shape. Like treasures. Like art. The clothes from many nations—"The Family of Clothes," she jotted down quickly—abounded in rich national differences and evoked other and past worlds. The worlds were as different from one another as these cases and their contents were from the monochromatic dormitory reconstruction she'd just seen. Madame Realism watched people as they gazed wistfully, even longingly, at the colorful costumes and household dishes. She wrote: Back to the future again or forward to the past. Access in representation only.

Madame Realism returned to the main first-floor exhibition, which she'd saved for last. Information, statistics, and demographics awaited in a huge room entitled "The Peopling of America." Charts and maps showed the population growth of the U.S. and the movement of various groups to and within the U.S. Rods of different sizes and colors indicated the numbers and kinds of immigrants within 20-year periods. The years 1900–1920 towered above all, followed by 1880–1900. Changing demographics were indicated, with Asian and Latin American immigrants dominating 1980–2000. The latest wave of immigration, Madame Realism learned, is expected to exceed even the previous record set in 1900–1920. No premature closure, she reminded herself. But would the new immigrants be valorized as American heroes the way the "Ellis Island immigrant" was in this museum? Would they become a permanent part of the idea of America?

Madame Realism was attracted to a large globe dotted with electric lights which tracked worldwide migration patterns—"Millions on the Move." But then she was distracted by a crowd that had formed in front of a big map of the U.S. It provided information about the dispersal of ethnic groups across the U.S. and called for audience participation. If you pressed the appropriate button for "Polish," for example, the map lit up, and in each state appeared the number of Polish-Americans currently living there. Some non-Iraqi schoolchildren pushed the button for Iraq—an effect of the Gulf War. But for the most part it looked as if Chinese-Americans pushed the button for Chinese, Romanian-Americans for Romanian, Italian-Americans for Italian and so on. There were oohs and aahs at the numbers, whether large or small. Madame Realism could have stayed there all day, watching people push buttons to see their group's numbers light up across the states. When people push "their" buttons, what are they trying to find out—how many of "them" there are? But what does that really mean to them? She stared at the map and a large hyphen seemed to light up in front of her eyes. What does it mean to be hyphenated?

Reluctantly Madame Realism moved on to another display. It wasn't electronic or three-dimensional; it was a sober, plain board with charts. On one side was "Forced Migration: The Atlantic Slave Trade." From 1700 to 1810 (though the slave trade was under way since the 1500s), "an estimated 6,000,000 Africans were enslaved and transported to cultivate cash crops—sugarcane, tobacco, indigo, later cotton.... North America imported less than 6 percent of the slaves, the rest going to

Brazil, Central America and the Caribbean." Six percent of 6,000,000 is 360,000 individuals who were violently separated from home and families, whose children were born to slavery. Madame Realism remembered Harriet Jacobs' extraordinary book, *Incidents in the Life of a Slave Girl.* She stared at the board. Hadn't there recently been a controversy about a professor of American civilization who insisted to his college class that there had been no accounts written by slaves?

On the panel's flip side was "Settlers, Servants, Slaves: 1620–1780." It was estimated that before 1710, "75 percent of white migrants were indentured servants." In other words, the majority of Europeans who arrived in America during that time were bonded into a form of slavery. A little farther away was a "First Americans" map, showing the distribution of 200 American Indian tribes: "Contact with Europeans brought disease, warfare, removal to reservations and destruction of traditional ways of life." The Native American population in 1500 was 5 million; in 1900 it was 250,000. All three exhibits were similar—no flash. Major parts of U.S. history, but nothing to put in lights; this past didn't lend itself to crowd-pleasing treatments in a theme park. National theme park, Madame Realism noted.

In the rear of the hall was an imposing U.S. flag made up of red, white and blue squares. When viewed from an angle, the colored squares changed into hundreds of faces of U.S. citizens, emphasizing the variety of ethnicities in the nation. To Madame Realism, "The Flag of Faces" was disconcerting; it turned people's faces into a flag. It wasn't exactly wrapping oneself in the flag, but it played on that. What does it mean to be part of a flag? Or part of a larger image—the big picture? And more, Madame Realism thought as she looked around the hall, what does love of country mean? Had the flag become identical with unconditional love? Madame Realism often considered that the strongest love was the most ambivalent. But does a symbol like a flag allow for ambivalence? What would a flag celebrating ambivalence look like? She recalled Malcolm X's words: "You can't hate your origin and not end up hating yourself."

Surfeited with statistics, facts, maps, globes, faces, dates, Madame Realism looked for the exit; there she noticed for the first time a sign for "The Peopling of America." "Statistics sometimes lack consistency and must be read in a critical light," it said. "Statistics...reflect changing attitudes about race, ethnicity and national identities.... There are no statistics on undocumented immigrants, even though in recent years they may have outnumbered the documented ones." Madame Realism started to wonder if she had visited two or three separate Ellis Island museums, so different were the approaches in it. This museum suggested as many reasons for division (wealth, class, race, forced or voluntary entry, for instance) as for unity (like economic opportunity, the desire for refuge, the wish for freedom from a greater servitude). Was this museum not only a house of national identities and emotions but also of contradictions?

Madame Realism felt split. The pictures of immigrants, relics, diaries, costumes, voices were the emotive engine of the museum; "The Peopling of America" was its mind, the control center. The brain. But, she reminded herself, hadn't the psychoanalyst D.W. Winnicott theorized that the mind was not just in the brain but all over the body?

The meal the museum had served up in many courses was curiously unsatisfying to Madame Realism. In a way the old, unreconstructed Ellis Island building had more profoundly impressed upon her the trauma of separation from home and entry into an unknown. There was something disturbing about the glut of information and the number of clever displays. Madame Realism shook her head from side to side. Perhaps the memories of trauma had had to be erased, or effaced, as quickly as they were memorialized and converted into the faraway past. Or the rupture had had to be covered over, disguised with mementoes and re-creations, the way the museum's new archway obscured the original facade.

Madame Realism walked outside, to get some air. Lots of people were milling about the Honor Wall of Names. Like the Vietnam Memorial, it is a wall of remembrance, a list of names, though this one is low to the ground and the names are etched in copper, not carved in granite. The view behind it, the background, was terrific—New York skyline, greenish gray water, ships coming and going. People were eagerly searching for their ancestors' names. But only if someone had paid $100 did the family name appear, which is very unlike the Vietnam Memorial. To be on that, Madame Realism thought, you just had to die for your country.

Suddenly Madame Realism was hungry; perhaps it was the sea air. The museum souvenir store was next to the cafeteria; Madame Realism bought postcards and another guidebook to the Ellis Island Museum, to read while eating. Under "visitor services," her eye alighted on "dining"; it listed "a cafe [that] serves American and ethnic food." But surely, Madame Realism thought, American food is ethnic food. What could American food be otherwise? Wouldn't a cheese sandwich be half-English for the Earl of Sandwich and half-Dutch, for the "kaas" or cheese? There was that hyphen again. This went to the heart—or perhaps the stomach—of one of the problems in determining the meaning of Ellis Island, with its emphasis on the "melting pot" of America and its underscoring of difference and unity. Was an American a hyphenated American or were all Americans just American? It occurred to Madame Realism that the museum and its exhibitions were as complex and contradictory as the object on exhibit—America seen through the lens of immigration.

It was late. After getting off the ferry at the Battery, Madame Realism caught a cab, which was driven by an African man who engaged her in conversation. He told her that he had learned prejudice in the U.S. He said he had never experienced racism in Ghana, his home. After a while, Madame Realism asked if he knew about the watches; why were watches, only watches, being sold out of attaché cases at the Battery? Madame Realism couldn't entirely resist, in her dioramalike mind, her playground, the verbal slide from history and time to briefcases and timepieces. The Ghanaian driver told her the watches were sold by the Senegalese. He said, "The Senegalese are lazy. They don't want to work. It's the same in Africa." More divisions and complications. That night Madame Realism dreamed of people climbing up and falling off ladders.

MADAME REALISM'S "1999"

It's a weird custom, seeing in the new year carrying around a pig. Madame Realism wasn't sure where it originated. Some say in the south of England before the Saxons invaded. According to tradition, a young pig is placed on a round table in the center of a room. At midnight, a handkerchief or scarf is dropped over the pig's eyes, symbolic of the wish that fortune in the coming year, like justice, be blind. Then everyone sings *Auld Lang Syne.* Pranksters change the words to acknowledge the pig. "Should old acquaintance be forgot, in the days of auld lang syne, should old acquaintance be forgot, in the days when swine were swine. We'll drink a cup of kindness, dear, in the days of auld lang syne."

When swine were swine, swine were swine, swine in 1999, swine in 999, swine throughout time. Madame Realism walked into the bar and pushed through the dancing crowd to a table not far from the one on which the young pig lay. Did everyone identify with the pig? Madame Realism was never certain what to expect.

"Expect the unexpected," her friend Ameena had advised months before, "and remember what Nostradamus prophesied: 'The year 1999, seven months, from the sky will come / a great

King of Terror: To bring back to life the great King of the Mongols, / Before and after Mars to reign by good luck.'" Expect the unexpected, Madame Realism repeated, laughing. And even though Madame Realism didn't believe in prophesy, she went to the library and looked up Nostradamus. That night she telephoned Ameena and asked, "How can he have predicted that and also that the world would end in 1996?" Ameena said, "You depend on reason." Madame Realism pondered that and replied, "I believe that Tertullian was right: 'It is certain because it is impossible.' But," she added, "I also believe the reverse is true: It is uncertain because it is possible." Madame Realism hoped Ameena would be at the party.

From across the room, the party's host, Kai, waved excitedly to her. He was the son of an African-American man, a soldier, and a Vietnamese woman, a bargirl, as she was called then. Kai had been born in Saigon during the war in Vietnam, which hardly anyone remembered except as movies about the loss of masculinity and national pride, shown on TV especially on Veteran's Day. It was like Kai to have chosen a neighborhood bar, which was known for its "territorial defensiveness," as Kai's friend, Eiko, put it, its emphasis on "small-group identity." Kai loved the poignance and irony of this quaint place, with its horseshoe-shaped bar, wooden tables, and Art Deco light fixtures. His guests had been invited to wear costumes, as if it were Hallowe'en. Kai and Eiko wore masks and were made up defensively, something like camouflage or obstacles.

Madame Realism had vacillated between dressing as a vestige or a ruin. Miming partial poses and ruinous expressions, she had rehearsed the unrehearsable. Perplexed, she even placed a chunk of concrete on her shoulder and secured it to her neck with rope. A ball and chain. That's the way history is, she reflected. But did she want to spend this coming New Year's Eve so burdened? As if one weren't burdened enough by attempting to distinguish the true new from the old new. After all, at the beginning of the 20th century, the Futurists had named and colonized the new, and nothing could be new that wasn't modern, and we weren't modern anymore, were we?

Instead Madame Realism outfitted herself as a Gypsy, her idea of one. Long ago Gypsies were supposed to have migrated from India. To Madame Realism the modern was inexorably connected to the nation state, but Gypsies, as far as she knew, had never agitated for their own. And now that the nation state was simultaneously on the rise and in collapse, the history of the Gypsies, in a sense, suggested past and future, before and after. Madame Realism knew she couldn't ever adequately explain this.

Prince's song *1999* was playing on the laser box. Whatever happened to him? she wondered as she watched Kai pat the pig. *1999* was popular when? 1984, 1985? "Tonight I'm going to party like it's 1999." 1999 had been like *1999*. Would 2001 be like *2001*? Madame Realism remembered that way back in the Sixties preparation had begun for the new millenium with *Space Odyssey: 2001*. And even in the middle of a noisy party, Madame Realism could recall the voice of *2001*'s computer, Hal. It was similar to an echo or an aural aura, something usually associated with epileptic seizures or migraines.

Memory was a game Madame Realism enjoyed. She was indifferent to virtual reality and surrogate travel. When she watched television, she didn't want to interact; she wanted to disappear into the screen. When Madame Realism traveled, she didn't want to project herself there before she left home. She hoped to get lost, to lose herself. The uncharted pleasures—mystery, oblivion, abandon—could never be mapped. Or could they?

"Absurd," Dorothy shouted to Madame Realism, "we are bordering on the absurb, irrelevance. Borders invite transgression, and religion's a border, don't you think?" She was a globe festooned with hot spots and religious symbols. It was awkward for Dorothy to move. Hard to think, Madame Realism thought. The two women studied the partygoers. John stood out—he was simulating extinction. "Look at Uncle Desmond," Dorothy urged, "in a Thirties outfit."

Uncle Desmond was resplendent in a threadbare tuxedo. Everyone called him uncle, though he was no one's uncle that Madame Realism knew. Uncle suited him; he was amiable and insistendy old-fashioned, which was a ruse, Madame Realism was sure. He was not a traditionalist yet he followed the pig ritual to the letter. In fact he had brought the pig. Madame Realism gazed at Uncle Desmond, now stroking the pig fondly. What would happen to the pig later? Imagine, she caught herself, worrying about a pig's future at the start of the year 2000.

Madame Realism tugged at her Gypsy costume, concerned that she or it would be misunderstood. She had once attempted to dress as a man and in that outfit hadn't recognized herself. Stymied, she came to realize that the greatest source of misrecognition and misapprehension resided in oneself. The sardonic pianist and wit, Oscar Levant, she read, once quipped when asked about playing himself in a movie: "I was miscast." It was probably Levant upon whom Uncle Desmond had modeled himself.

There was scarcely the right word to characterize Desmond, not one in her limited repertoire. Parodic, Roberto offered—he was dressed as a fan. Desmond was enigmatic, inaccessible.

Remote, Madame Realism decided, and already removed. Desmond had never set out to change the world. To life his response had been—just get on with it. Roll the dice. Shuffle the deck. Play your hand. Grab a few laughs. That's all you can expect. He wasn't easy to talk to. But no one really tried to talk to him tonight.

No one could talk tonight, not tonight. The future was inarticulate, inarticulable, dumb. Unspeakable desire longed for a wanton night. It demanded a wild, long night, a night to erase all other nights, an urgent night to end it all—the century, the millenium. A night to remember, and one to forget. You wanted to have been there and not to have been, just for the experience. "Like the sinking of the Titanic," Madame Realism whispered to Uncle Desmond, who grinned historically. It was almost midnight.

"Now, now," he murmured, to himself or to the pig, "now, now." And very gently he dropped the handkerchief over the eyes of the trembling animal. "Now it's time. It's over."

Madame Realism knew Uncle Desmond would not be remembered. His greatest inventions were practical jokes, a lost art. Practical jokers concocted elaborate plans to fool friends. During the Forties, Desmond and his crowd lived in cheap hotels; the desk clerk was often the inadvertent bearer of the joke. Once a Mr. Jello telephoned Mr. Riley every afternoon for a month and left a message: "Mr. Jello called." Every evening Riley complained—at this very bar—"Jello phoned again." No one ever let on. At the end of the month, Riley returned to his hotel. There was no message, which he'd come to expect. But when he got to his room, he discovered that his bathtub was filled with jell-O. Who would record that?

Auld Lang Syne was sung. People kissed and hugged and worried about catching something. Madame Realism wondered if this was Uncle Desmond's long good-bye, his swan song. Or, she brightened, swine song.

January 10, 2000: Can't decide whether to say two thousand or twenty hundred. Kai told me that in the Fifties Jell-O company was advised that its ads showing complicated molded shapes made consumers feel inferior. Tacked Dorothy's photograph of Desmond, pig, me, on wall. Might mean anything. Could suspect D. of bestiality or imagine he was about to kill pig. New photoelectronics computer process supposed to reveal thoughts at moment photo shoot. Called image busting. Don't believe D. would be be revealed. Can past (or future) be seen through present lens? Can present? My costume, no doubt, a dismal failure.

LUST FOR LOSS

What gives value to travel is fear.... This is the most obvious benefit of travel.

— Albert Camus

Though she didn't really like to travel, Madame Realism often wanted to be someplace other than home. Travel caters to the uncanny, to impulse and serendipity, and Madame Realism took chances. She gambled away some of the time allotted to her in life, and defiantly, almost wantonly, acknowledged and nurtured a craving to wreck her own schedule and daily routine. I am my own homewrecker; it is one of my freedoms, she told herself.

To Madame Realism the self-inflicted habits of a typical day were no comfort. She disliked the idea of a typical day. Though habits afford a reliable sanity, Madame Realism resented her own customs. She even resisted them, as if they were the amorous advances of a former lover. Easy, but who needs it, she thought. I'd rather be sitting on a crowded train, next to smokers, living dangerously.

Tainted by wanderlust, resigned to a permanent tourism, Madame Realism plotted journeys she might take. She indulged a fantasy, like envisioning a movie she longed to see, then set it into motion, which was akin to that movie appearing on the screen. First there was a desired setting and then there was an outcome, a reality—a hotel, a museum, an avenue, a beach, a cafe—all of which she'd conjured before. After all, Madame Realism mused, when you're watching a movie, it's your reality.

But she suffered the pangs of most thrillseekers—she hated departures. After one particularly lugubrious leave taking, she observed that train stations and airports were, like graveyards, watering holes for the sentimental. Or the mournful. She suspected that people who hung around might be waiting for no one or nothing but a good cry. There were always reasons to cry, she knew, but not as many places to cry as reasons.

I like it when I don't know where I am, or why, but it also terrifies me, she admitted to herself. Madame Realism was taking off, running away, going on a vacation or just roaming. Her destination was the coast of Normandy. She was curious about World War ll—she was definitely a postwar character—and had, if not a valid reason to be there, a valid passport. With it and money, she could get out of town. But just as she was suspicious of the reasons for following a routine, she was suspicious of the reasons for disrupting it.

Unsettled by her own vagueness, Madame Realism threw a bottle of aspirin into a bag. She tossed in another pair of underpants, too. The black silk underpants were an afterthought, a last-minute decision. Maybe all my decisions are, she worried, then closed her suitcase. She hummed an ancient tune: "Pack up your troubles in your old kit bag..." And do something. But she couldn't remember the lyrics. And what is a kit bag? She hesitated and cast last-minute glances about the room.

Madame Realism couldn't know what lurked around the corner, at home or abroad. From reading travel books and maps, from studying histories of particular locations, she could plan a course of action. But actually she yearned to be out of control in a place where she didn't know a soul. It's better to be a cliché, a reprehensible image, than not to venture forth, not to take a risk, she contended as she walked out of her apartment. Madame Realism might be both Sancho Panza and Don Quixote. She might also be their horse.

After having been asked by an airline representative if anyone had packed for her, if she was carrying a gift from a stranger, if she had left her suitcase unattended, Madame Realism boarded the plane, settled into a seat, and nervously considered, as the jet shot into the sky, what a first-minute decision might be. A decision of the first order. A crucial, life and death decision, which would certainly be made during war. That's why I'm going to Normandy, she concluded. To be alive in a place haunted by death and by great decisions. If that was true, if that was her motivation, Madame Realism felt even more peculiar and unreasonable.

What explains this mass mania / to leave Pennsylvania?
— Noel Coward

In a hotel not far from the beach, Madame Realism was standing on a small balcony. She was gazing out at the sea. Large, white cumulus clouds dotted the blue sky. The Channel changed from rough to smooth in a matter of hours. She found herself watching the rise and fall of the waves, the rush and reluctance of the tides, with fascination or dread. Or concern. Which characterization was most true she was not sure. Truth was so difficult to be told, small and big truths, she could never tell it completely. Much as she might try, she couldn't even adequately define the weird anguish she experienced at the sight of the placid stretch of beach that touched the sea. The five beaches of Operation Overlord—Juno, Omaha, Sword, Gold, Utah. She had memorized their wartime names. The code names intrigued her, codes always did.

The light blue water—maybe it was more green than blue—grew progressively darker as it left the shore. The sea was always mysterious, ever more so with depth. Unfathomable, she reminded herself, the way the past is as it becomes more distant and unreadable with every day, every day a day further away from the present or the past, depending upon the direction from which one is thinking. But is something that is regularly described as a mystery, like the ocean, like history, mysterious?

Puzzled, Madame Realism was never less contemporary than when she traveled. Each journey was the fulfillment of a desire, and desire is always an old story. Like everyone else's, Madame Realism's desires were born and bred in an intransigent past. Even if she imagined herself untethered as she flew away, she was tied. When she journeyed to an historic site especially, she kept a date with history. And when she trafficked in history, she was an antique. At least she became her age or recognized herself in an age.

Spread on the bed were histories and tourist brochures of the region. Military strategy appealed to her; secretly she would have liked to have been privy to the goings on in one of the D-Day war rooms. But there hadn't been any women in them. I'd have to rent a war room of my own, she laughed, and then recollected, in a rapid series of images, the war movies she'd consumed all her life—*Waterloo Bridge, The Best Years of Our Lives, The Longest Day, The Dirty Dozen.* Celluloid women waited and worried about men. They were nurses, wives, secretaries. Sometimes they drove ambulances, sometimes they spied. They grieved, they loved. Madame Realism learned from a TV program that the first woman to land on the Normandy beachhead at Omaha was an American named Mabel Stover, of the Women's Army Corps. Mabel Stover, earnest and robust, appeared on the program, exhorting World War II veterans to contribute money to a U.S. memorial, a "Wall of Liberty." "Your name belongs on this wall," she exclaimed. "It's your wall. Go for it, guys and gals."

> *You receive unforgettable impressions of a world in which there is not a square centimeter of soil that has not been torn up by grenades and advertisements.*
>
> — Karl Kraus

Early the next morning, restless and sleepless, Madame Realism left the hotel and went for a walk on the beach. There was hardly anyone around. The sea was choppy. With each barefoot step on the sand—the tide was out—Madame Realism concocted a battle story: Here a man had fallen. He broke his leg, he struggled, and a soldier he never saw before helped him, then he was shot. Both were shot, but both lived, somehow. Or, here someone died. But without pain, a bullet to the brain. Or, here a soldier was brave and sacrificed himself for another, but lived. They both lived. Or, here a man found cover and threw a grenade that knocked out an enemy position. Or, here someone was terrified, sick with fear, and could not go on.

At the phrase "sick with fear," Madame Realism kicked her foot in the sand and uncovered a cigarette butt. She wondered how long it had been buried. It was trivial to contemplate in a place like this, even absurd. But I can't always control what I think, she thought.

Madame Realism jarred herself with vivid images of thousands of soldiers rushing forward on the beach. She thought about the men who had been horribly seasick in the boats that carried them to shore. On D-Day, years ago, the weather was bad and the sea was rough. Madame Realism looked again at the water and toward the horizon. Imagine being sick to your guts and being part of the greatest armada in history, imagine being aware that you were making history in the moment it was happening, imagine having the kind of anonymous enemy who is determined to kill you—or being a terrifying enemy yourself. In the next moment she scolded herself: If you're throwing up over the side of a boat or scared to death, you're not thinking about history. You're just trying to stay alive.

At the horizon the sea was severed from the sky, or it met the sky and drew a line. As she did when she was a child, Madame Realism speculated about what she could not see, could never see, beyond that line, that severe border. She squinted her eyes and stood on her toes, hoping to see farther. It was impossible to know how far she actually saw. Still, she lingered and meditated upon the uncanny meeting of water and air, how it was and wasn't a meeting, how the touch of the air on the sea wasn't like the touch of a hand to a brow, or a mouth to a breast. It wasn't a touch at all. Just another pathetic fallacy. The sky doesn't kiss the sea. Jimi Hendrix must have been wildly in love or high when he wrote that line, "'scuse me while I kiss the sky."

Madame Realism licked her lips and tasted the salt on them. She loved that. She always felt very much alive near the ocean. She breathed in deeply. It was strange to be alive, always, but stranger to feel invigorated and happy in a place where there had been a battle, a life and death struggle. Maybe it wasn't weird, she consoled herself. Maybe it's like wanting to have wild sex right after someone dies.

Life wants to live, a friend once told her. Especially, Madame Realism thought, digging her toes into the sand, in a place where it was sacrificed. Death wasn't defeated here, but victory transformed it. That was the hope, anyway. Hope disconcerted Madame Realism. It was just the other side, the sweet side, of despair.

The soldiers landing, the planes dropping bombs, the guns shooting, the chaos, the soldiers scrambling for safety—she could envision it. But an awful gap split her comprehension in half, much like the sea was divided from the sky. It split then from now, actuality from memory, witnesses from visitors.

From time to time, Madame Realism forgot herself, but she was also conscious of being in the present. She was aware that time was passing as she reflected on time past. But even if she had not lived through it, the war lived through her. She was one of its beneficiaries; it was incontrovertible, and this was her war as much or even more than Vietnam.

Of course, she told herself, it's odd to be here. The past doesn't exist as a file in a computer, easy to call up, manage and engage. We can't lose it, though we are, in a sense, lost to it or lost in it. But was WWII being lost every day? she wondered. Everything was changing and had changed. The former Yugoslavia, the former Soviet Union, a reunified Germany. She recalled Kohl and Reagan's bitter visit to Bitburg. Was the end of the Cold War a return to the beginning of the century and an undoing of both world wars? It wasn't cold now, but Madame Realism trembled. Once history holds your hand, it never lets go. But it has an anxious grip and takes you places you couldn't expect.

And the wall of old corpses. / I love them. / I love them like history.
— Sylvia Plath

Suddenly Madame Realism realized that there were many people around her, speaking many different languages. Tourists, just like her. She shrugged and marched on. I go looking for loss and I always find it, she muttered to herself, a little lonely in the crowd. She reached Omaha beach and the enormous U.S. cemetery. The rows and rows of gravestones were rebukes to the living. That's precisely what entered her mind—rebukes to the living. She shook her head to dislodge the idea. Now, instead of rebuke, a substitute image, sense or sensation—all the graves were reassurances, and the cemetery was a gigantic savings bank with thousands of tombstonelike savings cards. Everyone who died had paid in to the system and those who visited were assured they'd received their money's worth. That's really crazy, she chastised herself. Over seven thousand U.S. soldiers were buried in this cemetery, and Madame Realism knew not a soul. But what if the tombstones were debts, claims against the living?

"I'd rather be," WC. Fields had carved on his tombstone, "living in Philadelphia." Sacreligious to the end, Fields was outrageous in death. And surrounded by thousands of white tombstones, Madame Realism was overwhelmed by the outrageousness of death itself. But since she was only a visitor to it, death was eerily, gravely, reassuring. Madame Realism looked at the dumb blue sky and away from the aching slabs of marble. But when she reluctantly faced them again, they had become, for her, monuments that wanted to talk. They wanted to speak to her of small events of devotion, fearlessness, selflessness, sacrifice.

Markers of absence, of consequence, of heartbreak, of loss, each was whispering, each had a story to tell and a silenced narrator. Madame Realism was astonished to be in a ghost story, spirited by dead men. But it was a common tale. Everyone hopes the dead will speak. It's not an unusual fantasy, and perfect for this site, even site specific, in a way. Though maybe, Madame Realism contemplated, they choose to be silent. Maybe in life they didn't have much to say or didn't like talking. Maybe they had already been silenced. What if they don't want to start talking now? That was a more fearsome, terrible fantasy. In an instant, the tombstones stopped whispering.

More people joined her, to constitute, she guessed, a counterphobic movement, a civilian army fighting against everyday fears. During the second world war, President Roosevelt had advised her nation: "There is nothing to fear but fear itself." War is hell, she intoned mutely, silent as a grave.

Haunted and ghosted, Madame Realism stared at the tombstones. The sun was shining on them, and they glared back at her. They glowered unhappily. And she had a curious desire. She wanted to sing a song, though she didn't have much of a voice. She wanted to sing a song and raise the dead. She wanted to dance with them. She wanted to undo death and damage. Even if it was a cliché, or she was, she gave herself to it. All desires are, after all, common, she reflected, and closed her eyes in ecstasy.

At last Madame Realism was spinning out of control in a place where she didn't know a soul. Maybe she was discovering what it meant to be transgressive. She wasn't sure, because that happened only when you couldn't know it. For a moment or two she dizzily abandoned herself to a god that was not a god, to a logic that was not logical. She imagined she'd lost something, if not someone. She had not lost herself, not so that she couldn't find herself again once she returned home. But she felt foolish or turned around, turned inside out or upside down. I'm just a fool to the past, she hummed off key, as the past warbled its siren song. And in a duet, and unrehearsed, Madame Realism answered its lusty call.

MADAME REALISM LOOKS FOR RELIEF

The sultry nights stretched credulity. Madame Realism stood up from the table and pushed her chair into a corner. She had been sitting in one position for too long and had become stiff. Her body was tense, as if it, like a body of work, were on trial. What was there wasn't enough, what might be there was beyond her. She could also be a body of water, affected by an autonomous, distant moon. With tides, not nerves. Her inventiveness was a sponge, and it was rock, scissors and paper, too. She wanted to play, but she didn't know which game. Then she turned on some music and danced. In motion, she produced a funny face. She jumped in the air and sang the lyrics: "I make my bed and I lie in it." She was weird, a character. I'm next to human, she supposed.

In an episode on TV Madame Realism hadn't watched, John Hightower played a poet, an educated man who lived in the country. The sun beat down on him. The field and he were parched. He didn't have many lines, and his part wasn't particularly distinguished or profound. Hightower hadn't received much attention as the poet, a kind of straw man, and even in a field where he was the only serious artist, he was overlooked. He took comfort in his uniqueness, he was one of a kind. His agent told him, you're great, an original. No one acts or interprets the way you do.

Madame Realism didn't know Hightower.

It was the second summer the Mets won the series. For Joe Loman it was the single event that made his day, his month, his year. It pierced the doom and gloom. Loman was more than a fan, he was a fanatic. He collected cards, autographs, attended every home game with his season pass. In the next world he wanted to play first or second base. He wore a Keith Hernandez pin on his shirt. To earn money Loman was a script doctor and a ghost writer. He kept his hand on the pulse. Loman was nobody's dummy. He played his cards close to his vest and suspected everyone. He didn't work cheap.

Madame Realism didn't know Loman.

She lowered the volume, but she could still hear herself think. She opened her messy closet. She couldn't throw anything out. There were shelves, compartments, boxes, drawers. A walk-in closet big enough to live in. Inevitably, she would be inundated by stuff, suffocated by the little things in life, submerged under the weight of kitsch and kultur. Madame Realism couldn't decide what was trivial, insincere, fake, inauthentic, frivolous, superficial, and gaudy; she herself was all of these. And crude, rude, stupid, obtuse and mean. And honest, real, prescient, dense, apparent, transparent, smart, and beautiful. In different situations she was different things and to different people she was different people. Reality was a decision she didn't make alone.

(What's real to you isn't to me, she mentioned inadvertently in another story. Madame Realism once found herself in a Guy de Maupassant tale, the one about a man who picked up a piece of string in the road, and because he did, because he saved things, he had a bad end. One thing led to another, what had seemed a nothing operation—picking up a piece of string in the road—changed the direction of his life. That's because you never know who's watching or what the consequences are. Life and fiction, Madame Realism thought, are a series of incidents and accidents. Everyone faced the possibility of a stupid end or of being stupid to the end.)

Bending down to save something and place it in her messy closet, Madame Realism wondered if one day she would be destroyed or defeated by her own desires and devices. She accumulated. But if she saved everything, there wouldn't be a place for herself. Maybe she could expand, move or change. But most of her changes were minor adjustments. She was set on her ambiguous course.

What Madame Realism didn't treasure affected her as much as what she did.

Somewhere else Hightower's sweating and ranting:

> People tell me, "Hightower, you're not capable of being understood. You expect too much." I don't want to talk to these people because they'll tell me their opinions. I'll be forced into comic book situations worse than the one I'm living. That would be death. I'm sick because I'm conscious. I'm important, but I'm not yet considered a genius. Art isn't recognized by everyone, it's not quantifiable or practical. It's for the fine and discerning. Beauty is the basis of quality. How many people do I need to please anyway.

When Hightower finished delivering his impromptu manifesto, which he performed impeccably and with passion, he looked over the field. He was far ahead of everyone, miles ahead, and heads taller. He raced away, aghast, like Hamlet's father's ghost.

Hightower phoned Loman. They were contentious buddies from way back.

Loman's at his computer, ghosting a self-help manual:

> You're asking yourself why you get up in the morning; why you go to the same job every day; why you live alone or with the same person even though you're bored out of your mind; you're wondering why life goes on without the great highs you had when you were a teenager. You were miserable then too. But probably you don't remember. You were doing drugs. You remember that you were young and a lot of life wasn't behind you. But don't think about that. That won't help you. That's why you're down. You can't control this stuff once it gets going. Ignore it. Deny it. Just hang out, exercise, be seen, never say die, diet, don't eat fat, don't admit anything, you're not unhappy, get lifted not uplifted, make money not love. Stop complaining.

Meanwhile Madame Realism left her apartment and her closet. She still had a shelf in her mind, where she stored and catalogued experiences and memory, so she felt safe to walk outside. It was a fantastic night. She pretended she could understand other people. When she entered her favorite bar, her neighborhood bar, Madame Realism saw two characters perched on stools in her usual place. Part of her didn't like being displaced, another part invited the unexpected, unanticipated, and unintended. She wanted to do the inviting, though, and the tables were turned. She was a guest.

What Madame Realism didn't apprehend might be more resistant than what she did.

Hightower and Loman were talking and gesturing, their hands and mouths furious implements. Madame Realism had to shove her barstool around and in, but finally she discovered a place at the counter. She wasn't going to let a couple of strangers push her around. She'd adjust, fight, or hold her own, though she wasn't sure what that was.

Unabashedly Madame Realism listened in. She had decided years ago that if she listened only to herself, she'd go crazy.

Loman growled:

> You're too subtle, Hightower. You have to reach more people. Appeal to a wider audience. The umpire behind the plate makes calls, instant decisions. Ball, strike, he stands for the people. You think baseball can be played for one person alone? Broaden your base. You can't expect people to get your performance. You have to deliver. Be obvious. What would a baseball game be like if there was only one person in the stands. What if one player ran from base to base, and no one had any expectations about his getting home, or stealing second, sliding over home base or getting a hit. You have to score.

Hightower glowered:

> Obvious? An umpire judges baseball. You want him to judge my performance? You think I should respond to, that's a ball, that's a strike? Not everyone in the stands likes the umpire's calls, there's a minority who argues. And some throw beer at each other. There should be a level of civilization, of civilized behavior we agree upon. Let people use dictionaries. Read the work of James Joyce. Everyone should know Shakespeare.

There's excellence, standards, otherwise democracy runs amok. Raise the level, don't wallow in it. You pander to the lowest impulses. Broaden my base! Limit your baseness!

Like a wedge between the two, Madame Realism inserted herself. It was characteristic for her to jump in and sink or swim, and sometimes she did both:

You say umpire, he says critic. You say ball game, he says theater. Who chooses the game? the umpire? the critic? Who decides on the players and the rules? I could go on and on.

Loman and Hightower looked at her. Loman thought Madame Realism struck out. She wouldn't even get to first base. Hightower dismissed her. He decided she wasn't very advanced.

Madame Realism went further:

If I were a sonata by Bach, or a song by Courtney Love or Ray Charles, an antique hourglass or a home page on the Web, a china figurine, or a painting by Caravaggio, who decides what I mean? What makes me valuable or lets me be thrown out in the garbage? My projection isn't yours even when you and I go to the same movie.

They ignored her.

Loman raved:

Your purity, Hightower, makes me sick. You wouldn't know what was great if it bled all over you. We're all just pitching balls or strikes....

Hightower reacted:

> You want to please everybody, Loman, anybody. You have no eye. No taste. You know nothing of beauty or the spirit that's necessary for seeking truth and creating art.

Loman bellowed:

> For values, I go to the marketplace. You don't have an audience, because you don't deserve one. Elitist!

Hightower countered:

> You disregard immutable laws that inspire all great endeavors and enduring work. Vulgarian!

Madame Realism wasn't sure what was really at stake. She'd heard it was Western civilization. She displayed her version of the pleasure principle:

> I seek pleasure, and I'll do anything to get it. We do anything to please ourselves, but we call it other names. Don't doubt that. I can be vicious in the pursuit of my pleasure. I fill my life with beauty, ugliness, happiness, despair, the cheap and the expensive, things are things. I need them, want them, I encounter them, they encounter me. I play them, they play me. We're all left to our own devices.

Madame Realism hated to feel that anything was insignificant. But her performance might be another exercise in futility.

Hightower and Loman couldn't continue to ignore Madame Realism even though she was obscure to both of them. There they were—three characters in a situation together. They came from different places and found themselves sitting on barstools in the same bar. It was a dialogue or a car crash. Any one of them could have been the piece of string, the narrator, or the man who bent down. Any one of them could've been somewhere else or in another position.

Loman slammed his icy mug of Miller High Life on the counter:

> I'm through handling you with kid gloves, Hightower. You'll never be major. Face it. You think you're ahead of everyone, but you've lost the race. You're a loser.

Hightower raised his glass and protested ironically:

> You have a mob mentality, you're trying to satisfy the lowest denominator. You speak down because you haven't an idea in your head. You're just a craven, trendy follower.

Madame Realism threw her drink to the ground. The glass shattered. Give me a break, an epistemolgical break, she declared. She pushed both of them away from her. They were crowding her. I don't have answers, but I need room. Her frustration showed, like a rash all over her body. I don't throw much away. I need to clear a space. You're tired, you're a couple of drunken clichés.

Hightower and Loman objected in unison:

> We aren't clichés. We're being unfairly caricatured.

What Madame Realism couldn't escape was bigger than she was.

Madame Realism reconsidered:

> I hear your words. But did you choose them or did they just come to you? I draw and withdraw, I get drawn, and I'm drawn into your argument. I try to keep my eyes open to see you, but I can't stop recognizing you as I do. I didn't organize the bar. I didn't organize your arguments. They've been around a long time. It's beyond my control, but you have become figures of speech. And I'm a condition like you. A piece of circumstantial evidence too.

When Madame Realism came face to face with characters and notions she didn't subscribe to, like a magazine she'd never ordered, she felt surrounded or blocked. Or thrown against a brick wall. Madame Realism sometimes wanted to respond in other ways. She wanted to rid herself of some beliefs, put them away like objects in her closet or toss them out for good, but she was never sure if she did or could. Completely. For one thing, she couldn't even keep track of all her opinions, prejudices, and points of view. They popped up at the weirdest moments. She couldn't always account for them. Worse, she didn't always believe her beliefs. She held some of them like a hand in cards or a script she didn't know she'd been reading. She tried to subject her ideas to analysis, doubt or possible evacuation. But every time she put one aside, or thought she did, another became bigger and moved into the vacancy. She wanted to shake free, but badly conceived and imperfect notions were clinging to her. She could smell them, like a sweet perfume named Sin.

Like sin, one's own history is not original, but it weighs heavy. Madame Realism's history was original only to herself. Engrained notions were stealthy and resilient. They were permanently dyed into her woolly identity. And since she couldn't easily step outside her own situation or context, it was improbable to ask others to step outside theirs instantly. This was why, she found, most discussions took effect long after they were over. And why she saw things differently later.

Loman bought Madame Realism a drink. She never turned down a free drink, on principle. She had more trouble because of her principles than anything else. And with the drink in her hand, Madame Realism became fully part of this moment or episode. It didn't matter that it might be another déjà vu or received idea. (In some quarters this event might circulate as a joke, a performance or a case of mistaken identity.) Whatever they were, whoever they were, the three of them were relating and in some way equivalent and unequal.

Madame Realism was intoxicated. She couldn't get rid of anything. Her closet was a mess. She could deposit Hightower and Loman in it. She considered bringing them home with her, but she didn't know where'd she'd place them. She might let time settle the argument, since time wasn't necessarily on anyone's side. That might be a solution, she brightened, if time were truly faceless and without envy. But time was also an idea, and it wasn't empty or free of constraints and human engineering. Madame Realism looked at Loman and Hightower. They were still baiting each other.

Madame Realism would never know where to put everything she owned, or collected, or that collected around her. She'd never know where to put everything that happened to her. She'd keep rearranging things.

Madame Realism looked around the smoky room. Stevie Winwood's "Bring Me a Higher Love" was playing on the jukebox, some people were kissing, some playing pool, and others were just staring straight ahead and drinking. Madame Realism's attention settled on the startling array of glasses behind the bartender. Small, large, thin, thick, short, tall, wide, narrow, plain, fancy. All shapes and sizes. If people were containers, she wondered what kind of glass she'd be, what kind of drink. A broad-mouthed Martini, a cool, narrow flute of Champagne, an impatient and short shot of Scotch. Or a mixed drink, a concoction served in a versatile shape. Smiling, Madame Realism bought a round for Hightower, Loman and the bartender.

She looked around the room again. She liked bars, all kinds of them. She thought she always would. They were a part of her. She hoped she'd always enjoy walking into one, taking a seat, seeing the shiny surface of the counter, watching a bartender mix a drink, and listening to strangers talk bar talk. It was a relief to her.

MADAME REALISM FACES IT

Madame Realism watched a documentary about an Englishman who kept great apes on his country estate. He had several children, too, and raised the apes and children together. They sat side by side, handling paints and brushes, concocting similarly artless or artful results. Humans and apes were developmentally comparable, Madame Realism learned, until the age of three. Then, suddenly, humans started drawing and painting faces. The apes continued their colorful abstractions. They never painted faces.

Human reflexivity manifested itself early, in baby line-drawings, in renderings of funny faces. Faces were funny, Madame Realism thought, and human was a funny word. Having the capacity for language and self-consciousness, which often warped into self-absorption, humans were licensed to name themselves human and ascribe to the word many flattering qualities and high-minded concepts. Lofty human animals concerned themselves with their humanity and humaneness, and humanism was the world according to humans.

Madame Realism liked it when aggrieved people insisted: I'm only human. It was impossible to understand what that meant, since, on its face, it was simultaneously obvious, grandiose and self-effacing. Hearing it said reminded her of Sammy "the Bull" Gravanno, who'd ratted on Mafia don John Gotti. Gravanno was once interviewed on Diane Sawyer's TV show.

Sawyer leaned forward, brow furrowed to mark her sincerity and perplexity, and asked him, one human being to another:

"How could you kill your wife's brother? Didn't you ask yourself, 'What kind of person am I?' Didn't you ask yourself, 'Who am I?'"

Like Atlas, Gravanno shrugged, nonplussed by doubts about his humanity, and said: "I'm a gangster."

Being a human idea, Madame Realism was interested in herself and in others like her. On walks around the city, she scrutinized faces and mentally tore them apart, rearranging features, the facial furniture, as if she were an architect from outer space. Facial parts lost their sense and meaning, like words repeated over and over lost theirs. On strangers' faces, Madame Realism could impose her thoughts or lose herself. On its face, a portrait was meant for her to do that, shamelessly.

These ruminations were occurring in front of a vastly larger-than-life-size portrait by one artist, Chuck Close, of another, Cindy Sherman. Sherman's monumental face peered down at Madame Realism. For years it had been disguised or hidden in Sherman's work, masked to represent women emblematically, in movies, paintings, and in scenes of horror and fantasy. Now it was uncloaked and gigantic. But did the huge portrait reveal her?

Madame Realism knew that things were often not what they appear to be, but now things appeared much larger. There were so many noses and words in the world, she mused to herself, little and big ones, as well as points of view. She knew she could never apprehend human diversity. She looked at people with sidelong glances or stared at them and thought that she wasn't. She made unconscious and conscious comparisons. They were like her, they weren't.

People were human by comparison with animals, but animals didn't seem to make comparisons, at least they seemed incapable of embarrassment, which was produced by making comparisons. Inescapably, humans had relational fates and faces. All relatives are trouble, Madame Realism thought, and moved farther back from the painting.

Sherman's super-large 1980s eyeglasses framed her eyes, like paintings within a painting. Or the eyes and frames were TV monitors, the eyes televisual, not windows to the soul. Sherman's head was tilted to one side, so Madame Realism mimicked the gesture, to feel what it meant. "Maybe," the position said, "I'm shy, modest, uncomfortable. Off-center." Madame Realism straightened her head.

Cultural production was centered on humans by humans. Art, novels, histories, movies, talk shows, sports, human studies were limitless; motives, reasons, interpretations endless. All versions were marked by irrationality, fantasy or contradiction. Much more was hidden than apparent. And, Madame Realism reflected, humans lie, animals don't. Probably. Too unaware to make themselves wholly readable in any form, humans were tar-pits of self-reflection, streaming subjectivities.

Madame Realism walked closer to the portrait. It stopped being a face when she was near enough to stick her nose against it, which she didn't do, because museum guards might pull her away from the painting. She feared embarrassment, but more, she feared being sent to jail.

Very close, the enormous face turned into a dotted surface, a molecular pattern, a map. If it were a map, she wouldn't know where she was, which suggested the experience of intimacy, when boundaries disintegrate or individuals collide in car-crash relationships. Up so close, the face dissolved into a field of inquiry, offering evidence that the subject of the painting might not be the sitter. Bigness indicated other business than traditional portraiture.

The portrait overwhelmed Madame Realism or any creature, except for an elephant, who stood before it. Its size exaggerated the individual it depicted. So maybe, Madame Realism pondered, identity as a concept was being pictured. Fragile, thick, multiple, identity was sitting in the witness box—a value, an obsession, a claim. Individual psychology and self-recognition weren't the portrait's aims, but questions it raised about those ideas. Madame Realism could never impose herself on this face.

She walked farther back. The painting might be saying: "Do you think you can know me?" "Can you actually see me?" "Get out of my face." But it was, of course, mute, its expression indeterminate.

What am I seeing? Madame Realism wondered. She had no immunity from how others saw her. Her hopes and intentions might be the result of a communicable disease. Madame Realism patted her smooth cheek.

To look like models, people had their faces sculpted surgically. Plastic surgeons were licensed counterfeiters of identity—deracinating, assimilating, de-aging it. Humans not only imitated faces, they also stole faces and names. Identity theft was easy. Photo IDs, fingerprinting, voice prints tried to protect "you" against another's claim on your face and good name. There was a lot of fraud and failure in the identity game.

Suspiciously, Madame Realism glanced behind her, then she looked again at the painting. It identified a specific person, but its implications were social and cultural—not psychological. Conceptualism peered through its nominal realism. Madame Realism narrowed her eyes. Now the portrait was a banner or flag, waving. Was it patriotic to human beings, defending their specialness, or subversive and treacherous? Madame Realism didn't know. She didn't trust herself, and before she left the museum, made sure she had her phone and wallet.

MADAME REALISM LIES HERE

Madame Realism awoke with a bad taste in her mouth. All night long she'd thrashed in bed like a trapped animal. The white cotton sheets twisted around her frenetic, sleeping body, and, like hands, nearly strangled her. Madame Realism pounded her pillow, beating it into weird shapes, and when finally she lay her head on it, she smothered her face under the blanket, to muffle the world around her. She wanted to tear herself from the world, but it was tearing at her. She wasn't ever sure if she was sleeping even when she was. Her unconscious escapades exhausted her. All restless night, her dreams plagued her, both too real and too fantastic.

She was in a large auditorium and a work of art spoke for her. Much as she tried, she couldn't control any of its utterances. Everywhere she went, people thought that what it said was the final word about her. When they didn't think it spoke for her, they thought it spoke about them. They objected violently to what it was saying and started fighting with each other—kick-boxing, wrestling. The event was televised, and everything was available worldwide. It was also taped, a permanent record of what should have been fleeting. Mortified, Madame Realism fled, escaping with her life.

In another dream, a sculpture she'd made resembled her. It didn't look exactly like her, but it was close enough. Friends and critics didn't notice any significant differences. But she thought it was uglier. Still, what was beauty? ugliness? Maybe she'd done something to herself—a nose job or face lift, her friends speculated. But the statue was much taller—bigger than life, everyone said—with an exaggerated, cartoonish quality. People confused her with it, as if they were identical. Madame Realism kept insisting, We're not the same. But no one listened.

In the last, she took off her clothes repeatedly, and, standing naked in a capacious and stark-white, hospital-like room, where experiments and operations might be performed, she lectured on the history of art. To be heard, she told herself, she needed to be naked, to expose herself. Nakedness was honesty, she thought; besides she had nothing to hide. But no one saw that. They just saw her body. And it wasn't even her own. It was kind of generic.

Madame Realism rubbed the sleep out of her eyes. Everything was a test, each morning an examination. She was full of delinquent questions and renegade answers. In her waking life, as in her dreams, she concocted art that confronted ideas about art. So life wasn't easy; few people wanted to be challenged. But Madame Realism had principles and beliefs, though she occasionally tried to disown them, and her vanity made her vulnerable. What if she didn't look good? Still, she didn't want to serve convention, like a craven waiter, or fear being cheap and brazen, either.

Things had no regard for the claims of authors and patrons, and Madame Realism's work wasn't her child. But, inevitably, it was related to her, often unflatteringly. Sometimes she was vilified, as if she were the mother of a bad kid who couldn't tell the truth. But what if art can't tell the truth? What if it lies? Madame Realism did sometimes, shamelessly, recklessly. She remembered some of her lies, and the ones she didn't could return, misshapen, to undo her. Uncomfortable now, she stretched, and the small bones in her neck cracked. The body realigns itself, she'd heard, which comforted her for reasons she didn't entirely understand.

Sometimes, in overwrought moments, in her own mental pictures, where she entertained illusions, she made art—no, life—perform death-defying feats. It wiped out the painful past. Life quit its impetuous movement into unrecognizable territory. She herself brutally punched treacherous impermanence in the nose. In her TV movies, art took an heroic stand, like misguided Custer, defeated criminal mortality, and kept her alive, eternally.

But Madame Realism, like everyone else, knew Custer's fate. So it wasn't surprising that her late-night dates with Morpheus had turned increasingly frantic. She didn't believe in an afterlife, and those who did had never been dead.

What if, Madame Realism mused, finally arising from her messy bed with an acrid, metallic taste in her mouth, what if art was like Frankenstein? Mary Shelley's inspiration for Frankenstein was the golem, which, legend goes, was a creature fashioned from clay by a Rabbi Low in the 17th century. The figure was meant to protect the Jewish people. But once alive, the golem ran amok, turned against its creator, and became destructive. Rabbi Low was forced to destroy the golem.

Madame Realism walked creakily into the kitchen and filled the kettle with water. She put the kettle on the stove. She always did the same thing every morning, but this morning she felt awkward. Then she walked into the bathroom and looked at herself in the mirror. She discovered a terrible sight. What she had dreamed had happened. There was a cartoonish quality to her. All her features were exaggerated. Her breasts had disappeared and her chest tripled in size, her ass was so big she could barely sit on a chair. Her biceps were enormous, and she flexed them. It was strangely thrilling and terrifying.

Madame Realism started to scream, but what came out of her mouth was the first line of a bad joke: "Have you heard the one about the farmer's daughter?" She recited this mechanically, when she really meant to cry: This can't be happening. She tried to collect herself. She could be the temporary product of her own alien imagination. She could be a joke that wasn't meant to be funny.

Tremulous and determined, she walked into her studio—actually shuffled, for with so much new weight on her, she couldn't move as quickly as she once had. Carrying the burden of new thoughts, she reassured herself, was weird and ungainly. Just as soon as she said that to herself, all the art in her studio metamorphosed. It was not hers, but she recognized the impulse to make it. Still, she was shocked. She'd never used rubber or stainless steel before.

Then, like golems, these monstrous pieces—which is what she thought of the invaders—became animated. A large, inflatable flower pushed her into a chair. And her ass was so big, she fell on the floor. When she looked up, there was a ceramic double figure staring down at her. It was Michael Jackson and one of his pet monkeys. Michael was crying. She'd never seen him cry before. Then he said:

> Call me tasteless, it doesn't matter. What you expect to see is just as tasteless. What is taste? Educated love? Don't you love me? After all this time, don't you know me...aren't we friends?... Don't be surprised—I might be Michaelangelo's *David.* I am popular and so was *David.* He protected his people and fought Goliath and won.

Well, Madame Realism heard herself say aloud, do you know the one about... She wanted to say something about ideas, but she couldn't stop kidding around.

Michael Jackson and his beloved monkey became silent, and suddenly she was overcome by a copulating couple. Madame Realism felt embarrassment creep over her new, big body. The lovers disengaged, and the beautiful woman spoke:

> Against death, I summon lust and love. Lust is always against death. It is life. Without my freely given consent and with it, totally, I'm driven to mark things out of an existence that will end against its will. It's a death I cannot forge, predict, violate or annihilate. Ineluctable death is always at the center, and like birth the only permanent part of life, central to meaning and meaninglessness. And to this meaning and meaninglessness, I ask, Why shouldn't you look at us in the act of love? What happens to you when you do?

The sculpted male partner nodded in agreement. The couple moved off and threw each other to the ground.

Madame Realism knew the word pornography meant the description of the life and activities of prostitutes, of what was obscene, and that there were drawings of prostitutes' activities in orgy rooms back in ancient times. Even now, the rooms weren't supposed to be seen. But what shouldn't be seen, and why? legendary New Yorker Brendan Gill, known as a man of taste, was asked why he watched pornography. He said: Because it gives me pleasure. Pleasure, Madame Realism said aloud, pleasure. Her biceps flexed.

With that, an enormous and brilliant painting appeared on the wall. Unlike the sculptures that had conversed with her, the painting remained mute. But it looked at her, it looked at her with an enormous unblinking eye, and it stared at her as if she were an object. It seemed to be the viewer, so she was being viewed by art. This had never happened before, she thought, with peculiar wonder. She felt naked in a fresh and violent way.

Art was a golem. It had taken over. It had a life of its own, and now she feared it was assessing her. What did it say about her? To be winning, she told it a joke, which more or less popped out of her mouth. But the painted eye kept looking. She followed its gaze and realized the painting wasn't really seeing her. She wanted it to, but it didn't. It stared past her, perhaps into the future or the past. It didn't speak, though maybe it spoke to her. It didn't offer an opinion of her. It said nothing at all about her. Nothing.

Madame Realism swooned and fainted. When she awoke, everything was as it had been in her studio. Her work was back in its place. She was no longer cartoonish.

She thought: My work can't protect me. I will be true to my fantasies, even when I don't recognize them. What I make is not entirely in my power, as conscious as I try to be. It's always in my hands and out of my hands, too. I like to look at things, because they make me feel good, even when they make me feel bad. I'm proud to be melancholic. I like to make things, because they usually make me feel good. I am not satisfied with the world, so I add to it. My desires are on display. What I make I love and hate.

Forever after, and this is strange to report, maybe unbelievable, Madame Realism saw things differently. Like Kafka's "Hunger Artist," who fasted for the carnival public who watched him waste away, until one day, when no one was looking or cared that he was starving, he wasted into nothing and died, she did what she wanted. She made a spectacle of herself from time to time, mostly in her work, trying to tell the truth and finding there's no truth like an untruth. She kept pushing herself to greater and greater joys and deprivations, which were invariably linked. And like any interesting artist, who can't help herself and is in thrall to her own discoveries, Madame Realism shocked herself most, over and over again.

MADAME REALISM'S TORCH SONG

The other night, as he sat near the fire in Madame Realism's study, in the place where chance had made them neighbors for a period of time, Wiley said: "Things go on we don't know about. They happen in the dark, metaphorically sometimes, but maybe you don't want to talk about dark stuff now."

"Marilyn Manson," Madame Realism said, "told someone on MTV that Lionel Richie was the heart of darkness."

"There's the light side. But it has a shorter life."

Wiley struck a match.

"It sparks, flares, burns, burns out."

He turned from the fireplace, where he was watching the fire, to her. Wiley looked grave or intent. Madame Realism felt strange, the way she often did. She hadn't known him very long, and, for a moment, he spooked her. Then he returned his attention to the hearth.

"Fire's positive, negative, amoral, not capable of reason, which reminds me of something..."

"Are you going to tell me a ghost story?" Madame Realism asked.

Wiley's large, almost childlike eyes were a silvery gray, like his hair, but his irises were flecked with brown and yellow, and especially when the fire caught them, they luminesced like a cat's. He stoked the fire, and it leaped higher into the air.

"Do you believe in ghosts?" he asked.

Tonight Wiley's manner or words or tone or bearing bordered on the dramatic. Did she believe in ghosts? She felt ghosted. Ghosts had a place in her vocabulary. Did it matter if they existed? She expected to be haunted by her past, and bodies kept turning up. Wiley might be someone who knew her differently from the way she knew herself, or he might be someone she once knew, disguised. His voice soothed and disquieted her. It was oddly familiar, but then lately everyone seemed familiar, which was a benign kind of horror.

"You and I are sitting together, talking. We came here to get away, and far off, in a place you've never been, or at home, something is happening that could undermine your plans, a lover is slipping out of love, or someone is scheming against you."

Madame Realism noted to herself that she'd found a dire soulmate, another paranoid. Wiley nodded circumspectly or as if he'd heard her thoughts.

"We have very little control, all our small plans can be overturned in..."

He snapped his fingers. It was an old-fashioned gesture. His fingers tapered elegantly at the ends. In another life, he might have been a Flamenco dancer.

"In politics, nothing is really hidden. In your life, if someone moves faster, or decides to play hard ball, or has a scheme and you have a small role, or you're a bystander, or an obstacle, your life changes. We're ants, or tigers, or rats, and we run from one place to another, avoiding or ignoring what's probably inevitable. Something, an enemy, could just..."

Wiley tended to finish his sentences with his hands, and this time he moved his left hand in the air, drawing a line through the space in front of him.

Madame Realism focused on the fire, because his eyes were becoming impenetrable, like colored contact lenses. She stared into it, seeing and not seeing, hypnotized or lulled. His words and pauses were the soundtrack to its chemistry.

"But it's important to let things develop, even in the dark, because surprise is like fire—positive and negative. So I like found poems and objects, and this may be crazy, but I make things disappear, just to find them. I study ordinary actions and reactions and all kinds of innocent signs. The collision of uneven things provokes a third element."

Wiley clapped his hands together.

The flames burned indifferently in the fireplace, and Madame Realism thought of alchemy, which usually never came to mind. There was a time, she supposed, when art and science were indivisible and the place where they fused might have been alchemical.

"Do you love fire?" he asked.

"I don't know if I'd call it love."

To herself she proposed: Imagine life without fire. But she couldn't. The world was raw, endless and empty. She got no further.

"I've considered pyromania," she went on, "but I don't know what it'd be in place of, unless there's an infinite parade and you could love millions of different things. Would pyromania substitute for heterosexuality? I could be attracted to men and want to start fires and see them burn, while watching handsome men put them out."

Wiley stared at her now, with open affection. She thought about the true marriage of opposites, attraction wedding repulsion, and a headline: Pyromaniac is a Firefighter.

Earlier she had started the fire that glowed now by twisting single pages of old newspaper into rodlike forms and placing kindling on top of them, arranging the thin sticks of dry wood into a configuration she'd never tried before, but which Wiley had employed, effectively, when Madame Realism first visited him. He was, in his words, "originally a country person, adept at firebuilding." His wife had disappeared two months or years ago, Madame Realism couldn't remember now, and he didn't say more about it or her. He went about building the fire, patiently teaching her his surefire method, which she hadn't yet perfected.

"What matters to me," Wiley said, "is the subtle experiment. It appears insignificant but breeds results no one would expect. Unexpected results from ordinary things are wonderful."

Not unwanted pregnancies, she thought, and poked the fire, which was alive and raised its red-hot head quickly. She always wondered what ordinary was. She always thought she would remember which was the best technique to start a fire, but she didn't. She didn't write anything down; she relied on memory. She didn't like tending a fire; she was easily distracted. She didn't like having to watch it to make sure it kept burning.

"I don't want my illusions to protect me," Wiley said, warming to his subject. "I need to protect them. I have to distinguish between fantasy and evidence, the world outside me. I want to produce fantastic things and control the things I make and do, but I also don't. I'm caught in that drama, a two-hander, but they're my hands, so I'm playing with myself."

The double entendre dropped plumply at her feet. Wiley didn't seem to notice; he was inside his own theater. Madame Realism hesitated.

"I don't want to be manipulated," she said.

It was an ugly word, but she pronounced all its syllables distinctly. Then she added: "But sometimes manipulation is fun. So maybe that's not true."

Tonight the fire caught easily, but she didn't know why. Yesterday she had placed the kindling in approximately the same way, and it hadn't. There was a blazing fire now when yesterday the fire had died out, because of the wetness of the wood or a slight difference in the configuration of the kindling and small logs with which Madame Realism always began or because she had become absorbed in other matters. Maybe she'd forgotten she'd started a fire.

"That's the battle," Wiley said, seemingly out of nowhere or out of no place she was. Was he thinking about manipulation? Or fire?

"What I love most I can't control," Madame Realism said.

Like conversation, the immediacy of it, and how she never knew why it had started, what its necessity was, where it was going to end up or what its lasting effects might be, if any. Conversation was ordinary, but it was also an unforeseeable element that allowed for eruptions in the everyday. Madame Realism saw herself vacillating inside the grid, with other creatures, temporary set pieces on a chess board. She often wanted to leap into the corny unknown. Something about Wiley and his wondrous eyes—Renaissance orbs—encouraged that longing. But escape, she'd been told a million times, was impossible. It also had predictable forms and outcomes.

"In ordinary encounters," he went on, "we expect people to hold up their end of the bargain. If you or I did something strange at dinner, didn't pass the salt, or if you didn't answer a friend's 'how are you?'—something as nothing as that—the whole situation would become tense, people would get angry, and all you'd done was not respond."

Madame Realism considered responses, his and hers, and the fire's. A fire dies out, when it's not tended, not responded to, but it could do the opposite; it could spread rapaciously, but if she were in the room, she'd notice it, because the heat would become overpowering. I'd sense it, she thought, though sometimes when Madame Realism was working or on the telephone, she did not notice something that could, if not checked in time, hurt her. A fire might spread quickly and overcome her. If she didn't escape fast enough, she could be badly burned, maybe suffer grotesque disfiguration, requiring costly surgery to return her face to relative normality—normality is always relative—though not ever again to be pretty or even attractive. Or she might die.

Madame Realism didn't know how much time had passed. A minute. Maybe more. Wiley waited quietly for her to return. His having come from the country implied reserves of patience, to her. But Madame Realism hadn't asked which country. Still, farmers everywhere wait for eggs to hatch, crops to ripen. Wiley seemed an unlikely farmer. She knew little about him; he could be anything. She wondered why his wife had left him, or if she even existed; she wondered if he missed her and still wanted her, if he would forever, no matter what her response to him was now.

When Madame Realism was no longer in love, her lover's eyes, which in the middle of an exacting passion she could not leave, whose every glance she scrutinized to discern greater meaning and which she thought unforgettable, when she was so far from any feelings of love or lust as to make recollection or meaning impossible, her lover's eyes and every other aspect of him lost interest, as if he and they had never been capable of exerting it. Bliss metamorphosed into disgust. In that sense, love was an experiment with unexpected results. Relationships were unpredictable. She had been told, by men, that men were more generous or more practical than women and could easily have sex again with anyone they once loved. She didn't feel she could ask Wiley about that, yet.

He bunched up a sheet of newspaper and placed it nonchalantly near the flames; it might catch if the fire moved its way. Then he dropped a chocolate-covered cherry into his mouth and straightened its crinkly gold wrapper on the slate floor as if he were ironing it. She liked the smell of clothes being ironed but wasn't sure if she liked that gesture and questioned how much meaning to give it.

"A fire changes all the time," he said, in an ordinary way. Madame Realism now watched it like a movie, whose characters she invented. She sat closer to it, wanting everything in close up. She tried to feel what she believed she was supposed to feel near a fire, heated by its quixotic flames.

The fire changed, but it also stayed the same, a blur of blue purple yellow orange red. Ephemeral, shifting, restless. With just a sheet of newspaper tossed casually onto it, it roared approval and grew bigger. She liked watching it, but it could also become boring, tiresome, the way anything could, especially when you were older and more in need of novelty. Sometimes she found herself feeding it like a child, until she lost interest, which she shouldn't if it were.

Wiley stood up, brushing off his black jeans.

"Do you think about beauty?" he asked.

"Sometimes, but I'm not sure how," she said, feeling a little melancholy, the way she did on her birthday. Beauty was the point, and it was pointless, too.

"Is your ghost story about beauty?" Madame Realism asked.

"Beauty's a ghost that haunts us," Wiley said, comically. Then he hunched his back and extended his arms, spreading them wide like the wings of a bat or an angel.

A figure of loss, she thought.

Together and apart, they looked inward, or at the hearth, and wandered silently into the past. The greedy fire, meanwhile, consumed everything.

"What ghost are you?" Wiley asked, finally.

"Everyone dead I've ever loved."

"Beautiful."

After the fire died, what remained were traces of its former glory, ashes and bits of coal-like wood. Wiley and Madame Realism walked outside, into the cold night. They went in search of shooting stars and other necessary irrelevancies.

MADAME REALISM'S CONSCIENCE

"Whatever it is, I'm against it."
— Groucho Marx, *Horse Feathers*

Way past adolescence, Madame Realism's teenaged fantasies survived, thought - bubbles in which she talked with Hadrian about the construction of his miraculous wall or Mary Queen of Scots right before the Catholic queen was beheaded. Madame Realism occasionally fronted a band or conversed with a president, for instance, Bill Clinton, who appeared to deny no one an audience. Could she have influenced him to change his course of action or point of view? Even in fantasy, that rarely happened. She persevered, though. In a state dinner thought bubble, Madame Realism whispered to Laura Bush, "Tell him not to be stubborn. Pride goeth before a fall." Laura looked into the distance and nodded absent-mindedly.

Over the years, Madame Realism had heard many presidential rumors, some of which were confirmed by historians: Eisenhower had a mistress; Mamie was a drunk; Lincoln suffered from melancholia; Mary Lincoln attended séances; Roosevelt's mistress, not Eleanor, was by his side when he died;

Eleanor was a lesbian; Kennedy, a satyr; Jimmy Carter, arrogant; Nancy Reagan made sure that Ronnie, after being shot, took daily naps. When Betty Ford went public with her addictions and breast cancer, she became a hero, but Gerald Ford will be remembered primarily for what he didn't do or say. He didn't put Nixon on trial; and, he denied even a whiff of pressure on him to pardon the disgraced president. Ford's secrets have died with him, but maybe Betty knows.

> The Pope, President Clinton, Henry Kissinger, and an Eagle Scout were on a plane, and it was losing altitude, about to crash. But there were only three parachutes. President Clinton said, "I'm the most powerful leader in the Free World. I have to live," and he took a parachute and jumped out. Henry Kissinger said, "I'm the smartest man in the world. I have to live," and he jumped out. The Pope said, "Dear boy, please take the last parachute, I'm an old man." The Eagle Scout said, "Don't worry, there are two left. The smartest man in the world jumped out with my backpack."

Whatever power was, it steamrolled behind the scenes and kept to its own rarefied company, since over-exposure vitiated its effects. So, when a president came to town, on a precious visit, people wanted to hear and see him, but they also wanted to be near him. They stretched out their arms and thrust their bodies forward, elbowing their way through the crush for a nod or smile; they waved books in front of him for his autograph, dangled their babies for a kiss, and longed for a pat on the back or a handshake. Madame Realism had listened to people say they'd remember this moment for the rest of their days, the commander in chief, so charismatic and handsome. And, as fast as he had arrived, the president vanished, whisked away by the Secret Service, who surrounded him, until at the door of Air Force One, he turned, smiled, and waved to them one last time.

Without access to power's hidden manifestations, visibility is tantamount to reality, a possible explanation for the authority of images. Everyone comprised a kind of display case or cabinet of curiosities and became an independent, unbidden picture. Madame Realism dreaded this particular involuntarism; but interiority and subjectivity were invisible, they were not statements. Your carriage, clothes, weight, height, hair style, and expression told their story, and what you appeared to be was as much someone else's creation as yours.

You never get a second chance to make a first impression.

If the President of the United States—POTUS, to any *West Wing* devotee—dropped his guard, power itself shed a layer of skin. Ever cognizant of that, one of the great politicians of the twentieth century, Lyndon Baines Johnson, called out to visitors while he was on the toilet. Suddenly, Madame Realism took shape nearby, and seeing a visitor's embarrassment, she shouted to the president, "Hey, what's up with that?" LBJ laughed mischievously.

It gave her an idea: maybe he had consciously made himself the butt of the joke, before others could. A Beltway joke writer had once said that self-deprecating humor was essential for presidents, though Johnson's comic spin was extreme and made him into a bathroom joke. Presidential slips of the tongue, accidents and mishaps supposedly humanized the anointed, but the unwitting clowns still wielded power. Laughter was aimed at the mighty to level the playing field, but who chose the field? To her, the jokes also zeroed in on powerlessness; and, Madame Realism trusted in their uneven and topsy-turvy honesty. To defame, derogate, offend, satirize, parody, or exaggerate was not to lie, because in humor's province, other truths govern.

> "Any American who is prepared to run for president should automatically, by definition, be disqualified from ever doing so."
>
> — Gore Vidal

She herself followed, whenever possible, G. K. Chesterton's adage: "For views I look out of the window, my opinions I keep to myself." But presidents were nothing if not opinions, and, at any moment, they had to give one. Maybe since they were kids, they had wished and vied for importance, to pronounce and pontificate, and they had to be right or they'd die. The public hoped for a strong, honest leader, but more and more it grew skeptical of buzz and hype, of obfuscation passing as answer, of politicians' lies. Yet who one called a liar conformed to party of choice.

> Some people are talking, and one of them says, "All Republicans are assholes."
>
> Another says, "Hey, I resent that!"
>
> First person says, "Why, are you a Republican?"
>
> Second person answers, "No, I'm an asshole!"

Some jokes were all-purpose, for any climate. Madame Realism first heard the asshole joke about lawyers, but most proper nouns would fit, from Democrats to plumbers, teachers to artists. Jokes could be indiscriminate about their subjects, since the only necessity was a good punchline that confronted expectation with surprise, puncturing belief, supposition, or image.

> "Mr. Bush's popularity has taken some serious hits in recent months, but the new survey marks the first time that over fifty percent of respondents indicated that they wished the president was a figment of their imagination."
>
> — Andy Borowitz, *The Borowitz Report*

Her fantasies often skewered Madame Realism, threw her for a loop, but at times they fashioned her as the host of a late-night talk show, when, like Jon Stewart and Stephen Colbert, she held the best hand. Madame Realism imagined questioning presidential also- rans, who had sacrificed themselves on the altar of glory and ambition—Al Gore, John Kerry, the ghost of Adlai Stevenson. Suddenly Adlai stated, out of nowhere, "JFK never forgave me, you know, for not supporting him at the Democratic convention." Then a familiar, haunted look darkened his brown eyes, and pathos quickly soured their banter. Pathos didn't fly on late-night TV.

Anyone but an action hero understood that even a rational decision or intelligent tactic might awaken unforeseen forces equipped with their own anarchic armies, and some presidents agonized under mighty power's heft. In portraits of him, Abraham Lincoln morphed from eager Young Abe, saucy, wry candidate for Congress from Illinois, to a father overwhelmed with sadness at his young son's death, to a gravely depressed man, the president who took the nation to its only civil war. Madame Realism treasured soulful Abraham Lincoln, because he appeared available to her contemporary comprehension, a candidate ripe for psychoanalysis. She pictured speaking kindly to him, late at night, after Mary had gone to sleep, the White House dead and dark, when words streamed from him, and, as he talked about his early days, his ravaged face lit up, remembering life's promise.

> Q: What do you call Ann Coulter and Jerry Falwell in the front seat of a car?
> A: Two airbags.

In the nineteenth century, even Thomas Carlyle believed that "all that a man does is physiognomical of him." A face revealed a person's character and disposition, and with skillful readings by physiognomists, the natural science proponents of this idea, why human beings acted the way they did could be discerned. Also, their future behavior might be predicted. Criminals and the insane, especially, were analyzed, because the aberrant worried the normal, and, consequently, deranged minds had to be isolated from so-called sane ones. The sane felt crazy around the insane.

Though face-reading as a science had gone the way of believing the world was flat—poor Galileo!—facial expressions dominated human beings' reactions; each instinctively examined the other for evidence of treachery, doubt, love, fear, and anger. Defeat and success etched an ever-changing portrait of the aging face that, unlike Dorian Gray's, mutated in plain sight. Animals relied on their senses for survival, but beauty made all fools, democratically. And though it is constantly asserted that character is revealed by facial structure and skin, plastic surgery's triumphal march through society must designate new standards. For instance, Madame Realism asked herself, how do you immediately judge, on what basis, a person's character after five facelifts?

> "Images are the brood of desire."
>
> — George Eliot, *Middlemarch*

Before appearing on TV, politicians were commanded: Don't move around too much in your chair, don't be too animated, you'll look crazy, don't touch your face or hair, don't flail your arms, don't point your finger. Their handlers advised them: keep to your agenda, make your point, not theirs. The talking heads tried to maintain their pose and composure, but these anointed figures faltered in public, and, with the ubiquity of cameras, their every wink, smirk, awkwardness, or mistake was recorded and broadcast on the Internet, the worse the better.

At a political leadership forum led by his son, Jeb Bush, the elder President Bush wept when he spoke about Jeb losing the 1994 governorship of Florida. Madame Realism took a seat next to him after he returned to the table, still choked up. "Did you cry," she asked, "because you wish Jeb were president, not your namesake?" President Bush ignored her for the rest of the evening.

Q: Why are presidents so short?

A: So senators can remember them.

A happy few were born to be poker-faced. A rare minority suffered from a disease called *prosopagnosis*, or face blindness; the Greek *prosopon* means face, and *agnosia* is the medical term for the loss of recognition. An impairment destroys the brain's ability to recognize faces, which usually happens after a trauma to it; but if the disease is developmental or genetic, and occurs before a person develops an awareness that faces can be differentiated, sufferers never know that it is ordinary to distinguish them. They see no noses, eyes, lips, but a blur, a cloudy, murky space above the neck. What is their life like? Their world? How do they manage? But she couldn't embody their experience, not even in fantasy.

> He wants power
> He has power
> He wants more
> And his country will break in his hands,
> Is breaking now.
>
> — Alkaios, ca. 600 BC, from *Pure Pagan*, translated by Burton Raffel

Those who ran for president, presumably, hungered for power, to rule over others, like others might want sex, a Jaguar, or a baby. Winning drives winners, and maybe losers, too, Madame Realism considered. Power, that's what it's all about, everyone always remarked. But why did some want to lead armies and others want to lead a Girl Scout troop, or nothing much at all? With power, you get your way all the time.

She wanted her way, she knew she couldn't get it all the time, but how far would Madame Realism go to achieve her ends? She wasn't sure. And, why were her ends modest, compared, say, with Hadrian's? Like other children, she'd been trained not to be a sore loser, to share, not to hit, but probably Hadrian hadn't. And, what a joke, she laughed to herself, the power of toilet training.

> "Things are more like they are now than they ever were before."
>
> — Dwight D. Eisenhower

Thought -bubbles gathered over her head, and she attempted, as if in a battle, to thrust into those airy-fairy daydreams fates that she didn't crave, like serving as a counselor in a drug clinic or checking microchips for flaws. In fantasy only, Madame Realism ruled her realm, and she could go anywhere, anytime. She would be lavished with awards for peace and physics and keep hundreds of thousands of stray animals on her vast properties. Fearlessly and boldly, she would poke holes in others' arguments, and sometimes she did influence a president. She did not imagine having coffee with the owner of the local laundromat, she didn't make beds or sweep floors. Though she believed she didn't care about having great power, her wishes, like jokes, claimed their own special truths.

> "The King of Kings is also the Chief of Thieves. To whom may I complain?"
>
> — The Bauls

There was a story that standup comic Mort Sahl told about himself and JFK. Mort Sahl was flying on Air Force One with

Kennedy, when they hit a patch of turbulence. JFK said to Sahl, "If this plane crashed, we would probably all be killed, wouldn't we?" Sahl answered, "Yes, Mr. President." Then JFK said, "And it occurs to me that your name would be in very small print." The comic was put in his place, power did that. Madame Realism wondered how wanting power or wanting to be near it was different, if it was. Maybe, she told herself, she would give up some of her fantasies and replace them with others. But could she?

TWO

THE COMPLETE PAIGE TURNER STORIES

LOVE SENTENCE

O, know, sweet love, I always write of you, / And you and love are still my argument; / So all my best is dressing old words new, / Spending again what is already spent; / For as the sun is daily new and old, / So is my love still telling what is told.

— William Shakespeare, Sonnet 76

Evelina lowered her lids while he read. It was a very beautiful evening, and Ann Eliza thought afterward how different life might have been with a companion who read poetry like Mr. Ramy.

— Edith Wharton, *Bunner Sisters*

It's strange... it's strange! / His words are carved in my heart. / Would real love be a misfortune for me?

— Verdi, *La Traviata*

I wrote and told you everything, Felice, that came into my mind at the time of writing. It is not everything, yet with some perception one can sense almost everything.... I don't doubt that you believe me, for if I did you would not be the one I love, and nothing would be free of doubt.

— Franz Kafka, to Felice Bauer, July 13, 1913.

Everything Paige thought about love, anything she felt about love, was inadequate and wrong. It didn't matter to her that in some way, from some point of view, someone couldn't actually be wrong about an inchoate thing like love. "An inchoate thing like love" is feeble language. If my language is feeble, Paige thought, isn't my love?

Love, are you feeble?

It was spring, and in the spring a young man's, a young woman's, heart turned heedlessly, helplessly, heartlessly, to love. Were those hearts skipping beats? Were eager suitors walking along broad avenues hoping beyond hope that at the next turn the love they had waited for all their lives would notice them and halt midstep or midsentence, dumbstruck, love struck? Were women and men, women and women, men and men, late at night, sitting in dark bars, surrounded by smoky glass mirrors, pledging their minds and bodies?

In her mind's eye, Paige could see the lovers in a bar, where plaintive Chet Baker was singing, "They're writing songs of love, but not for me," and Etta James wailing, "You smile, oh, and then the spell was cast.... For you are mine at last." And what did the lovers sing to each other? Did they, would they, utter the words "*I love you*"?

On the computer screen, "I love you" winked impishly at Paige.

I love you.

Paige wondered whether words of love, love talk, would survive, whether that courtly diction would rest easy on the computer screen, where words appeared easily, complacent and indifferent, and disappeared more casually, deleted or scrolled into nothing or into the memory of a machine, and so wouldn't the form dictate the terms, ultimately? Wouldn't love simply vanish?

Even so, I love you.

Once upon a time the impassioned word was scratched into dirt, smeared and slapped onto rough walls, carved into trees, chiseled into stone, impressed onto paper, then printed into books. On paper, in books, the words waited patiently and were handy, always visible, evidence of love. In that vague, formative past, love was written with a flourish, and it flourished.

Is the computer screen an illuminated manuscript, evanescent, impermanent, but with a memory that is no longer mine or yours? Is love a memory that is never mine, never yours?

Remember I love you.

Paige thought, I give my memory to this machine. I want ecstasy, not evidence. Can a machine's remembering prove anything about love? If she points to its glowing face, could Paige attest, as one might of a poem written on the finest ivory linen paper: Here, this is evidence of my love.

> "For you are so entirely fair, / To love a part, injustice were; / ... But I love all, and every part, / And nothing less can ease my heart."
>
> — Sir Charles Sedley, "To Cloris"

Paige glanced at the little marks, letters in regular patterns making words and paragraphs, covering sheets of paper that were spread haphazardly around her on the desk and on the floor, and she gazed at the computer's face, as comforting and imperturbable as a TV screen.

Love, my enemy, even now I love you.

Romantic love arrived with the singer, the minstrel, who traveled from court to court, from castle to castle, relaying messages of love, concocting notions of love, torrents of poetic emotion, and in the courts men and women listened to these plaints and added more, their own. The singer heard new woes and put them into song, fostering a way to woo, but why did the minstrel sing in the first place, and how did traveling from one place to another inspire him to produce songs of love? And later, did the printing press change love? Did the novel, offspring of Gutenberg's invention, transform love? Did love become an extended narrative with greater expectations, not a song but an opera?

> "When people used to learn about sex at fifteen and die at thirty-five, they obviously were going to have fewer problems than people today who learn about sex at eight or so, I guess, and live to be eighty. That's a long time to play around with the same concept. The same boring concept."
>
> — Andy Warhol, *The Philosophy of Andy Warhol*

Dearest,

I don't think I've ever felt this way before, not exactly. Not like this. Is it possible? I thought about you all day, and then in the night too, and I felt I was going to die, because my heart was beating so fast, as if it were a wild bird caged in my chest, flapping its wings madly, trying to escape. Even if my heart were a wild bird, it would fly to you.

Paige wondered if love disinvented, too, undid her and him. She moved from the computer, which seemed now to glower, into the kitchen and turned on the cold water. She watched the water flow into the teakettle, and then she put the kettle on the stove.

Dearest,

I love you especially when you're far away. I can feel you most when I don't see you. I carry you with me because your words carry, they fly, and yet they stay with me, stay close to me, the way you do even when you're not beside me. To be honest, love, sometimes words are all I need, words satisfy, your words, your words.

> "Does that goddess know the words / that satisfy burning desire?"
>
> — Puccini, *Madama Butterfly*

> "I can love the other only in the passion of this aphorism."
>
> — Jacques Derrida, "Aphorism Countertime"

Paige thought writing might be an act of love, a kind of love affair, or a way of loving. She hoped it was a possibility, because even more, more horribly and wretchedly, she knew that it was also an incessant demand for love, enfeebling and humiliating. Always wanting, writing exposed its own neediness, like unrequited love, which might be the same thing, she wasn't sure.

Except that when her own worthless desires rebuked her, her writing turned derisory, dissolved into worthlessness, and then became transparent.

> "My Love is of a birth as rare / As 'tis, for object, strange and high; / Iit was begotten by Despair / Upon Impossibility."
>
> — Andrew Marvell, "The Definition of Love"

Dearest,

Maybe I'm always writing love, to you. That's the only way I can love you. What if love, like writing, was a rite enacted and re-enacted, or a habit, or a disguise to cloak a vacant lot near the streetcar named desire. Sometimes I think it would be better to remain silent, to let emptiness, vacancy, and loss have its full, dead weight, and that it would be better to let love and writing go, but, love, I don't want to stop writing or loving you.

It was nearly night. Paige visited old haunts, without going anywhere, and she wallowed in dead loves and called upon memory, which competed with history, dividing her attention. Paige indulged herself, as if eating rich chocolates filled with her romantic past, and looked at pictures of former lovers stuck between pages in journals and albums. She mused and cut hearts out of paper towels, she held up one, then another, to the light. The hearts were large and ungainly, imperfect shapes meant to represent a romance or two or four. What would she write on a cheap paper heart?

"I wrote you in a cave, the cave had no light, I wrote on pale blue paper, the words had no weight, they drifted and danced away before my eyes. I couldn't give them substance. I could not make them bear down. I keep failing at this poetry, this game of love."

> "O love is the crooked thing, / There is nobody wise enough / To find out all that is in it…"
>
> — W. B. Yeats, "Brown Penny"

Dearest,

I know you think I have no perspective, and I know without perspective, everything is flat. Our love exists on available surfaces, beds, floors, on table tops, on roofs. Tell me to stop. I can't help it, I want more, I want everything now. I love you, silently and stealthily. I love you as you have never been loved. I love you because I cannot love you.

> "True hearts have ears and eyes, no tongues to speak; / They hear and see, and sigh, and then they break."
>
> — Sir Edward Dyer, "The Lowest Trees Have Tops"

I love you.

It was just a sentence. Paige was struck by it and, she thought, stuck with it. Three ordinary, extraordinary, diminutive words, I love you, and just eight sweet letters. "O" repeats, oh yes. So little does so much, three little words, three little piggies make a sentence: I love you. The love sentence, arrêt d'amour.

Dearest,

What if I were sent to love you? What if I were the sentence "I love you"? Do you or I ever think of love as a sentence? I don't think so, you and I can't stop to do that, we don't bother with its syntax, or who is sentenced, and for how long. I think you and I can't think love at all. I can't now.

> "What voice descends from heaven / to speak to me of love?"
>
> — Verdi, *Don Carlos*

> "Wild thing, you make my heart sing. / You make everything, groovy. / Wild thing, I think I love you. / But I want to know for sure. Come on and hold me tight. I love you."
>
> — The Troggs, "Wild Thing"

Feeling stupid, Paige tore up one of the hearts. She crumpled the others and looked at the mess. With hardly a second thought, she took each newly crumpled heart and straightened it out, then patted down all of the hearts until they were more or less flat and unwrinkled, and lined them up like place mats on the table in front of her. Paige smiled at the hearts, paltry emblems of couplings gone. She even liked the hearts better with creases, because she liked her lovers to have lines around their mouths and eyes. So strange to concoct emblems, to want signifiers of old loves, but it was, she thought, stranger not to keep faith with memory and to desire, as obsessively, to forget.

Dearest,

I love you trembles inside me. It trembles and I can feel it just the way I can feel you. You can't think love, I know you can't, not when you think about me. I'm the one who loves you, no matter what, and I love you, no matter that I want to take apart "I love you."

> "But, untranslatable, / Love remains / A future in brains."
>
> — Laura Riding, "The Definition of Love"

I love you.

What or who is the subject of this sentence, the object or the subject? Love confuses by constructing a subject/object relation that forgets what or why it is—who subject, who object. "You" never refuse "I," my love.

To Paige, a torn-up heart, its pieces scattered on the table top, represented all the broken hearts, not just hers. There were too many to name and count, countless numbers.

"My first broken heart wasn't a romance. My heart broke before I even thought about love. It broke when I wanted something and couldn't have it, and I don't even remember when or what that was."

> "...When the original object of an instinctual desire becomes lost in consequence of repression, it is often replaced by an endless series of substitute objects, none of which ever give full satisfaction."
>
> — Freud, "The Most Prevalent Form of Degradation in Erotic Life"

Paige worried that memory, like love, was something she couldn't make decisions about, even when she made sense of the past, or it made some sense to her. Unlike love, memory was constant, and she was never without it. It was holding her hand as she tailored hearts.

Dearest,

I can't think straight, I can't do what I'm supposed to do. I can't eat or write or wash or cry or scream or die or decide, since loving you. Now "I love you" becomes a suffocated gasp, an involuntary gush. When you touch me, I can't swallow, when you touch me, everything's a movie, and everything in me moves over to sigh. I gasp, I suffocate, I gush for you. If "I love you" becomes a lament, then I will gag on love and die.

> "Know you not the goddess of love / and the power of her magic?"
>
> — Wagner, *Tristan and Isolde*

> "'Cause love comes in spurts / In dangerous flirts / And it murders your heart / They didn't tell you that part. / Love comes in spurts / Sometimes it hurts / Love comes in spurts / Oh no, it hurts."
>
> — Richard Hell, "Love Comes in Spurts"

I love you is the structure through which I love you. "I" is such a lonely, defiant letter. In this fatal and fateful sentence it's the first word—in the beginning, there was I—a pronoun, the nominal subject. In the love sentence, "I" submits to "you." That I is mine. That I is yours. That I is for you.

Dearest,

I'm the one who loves you better, longer, stronger, whose passion robs you of passion, whose daring steals your courage, whose boldness provokes your fear, whose gentleness savages you, whose absence electrifies you.

Paige waved a paper heart in the air and pretended to enact an ancient, time-honored ritual. She considered burning the heart in a funeral pyre and laughed out loud, a hollow sound with reverberations only for her. You never see yourself laughing, Paige realized. Once upon a time a man she loved caught her looking at herself in a mirror and noticed something she didn't want him to see.

> "I'll be your mirror / Reflect what you are / In case you don't know."
>
> — Lou Reed, "I'll Be Your Mirror"

"The woman who sang those lines died in a bicycle accident on an island. When she first sang the song, she was beautiful and somber and lonely, but not alone. She died in what's called a freak accident, and, at the time of her death, her body was swollen from years of shooting heroin, so she was no longer beautiful, but she was always, or still, lonely. It was spring when she died, it may have been summer."

I love you.

Love, the second word in the sentence, is the verb and acts by joining the two pronouns, pro-lovers, you and I. Love melts "you" into "I" or is it just grammar that bends "I" into "you," just that old subject to object-of-the-verb magic? Love dissolves disbelief, since it defies credulity. Love establishes an impossible, enduring, tender, spidery bridge between us, two poor pronouns. You and I are simple, one-syllable words; you and I need love.

"We do not see what we love, but we love in the hope of confirming the illusion that we are indeed seeing anything at all."
— Paul de Man, "Hypogram and Inscription"

"Stereotype / Monotype / Blood type / Are you my type?"
— Vernon Reid, "Type"

Paige shuffled the hearts and named each of them, and while she did, forced herself to remember him and herself with as much detail and vividness as she could bear. It's often hard to bear your own history. A languid heaviness coursed through her and then settled like a stone in her stomach.

"I walked across the Brooklyn Bridge with him. The cars and trucks rumbling and tearing beneath us were terrifying. He thought it was weird that I didn't find any security in the fact that there was something solid under our feet. He held my hand, the way I hold this heart. Later, we went for Indian food. It was the first time I ever ate it. Then we went back to my place and made love for the first time, too. He stroked the insides of my thighs."

"Love u more than I did when u were mine."
— Prince, "When U Were Mine"

"The heart you betrayed, / the heart you lost, / see in this hour / what a heart it was."
— Bellini, *Norma*

Dearest,

I'm afraid now too, though I'm not actually walking over a bridge. There isn't anything beneath my feet. I can't breathe or yawn or laugh or smile or cook or move or run or jump or stand or sit. I am restless. Bedeviled angel, sweet oxymoron, I ask questions you can't possibly answer. I'm not reasonable, absolutely not, why should I be, why should you?

Really, I only have questions and you are a question to me, you are the question. I ask myself—you—what is it you want and what is it I want. Our wanting isn't going to be enough, though it is for now, wanting you is enough now. I can't live without you. See how you have destroyed me?

> "For love—I would / split open your head and put / a candle in / behind the eyes."
>
> — Robert Creeley, "The Warning"

Even so, or even more, I love you.

"You" is, you are, the last word, the last word and the first one too. In "you" there are two letters more than "I"—the difference is a diphthong, two vowels to create one sound—ooh, you-ooh. The vowels demand each other, they nestle together to make their sound.

Dearest,

My love clings to you. It is silent and dark, hidden from everyone else but you. Love is silent, sex is noisy. To write love, that's what I really want, and to write it to you must be finding silence also. Soundlessly, I'd put everything into words, and though the words are not actually love but how love would speak if it could—if my heart could talk—the words would make no sound. Yet, through my desire, with my will, they would strike a chord inside you. My words would creep and slither into you, if I had my way, and I want my way with you, and words once inert on paper would suddenly wing through the air like missiles. Silly or profound, they would fly into you, and you would embrace them or, more perfectly, they would embrace you. You would be entered, love, you would be my precious entrance to love and also my final destination, eternal enchantment.

> "What is the use of speech? Silence were fitter: / Lest we should still be wishing things unsaid. / Though all the words we ever spake were bitter, / Shall I reproach you dead?"
>
> — Ernest Dowson, "You Would Have Understood Me"

Paige drank green tea and wondered what had happened to him, the lanky, green-eyed young man who hated himself, who said, I don't know why you like me. She hadn't liked him but had loved something about him.

"He was living on West Fourth Street and had been suicidal for years. He told everybody his brother was a movie star, and that was true. His room was in the back of a store and on the floor was a single mattress. The mattress looked like an unopened envelope. He said he had not made love in three years, and after he came, he cried, and the next day he hovered in a doorway, there was a violet gash on his neck. Then he disappeared forever."

Obliviously, I love you.

She was becoming stiff and rose from the table, and walked from room to room, imagining she was a ferocious animal. Paige paced back and forth, back and forth, not sleek as a tiger or cunning as a fox but on the prowl. She felt a little hungry.

> "Even today love, too, is in essence as animal as it ever was."
> — Freud, "The Most Prevalent Form of Degradation in Erotic Life"

Paige took up the scissors again. Love, she considered with affection, should be generous, at the very least it should appear to be. She smiled absentmindedly as she cut more hearts, attempting to keep them attached like a chain of paper dolls. Was she fashioning love? Wasn't the memory better than the love? The shapes grew progressively more uneven and awkward.

"You planted yourself in my garden, taking up room, then, oh, you grew, you became a weed, you were so tall, with such nerve. Your satin trousers and you were much too sleek. I tried to escape, but you insisted. You kept on insisting, about what, toward what end, I can't remember. I wish flowers had never been looked at before. When we stood up, I felt taller, as tall as you, no, taller. You were awkward, but I remember all your questions."

Awkwardly, I love you.

Dearest,

I can still say it, common as it is, common as mud and as thick and undecipherable. In my dreams I cleave to you, I hold you, your body bent to mine, your body reminding me of someone else who is no longer here to love me, but then that's love, one body replaces another. I don't mean that, not just any other, yours, only you. And only you understand me, the me who loves you. You and I make meaning together, that's how love is, what love is—meaning. Meaning I love you. Meaning, I love you. "I love you" means I won't listen to reason.

> "Everybody has a different idea of love. One girl I knew said, 'I knew he loved me when he didn't come in my mouth.'"
> — Andy Warhol, *The Philosophy of Andy Warhol*

Paige thought about coloring the hearts and affixing titles to them. I'm glad no one can see me, she thought, and hummed aloud: I'm a little teapot, lift me up, pour me out. I'm a common heart, a commoner, a common metaphor, a cup of tea, a loaf of bread, a bouquet of posies. I am also beside myself. Hush, Paige admonished, be still, useless heart. Then she uncorked a bottle of red wine.

Commonly, I love you.

Since childhood, Paige had read poets and listened to the music of composers and songwriters who ordinarily took love as their subject. It made sense because love is mute, nearly unspeakable, so it needs a voice; still, it's impossible to give it fully or sufficiently. So, no one can say enough about love or for it, and it cannot be encompassed or conquered, since it's abstract, constantly inconsistent, outrageously ineffable, obdurate, and evasive. Therefore, Love endures as a subject worth taking up.

Paige allowed these sentiments and others entry, yet feared that whatever she had experienced and read, the cautionary tales she imbibed, couldn't protect her. She hoped, desperately, to invest in knowledge and gain strength for the lovesick nights, for those raw, endless hours that robbed her blind and stole her reason.

> "The night murmurs / Its thousand loves / And false counsels / To soften and seduce the heart."
>
> — Puccini, *Tosca*

> "There was a time when I believed that you belonged to me / But now I know your heart is shackled to a memory /...Why can't I free your doubtful mind? / And melt your cold, cold heart."
>
> — Hank Williams, "Cold, Cold Heart"

Blindly, I love you.

Dearest,

Even when my eyes hurt and everything's blurred, I keep writing and reading. Weak eyes still love stories. Remember when you said I'm full of stories. You are too. Isn't this how you seduced me? Wasn't it your story, how you told it, how I sank into it, submitted, and collapsed into the superb rendition of your life—into you? I thought I saw you in your story. And isn't this how I seduced you? It wasn't my beauty, was it? It wasn't my youth, was it? I think it was my story, one word after another after another, circling around you, gathering you to me. My lines roped you in, the way yours did me, our lines—to continue this pathetic figure of speech—tangled, and we became one story. I have a French friend who always said about her love affairs, I'm having a little story with him. With words like sticky plums, I drew you close.

My grip, on you, on my own tales, is sometimes tenuous. I might slip, but I always love you.

Paige drank the wine, but she barely tasted it, she was transfixed. In her red bathrobe she looked comical, like a giant valentine.

From time to time she glanced at the clock on the wall, but she wasn't sure what time it was. Every month the clock needed a new battery, but she forgot to change it. It was good that actual hearts didn't have batteries to be changed or recharged. Except there were pacemakers. Maybe that's why she felt run down, her heart was mimicking a machine. Paige stacked the paper hearts like honeyed pancakes.

Sweetly, I love you.

"She was so much in love, she wanted to make love all the time. He was away. She left their house and walked to a canal and saw a man standing on a bridge. She liked him, and it was easy to make love. Her exciting, grand passion threatened to make negligible any differences between one man and another. And, also, her love made her expansive, bigger than she was. She abandoned herself to the threat of self-annihilation—that's what love is—and spent the afternoon with the stranger. There was no restraint, she gave him everything he wanted, without regret. He gave her his address, and she tore it up later."

> "Such wayward ways hath Love, that most part in discord / Our wills do stand, whereby our hearts but seldom do accord." — Henry Howard, Earl of Surrey, "Description of the Fickle Affections, Pangs, and Slights of Love")

Discordantly, I love you.

You are everything. "You" is everything to the sentence, I love you, for without "you," could "I" love?

Dearest,

It's strange to write "I love you." I don't mean to you, what's strange is to write it, to commit it to paper or the screen. I don't mean that it could be anyone but you when I write, "I love you." Only you could be the "you" that I love. That's obvious. Isn't it obvious that I love you, and that, without you, I cannot love? You alone will see where I'm leading, where my thought carries me, because my thought carries me to you.

"The air is fragrant and oddly pure this morning. It wafts into my room and reminds me of days when I played for hours in the forest down the road, our jungle, or maybe it was next to the house then, back then. I can't remember. I remember how in the winter the pond would freeze over and all of us kids would ice skate, our hands tucked into our sleeves or sheltered safely in woolen mittens. Mittens are for little creatures who need shelter all the time. With mittens we are small animals with paws. The boys I played with—were you one of them? Even then? Steve, Ronnie, Jerry. They were always around the house. Jerry was dark and round. Ronnie, tall and blond, angular and angry, a bad boy. He became a lawyer. Steve stood apart and sulked. I wonder what happened to him."

Abruptly Paige jumped up from the table. At the sink she poured out the dregs of the tea. It was late, and the city was quiet, sleeping. Does a city sleep when it can't close its eyes?

Isn't everyone wrong about something like love?

Above her, in the upstairs apartment, a man strode heavily across the floor, from the refrigerator to the toilet, to the bed, or in a different order. He stomped around like an enraged elephant, like a lover floundering from betrayal.

Love is not silent, love is loud and violent and vicious with a lovely, unsatisfactory language entangled on a wet tongue that entices. Paige danced around the kitchen, one hand gently patting her stomach.

> "I danced on '"Shop Around' "/ but never the flip side / '"Who's Lovin' You' "/ boppin' was safer than grindin' '/ (which is why you should not come around)"
>
> — Thulani Davis, *Telepathy: Poetry/Music Suite*

The language of and for love explains and isn't explanatory enough. If it's not learned well or early, but if one is a quick study, one could, with diligence, pick it up later. Paige wondered: Is psychoanalysis the way to learn to love later?

> "The analyst's couch is the only place where the social contract explicitly authorizes a search for love—albeit a private one."
>
> — Julia Kristeva, *Tales of Love*

Childishly, I love you.

Dearest,

I don't want to love you badly. It's intangible, I suppose, how to love, but since it resides in language and the language of the body—can touch be taught?—it has a presence and effects, and it also exists with words. Love is a grammar, a style, replete with physical gestures and utterances and yellow marks flashing on gray-green computer screens. What if my hard drive crashes? What if you stop loving me? What if I stop loving you? What then? What words would ever be enough?

> "I think that once you see emotions from a certain angle, you can never think of them as real again. That's what more or less has happened to me. I don't really know if I was ever capable of love, but after the '60s, I never thought in terms of 'love' again."
>
> — Andy Warhol, *The Philosophy of Andy Warhol*

Dearest,

I hate this something you and I didn't name. It's gone out of control. With time, with time weighing us down, with no time to think about the future, with every fear about time passing—when will love come?—we grab love and hold it tight. Now we have it, now we have it, here it is, do you see it? I give it to you. I will forget everything else to love you.

> "Let us forget the whole world! / For you alone, dearest, I long! / I have a past no more, / I do not think of the future."
>
> — Verdi, *Don Carlos*

> "Love is begot by fancy, bred / By ignorance, by expectation fed, / Destroyed by knowledge, and, at best, / Lost in the moment 'tis possessed."
>
> — George Granville, Baron Lansdowne, "Love"

Impossibly, I love you.

"Love incapacitates me, my language is never enough. The language is the matter, language is matter, it matters, it doesn't matter, we matter, we are matter, you and I are the matter, the matter of love, the stuff of it, you and I. We are not enough, neither is love, there's no sense to it, it doesn't make sense to you or me that this is what we are in, love, a state of temporary grace with each other. It doesn't make sense, it's not sound. It is a sound. It's your voice."

Dearest,

You wanted to know, when you phoned (I love the sound of your voice), what was on my mind. Just as you called I was thinking (I had pushed you out of my mind in order to think), Some days it doesn't pay to get out of bed. Then the telephone rang. Anyway it's Sunday, and I was thinking of Lewis Carroll and Edith Wharton, who wrote in bed, enviable position, with a board on her lap, traveling or at home, every morning. As she finished a page, she let it drop to the floor, to be scooped up later by her secretary who typed it. Lewis Carroll (I don't know where he wrote) and Wharton, it was something about her love letters to Morton Fullerton, and Carroll's love of Alice, his desire for young girls. Was his sense of the absurd best exemplified by the ludicrous position he fell into, his love for such a small being? How crazy it must have felt to him, spending Sundays with Alice, bending down to hear her speak all day long, looming over the tiny object of his illicit affections. Even stranger to him must have been his wild, prohibited longing, if he actually felt it, to insert his penis into that girl's vagina. He must have felt so small and so big, and there it was, the topsy-turviness of his intimate world which he then concocted into words, and with words published (in the old sense), though no one knew, or wrote his body, I think, and its occupying desires. Alice had to become small to become big. Carroll had no sense of scale, did he? No proportion. Did he ever tell Alice, I love you? Did Lewis Carroll love Alice the way I love you or very differently? Is love the same for everyone, from its beginning to its end? If I wrote to you the way Wharton wrote her lover, would you like it? Please tell me, I want to give you what you want, I want to be everything you want me to be.

Now I'm crimson. I don't want to feel like this, but I can't help it, my words stall on my tongue, they won't come, and then they can't stop coming.

> "I'm so afraid that the treasures I long to unpack for you, that have come to me in magic ships from enchanted islands, are only, to you, the old familiar red calico & beads of the clever trader.... Well! and if you do? It's your loss, after all!"
>
> — Edith Wharton, to Morton Fullerton

Alone with longing, Paige verged toward alienation, like a spectator in her own amorous theater, where she could no longer play the ingenue. Now the paper hearts were actors, and some had important roles and others minor parts, just a line or two appended to a sexy action. Some characters were walk-ons, others appeared as comic relief.

Still, Paige fell in love, and, when she fell, plummeted into a lavish set of conventions. The modes were intractable and not her own, yet sensation maintained that her love was unique. Paige was capable of holding contradictory ideas and emotions, and, as ridiculous as it all was, she bore the irony. People bore it all the time, and some were so experienced in love's disappointments, they had discarded or discredited it. But Paige couldn't let it go, and, for its part, love wouldn't leave her alone.

> "Mother, I cannot mind my wheel; / My fingers ache, my lips are dry; / Oh! if you felt the pain I feel! / But oh, who ever felt as I!"
>
> — Sappho, "Mother, I cannot mind my wheel"

Ironically, I love you.

Dearest,

Your love proposes and then marries me to a different idea of me, a new identity with its own poetic license, so now I'm different from myself but joined with your self, and you are different from yourself, at least from the way you have been, and the way your life has gone, and our love is the best difference that you and I will ever experience. Isn't it? Won't our love mark, cloud, inflect, protect, deform, consume, and subsume us? Won't it cast shadow or sunlight over all other experience? Isn't love the limit? Or, more gravely, like death, an inconsiderate end parenthesis.

> "Do you not hear a voice in your heart / which promises eternal happiness?"
>
> — Bellini, *Norma*

> "Who needs a heart when a heart can be broken?"
> — Terry Britten and Graham Lyle, "What's Love Got to Do with It?"

Paige knocked her leg hard against the table. It hurt. Then a voice whispered: I don't want to die. Paige swung around in her chair, her solitude broken by a strange visitor, the voice an interruption or maybe a discovery, a sensation inside her. But nothing shakes or reaches the vicissitudes of the imaginary inside. I don't want to die, it repeated. She wasn't sure if it actually spoke, it was barely a voice, but she believed she'd heard it before.

Immortally, I love you.

"She wanted to be saved. She wanted to tear his eyes out. She wanted to eat his flesh. She wanted to carve her name on his forehead. She wanted him dead. She wanted him around. She wanted him to stand like a statue. She wanted him never to be sad. She wanted him to do what she wanted. She wanted him invulnerable and invincible. She wanted to look at him. She wanted him to get lost. She wanted to find him. She wanted him to do everything to her. She wanted to look at him.

"She had no idea who he was or what he was thinking. She only pretended that she knew him. He was an enigma of the present, the palpable unknown. He was the loved one, and he wasn't listening to reason. He would save her, and she would never die.

"She didn't want to die. She wanted to be saved."

Irrationally, I love you.

Paige turned off the computer. "She wanted to be saved" winked one last time. She tore up all the hearts and threw them in the garbage and, days later, wondered if they should have been recycled with the newspapers. She liked recycling.

> "...For the transaction between a writer and the spirit of the age is one of infinite delicacy, and upon a nice arrangement between the two the whole fortune of his works depend. Orlando had so ordered it that she was in an extremely happy position; she need neither fight her age, nor submit to it; she was of it, yet remained herself. Now, therefore, she could write, and write she did."
>
> — Virginia Woolf, *Orlando*

She sorted through some papers, closed her books, drew the covers off her bed, and undressed. She laid her head on a pillow and shut her eyes. Paige dismissed the present, and then the dead sat on chair and talked, and love and hate gamboled, trading blows and kisses. Friends and enemies mingled, and her neck out of joint, Paige awoke just before the sun did. She rubbed sleep from her eyes and turned on the computer.

"Love is a necklace around the throat, it needs a durable clasp, so it can be put on and taken off again and again. Some necklaces you never want to take off, though."

Paige Turner is writing to you.

I love you.

TO FIND WORDS

The mechanism of poetry is the same as that of hysterical phantasies.
— Sigmund Freud

I have nothing to say. There is nothing to say is another way to say it. Or, still another way, there is so much to say, and so many ways, should I begin? May I begin? Do I need to ask your permission? I promise you delight. I promise you a real good time. I promise you the best. This will be the very best, the best you've ever had. I am a ride, a roller coaster, the fun house. I'm what frightens you in the palace of horror. I'm pleasure. I'm a drive in the backseat of a car late at night when the moon is full and everyone else is asleep. I'm sex. I'm compassion. I'm the tears on your cheek when you say goodbye forever to that handsome but pitiful character in the movie you love. Now I'm anger and outrage, fire engine red inside your brain. I'm choking you with rage. I'm the pain that dwells in your gut which you cannot express to anyone. I'm the ache in your heart. It hurts. You hurt. You cannot speak. Lie down, make yourself comfortable, adjust the light. I'll speak for you.

That's the problem. And I could go this way or that, tell this story or that. I could seem to believe in words, I could pretend to believe in words and in the power of stories. I could insist: I am a storyteller. I could take comfort in conventional wisdoms and make many references, shoring up my position, to defend myself to you and from you. I could hate words, distrust language, forego stories. I could do all this, everything. I could use everything, I could try it all.

I could, but I don't want to. I don't care, though that's not entirely true. It is partially true and partial truths are after all what one must settle for. If one settles. I don't know about you, but I feel like hell. The country is falling apart, what does anything matter, people are dying, starving, being blown out of the sky, people are suffering, and what does anything matter, what difference does this nothing make, what matter do words make?

When she awoke, she could not speak at all. I didn't let her swallow, she felt she could not breathe, her throat was dry, she drank many glasses of water, she went back to bed and fretted silently. Words danced in front of her, a ballet that no one would comprehend. This word partners that? She could not swallow, that damned, fucking, horrible lump in her throat. It is not the first time. It happens often. Such a weird sensation.

It's terrible that I am her voice because she depends on me. She is to be pitied. She looks sad, lying there in her mother's nightgown. Her mother is dead. Suddenly she sits up, puts a notebook on her lap, and finds a pen on the floor, the pen she threw away last night (oh last night). She writes in her notebook. Her other hand is wrapped lightly about her throat as if she were gagging herself.

The Body has a Mind of its Own
The Mind Speaks through its Body
The Body Speaks its Mind
The Mind has a Body of its Own

"To write a story is to be in a state of hysteria. Writers call up from their minds and bodies (I do not make a separation) memories, ideas, fragments of thoughts, images. The fragmented story is symptomatic, and like a symptom of the hysteric, who cannot retrieve the whole, it is stymied by a regrettable and important loss from a particular scene that would make the story complete. But even the narrative that we think of as well-formed, the traditional narrative, with a beginning, middle and end, that too is of necessity a fragment, which the writer, to counter loss, is impelled to produce. All writing is hysterical. The body always speaks."

This was the voice that Paige Turner initially chose, from many possible voices, I might add, to begin a story about hysteria. She had studied and studied, thought and thought, and from all that she had read, and from all that was in her, so to speak. Paige decided to sally forth with a jab at the problem of writing itself. It is one possible approach. Sally go round the roses.

It doesn't seem to me that it is exactly the right voice or precisely the right way to begin. The first line of a story is like the first impression one can never make again. You never get a second chance to make a first impression. I am not completely sure and neither is she. And it is this that I have reminded her: Is this your voice? Couldn't anyone else have written this? Who is speaking? And, of course, who cares?

Paige Turner is a tall woman, with bright red hair. She is a petite woman with jet black hair. She is of middling height, has blond hair and is known to diet strenuously and laugh loudly. Today her cough is constant; she hates what she has written. She will not begin her story that way, but it will plague her. Paige worries that the ideas she thinks urgent won't be understood. On the other hand overstatement worries her more. She thinks this and glances at her other hand. There is dirt under two of her nails. Red nail polish peels off both thumbnails. Her hands look injured, as if they've been to war. She will apply more red polish to her short, dirty nails. One hand is shaking. This is beyond her control.

When Paige was just a child, she would shake at the kitchen table, shake her leg so vigorously that her father would joke: Will that be a chocolate or a vanilla milk shake? Paige shakes her head, to forget the moment and his expression, what he said as well as the look on his face. A look of bemusement, mockery or tenderness. The look that she remembers, the look she invents again and again, is a jumble in her mind which she thinks of as a kind of messy store where her trinkets and junk are displayed, where other people's souvenirs, other people's pasts, are represented, all as small objects. Precious memory. Her throat hurts. She swallows hard. She cannot speak.

I call her Little Miss Understood. Naming is everything. Sticks and stones will break your bones and names will always hurt you. Names will make you cry. A comic and ominous taunt to Little Miss Understood sitting at her Underwood. On days that are wet and grey or on bright blue ones, it drives her crazy. Mad, wack, nuts, bonkers, ape shit, and so on. I drive her out of her mind. She wants to do the driving herself. She walks back and forth mumbling aloud, speaking to herself. She tells herself that it is a mark of intelligence to talk to oneself—she read this in a popular psychology column written by Dr. Joyce Brothers, for *Vogue* magazine. She takes comfort in such reassurances. She sits at her desk, pulls at her hair, jerks her leg and sorts through paper. She opens books and stares into space. She looks at old photographs of herself and her family, of lovers and friends. Sometimes she imagines she is staring inward, as when she pretends that the outside is the inside. Have you ever tried that? At other times she gazes at the pictures on her walls to invigorate her mind, to catch herself unaware, to startle herself with new meanings. There is a lump in her throat.

"I look for a hair that might have lodged between my lips when eating. It has been swallowed and sits in my throat, tickling me, tickling my fancy. I have eaten hair. Disgusting? Disgust is interesting. Voices can be disgusting. Insinuating, dirty. A voice from the past. I will tell the dirty old man story. Every woman has a dirty old man story."

She is hoarse, her voice deep in her raw throat. But she begins to write, which I think takes pluck, shows stubbornness or demonstrates a kind of silliness, a deep silliness deep in her deep throat. I ought not trivialize the task before her, but how can I not? I remind her how foolish she is. She glances at the ceiling, distracted. She touches her throat and coughs. She calls to me, her disembodied voice. Be still, lie down, rise up, die, live.

"She was sick to her stomach. The bus ride was supposed to take five hours, but it was raining and the slick roads caused the driver to go slowly. Time was dragging, moving along with the labored swish of the window wipers. Time was dumb and slow. She liked buses better than trains because the lights were always off in buses if you rode late enough at night. She was returning to college. She'd eaten so much during the weekend at home that she could barely move. She opened the button at the top of her pants. Her mother had made a chocolate cake which she'd finished when her family had gone to bed. She vomited in the morning but she knew she'd gained weight anyway.

"The man next to her stirred. He'd been sleeping since the beginning of the trip. Now he was awake. He was old and his face was covered by stubble. He was fat too. He started to talk to her. He ran a fast-food chicken place on Second Avenue, he asked if she'd ever been there. She said no. She was glad to talk even though he was ugly. In the light he would be even uglier so she was glad it was dark in the bus. After a while she didn't know what else to talk about because she didn't think he'd be interested in what she was studying or the fact that one day she was going to be a writer. She was too self-conscious to say any of it anyway. It seemed stupid.

"So she closed her eyes. She covered herself with her coat and pretended to go to sleep. He didn't do anything for a while. Then he placed his hand on her pants, first on her thigh, and then he moved his hand there. He began to rub her. No one had ever done that. She didn't know what to do. She didn't think she wanted him to stop because the feeling was strange and nice. She knew it was wrong but it didn't matter what it was. She watched the feelings she was having. She felt very far away. Then she became more and more uncomfortable. She felt hotter. She pretended to wake up and went to the bathroom. There are always bathrooms on Greyhound buses. Everyone else was asleep. She was really alone. Inside the small toilet she felt her underpants. They were wet. She went back to her seat and told the dirty old man, 'I know what you were doing and it was wrong. Don't do it again.' The words came from outside of her, as if spoken by an intruder. It was a strange voice, almost unrecognizable."

I disgust her. She returns to bed. She is discontented. The story may not be right, the voice off. Unsure, she shrinks from herself. She is too little to live. To love. She is too big. There is no time to be content. I disgust her. The hair tickles her throat, her fancy. Her fancy is a lump in her throat.

The saying, I have a lump in my throat, is used generally, in English anyway, when someone feels a great burst of sad emotion, a swelling of emotion. Emotion seems to swell and gets stuck in the body, odd though that may be. The swelling becomes physical, something is stuck in one's throat. Often I become a thing in her throat, as if she'd swallowed a great obstacle and it lodged there. I don't mean she actually swallowed an obstacle. I mean I am the lump in her throat, which is an obstacle. As she writes the dirty old man story, she loses her voice—a case of laryngitis. She cannot speak above a whisper. She wonders if her loss is also her gain, one voice for another. She wonders if she is a whispering woman. She coughs.

"A woman I know attended a private screening of a film. Jackie Kennedy Onassis entered the small cinema, with another woman. Jackie Onassis stood close to my friend who was sitting at the end of the row. She had never seen Jackie O. in person. It was peculiar because she felt she had grown up with her. Jackie

O. had recently had a facelift and she looked much younger than she was. That was peculiar too. Jackie O. whispered loudly to her friend, who had red hair and was as tall as she. The whisper was a stage whisper. It could be heard all through the room. When the two sat down in front, Jackie O. kept whispering, her head inclined close to her friend's. But when the movie started, she stopped and sat absolutely still in her seat, not moving. Not once during the entire movie did she move. She was fixed in her seat. That too was strange. The movie ended and Jackie O. and her friend walked out behind my friend. Jackie O. was still whispering. Afterward there was a lavish reception. My friend took a seat on a couch and drank wine. She saw Jackie O. talking to some people. My friend thought, I'm glad not to be introduced to her. What could I possibly say to her? Later she mentioned this to her lover. He said, 'You could have asked her if she saw anything on the grassy knoll.' They laughed for a long time, imagining how Jackie O. might respond. They knew she wouldn't. I told my friend I'd once heard that Mary Todd Lincoln also whispered. But whether she whispered after Lincoln's assassination or whether she whispered all her life, I didn't know.

"The next day I read in *The New Yorker* magazine about a woman who had placed her mother in a nursing home. The woman's mother warned her, 'If you do this to me, you'll never sleep again.' The woman developed insomnia on the day her mother entered the home. She has not slept regularly since."

Paige might call this The Whispering Women. I remind her that the mother did not warn her daughter, You will lose your power of speech or stutter for the rest of her life. That would be germane. But Paige likes the insomnia story. It gives her goosebumps just to think of it. It makes her flesh crawl. It makes her look behind her to see if someone is standing there. She has a coughing fit. She is thinking and she is not thinking. She may be dreaming.

Paige's mother is in a nursing home. On the day she left her there, and after parting from the reluctant, tearful, elderly woman, Paige came down with the flu. It turned into strep throat. And she lost her voice. Who could she have talked to about it anyway, she thought.

To find words, to find words from all the possible words. It's a game, like Stick the Tail on the Donkey or Treasure Hunt. The hunt may or may not offer a reward at its conclusion. The game cannot be Monopoly. You know that. To find words and place them in sentences in a certain order. Syntax.

"There is a sin tax in the U.S. on liquor and cigarettes, on luxuries, but what are luxuries. What isn't necessary and who decides that?"

If I let her find words, she will rush to form sentences. She will rush to judgment and will try to make sense. Can she?

She persists. Sense and nonsense. Words free, unfixed. Paige longs to make music with words, to discover the moment when words vibrated in the body. She wants to discover time inside herself, to give rhythm to her sentences. Style is rhythm. Rhythm is style. She hears a drumbeat, then a bass line, tough and funky. She imagines the inside is the outside. She is greedy for everything. She opens her mouth wide. If words could make wishes come true. If wishes were horses she'd ride away. Paige wants a voice like the wind.

I tell her: The wind has a voice but I cannot mimic it. The wind has its own music. The wind howls, everyone says so. It is a wolf. I cannot be a wolf. I cannot howl. When I give voice to a thought—do you like that?—it may sound scratchy. Her voice may sound thin, a scream vibrating at a frequency unbearable to dogs or wolves. Do you find that amusing? I had to urge those words from the local box into the mouth and onto the tongue. She repeats them. Her tongue is pink and whitish and scalloped at the edges. She is neither proud nor ashamed of her tongue. She can't touch her chin with her tongue. She rarely thinks of her tongue but when she does, she begins to imagine that her tongue is too large for her mouth. When she realizes this feeling, she gets small sores on the sides of her tongue. Then she remembers her mother telling her, when she was little, Don't get too big for your britches. Paige didn't know exactly what britches were, then.

"I dreamed that I was a man who was a psychoanalyst. We were sitting in a circle, I was opposite him. There were other people in the circle, too. He told me that he had been looking up my skirt. He spoke indifferently. I said to him indignantly, surprised, 'I'm used to wearing pants, not skirts. I am very angry that you continued to look up my skirt and didn't warn me.'"

Her sister takes her to a shopping mall which turns into a medieval castle. Paige doesn't remember this part of the dream. Anyway, if she publishes it, it's not her dream anymore. She shakes her head, rubs her eyes, pours a cup of tea and has the sense—sensation settling in her throat, words are stuck there—that she's forgotten to telephone someone. Or that she's lost something of importance. She shakes her head again. A friend who does Yoga once insisted it was possible, with a vigorous shake of the head, to rid oneself of bad thoughts. Paige doesn't believe it but she does it anyway. She intones silently: Let it go, let it go, let it go.

She blows her nose. Crumpled up tissues, the day's detritus, are strewn about the room. In a drawer, the second drawer in her dresser, the dresser she inherited from her grandmother, there are handkerchiefs with "Paige" embroidered on them. She likes to blow her nose into linen handkerchiefs, especially those bearing her name. She runs to the dresser and does just that. She laughs out loud. She feels unwell. Then she telephones a friend but there is no comfort, no release. Her friend says she can barely hear Paige, and why doesn't she see a doctor? They say goodbye. Paige's throat aches. She sits down at her desk.

Words plague her and push through her body, brazenly, hazardously, forced by the breath, the break of life. Her lungs work furiously, her heart beats rapidly in a kind of rhythm, a pulse beat: I love you, I love you, I do. I'm thinking of you all the time. Can you hear my heart beat? It's a furious melody, it's a cacophony, this insistent incessant crazy love I have for you. You're always near. You never go away. Paige thinks she's going to scream. She might not be able to restrain herself. But can she scream? Does she have it in her? If she screams, the neighbors might think she was being murdered.

"A scream ripped from her, tearing the air, renting it as if it were silk. A scream—in the middle of the night, in the middle of a party. Everyone sat there, their hands shaped like cups and saucers. They were indifferent to her, preening. It was not unusual for people to watch themselves in mirrors and admire their images. Oddly enough those people who looked longest were considered the most beautiful. The scream, everyone said, meant nothing.

"She was not without charm. Silky hair fell in waves about her face, covering one of her clever eyes. She clasped her pale hands, crossed her long legs, held herself erect. She lowered her gaze, embarrassed and yet oddly proud. He danced toward her, embraced her and then regaled her with stories of places she had never been. After this she did a slight dance that went unobserved by everyone but the tea drinker. The tea drinker gestured, beckoning with compassion. She caught the look but acknowledged it a little too seriously. Both grew uncomfortable.

"In the corner, too close to her, was a man who repeated himself endlessly. He had a square jaw. She listened to him and could not listen to him. He spoke in a monotone but even so he was sometimes perceptive and entertaining, in a tragic sort of way. They had once been lovers for reasons she could not fully remember. And one day, suddenly, she no longer wanted him to penetrate her. The very thought of making love with him became abhorrent to her. He could not understand her reluctance to engage in an act they had done many times before. But then he repeated himself endlessly, so how should he understand?

"Her brothers strode into the room. The sight of them caused her a simultaneity of pain and pleasure. She was speechless. She wished they would leave. An old feeling, a dusty antique gown, wrapped her in perpetual childhood."

She feared she must stay there always. She wanted to believe something else. The room enclosed her. She could not breathe. She was a fish out of water. She was an uninvited guest. A stranger, a madwoman, a whore. She was an explorer who didn't like what she found. She swooned. She screamed.

"The scream came from someone she did not know, as if a lodger had taken a room in her without her consent. The scream was unpleasant, though not completely unmusical. It was pitched high, at the top of a tall tree, at the top of a winter tree, bare of leaves, stark against a steel-grey sky. Naked branches, fingers pointing to the abyssal sky, would scream the way she did if they could."

The words lie there and they may be lies. They lie on the page. They are little worms. Once she dreamed, on the night before a reading she was to give, that rather than words on paper, there were tiny objects linked one to another, which she had to decipher instantly and turn into words, sentences, a story, flawlessly, of course. Funny fear of the blank page. Didn't she recently explain that writing was erasure, because the words were already there, already in the world, that the page wasn't blank.

In the room there is no sound other than her own breathing and the rattle of the windows. An eerie sound. The wind is blowing hard against them. The windows may shatter. Their rattling is like a wheeze from a dying person. A death rattle, a wail. The buffeted windows emit a sad human sound. Paige is sensitive to sound, the way some people are sensitive to smell. Her mother was an opera singer, a soprano who quit midcareer to marry Paige's father. Sometimes her mother would sing when she did housework. When Paige was little she disliked her mother's voice. Later she admired it.

Paige doesn't like the sound of her own voice. When she has laryngitis, her voice settles deep in her throat and sounds raspy.

Call it sexy. Do you think so? Perhaps the voice intimates a threatening possibility. It may be saying: I come from down here.

I am in your body. I am, like you, from an animal. I growl. I am covered by soft hair. I go out of control, I like to be touched, and were you to reach inside me and find that hidden place, it would surprise you. It would terrify you. The urgency is raw and harsh, like this voice that has been taken away, taken by the wind or gods or ancestors. When I cannot talk at all, will you listen to me?

"It is the night of the world. Life is dark and hidden from me. The animals cannot sleep. The mountains are complacent and stalwart. The caves are shy, without light. The plains don't want to be flat. The desert is listless, waiting. I have been sitting here a very long time listening to the wind as it races past. It is howling and wailing, it is crying. It pules. It shakes the glass in the windowpanes. I stare out into the dark night. I am completely alone, my hand caresses my neck. The beauty of the world stretches away from me."

Page pats her left shoulder absentmindedly. She strokes her neck. She has a long thin neck upon which her head balances precariously, like an exotic bird's might, a salmon pink bird that can be found only in a hot southern clime. Paige. has never been to the tropics. It is cold in the room. Her throat is sore. It hurts like a broken window.

"Where does the wind rush and why does it gallop away? How to describe the fascinating horror of natural forces, to describe the body of the world which envelops me and exists outside my body? The house is old. It is old enough to be an antique. The shadows in the room obscure the objects in it. I sit on a chair made of dark wood. I am wearing blue cotton pajamas that my father once wore. Blue is the color of hope. I nursed my father for many years before his death. He died of throat cancer. At the end he could not speak. I have my memories. They are fixed and still like his dead body. It is almost morning but the sun has not yet completely risen."

The effect wasn't what she wanted. Paige probably ought to weave these paragraphs into the scream story. It might work. It might fit. It might be fitting but she cannot decide. She is lost at sea and cast in doubt. She is scrambling for words and glances helplessly at her books. Her guard is down. Right now, were you to criticize her or, worse, insult her, she'd be stunned, crushed. Look: She crumples before your sharp eyes, her face falls, actually falls, as if the bones that construct it and the skin that the bones support had given up, given her up, given up on her. Crestfallen, she is as helpless as an animal that has had the misfortune to be shot with a tranquillizer dart.

Have you ever seen an elephant go down when injected with such a drug? A sorry sight. The elephant drops like a sack of concrete; it falls like a building exploded by dynamite. One can watch it happen in nature films, which Paige likes very much. Animals move her in a way that human beings never do. She will not admit this nor will she write about it. Her parents gave away her dog. She didn't talk for weeks. Her calico cat ate her powder blue parakeet. The cat was given away. She was beyond words and didn't even write about it in her diary. Her father asked: Cat got your tongue, Paige?

"It is in the unconscious that fantasy, moments of the day, and memory live, a reservoir for the poetry of the world. Is everything else prose? Is what's conscious ordinary prose, the prose of the world?"

Or, I tease, the pose of the world. She is separating much too neatly the world she knows—I nearly wrote word for world—from the world she doesn't know, the one that owns her and to which she is a slave. She is a slave to what she can't remember and doesn't know and she is a slave to what she remembers and what she thinks she knows. Her education has damaged her in ways she does not even know.

Paige suffers mainly from reminiscences. Memories come in floods, in half-heard phrases, in blurry snapshots. They merge into one another. They have no edges. They emerge in the mountains, in movie theaters, in fields, on the road; they erupt in rooms, in cafes, when she walks, they come all the time. They come when she is talking to friends. They come and her friends disappear in front of her as she fights to clarify a faded image, reassemble a dubious moment, inhale a familiar scent.

Impossible past, what did that perfume smell like, what did his voice sound like, where does the air linger so sweetly, where did her train set go, where was the playground, who are the small people playing funny, frightening games, who called her name. What is whispering? She is captive to impossibility. She opens her notebook, then turns on the radio. An advertisement asks: "Would you like to speak French? It's easier than you think." On the news a missile is referred to as a "technological hero." She turns off the radio. She chooses music from many cassettes which are piled one on top of the other. Her hand covers her mouth, an old gesture, and she coughs; then her index finger slides free and touches her top lip. She looks as if she is musing, being her own muse.

One of Paige's favorite songs, "I'm Your Puppet," was recorded by James and Bobby Purify. It was popular years ago, but she didn't know when it was written, and maybe the Purifys—purify, could that really have been their name?—maybe they were no longer alive. No matter when she heard the song, morning or night, and no matter where she was, she always felt what she felt when she heard the song for the first time. Paige can even remember where she was and with whom: near her high school, in a fast-food joint, with a rock and roll musician; and she even remembers what he said to her about the song—he was curious why she liked it so much, wasn't she perverse? She remembers how she felt when the tune ended and also when the relationship ended, curiously and insignificantly.

> Pull a string and I'll wink at you
> I'm your puppet
> I'll do funny things if you want me to
> I'm your puppet
> I'm yours to have and to hold
> Darling, you've got full control
> Of your puppet...

Paige is dancing in front of the mirror. She is moving her hips. She is swaying, her eyes are closed, she is traveling, she is faraway. Sinuous motion. She is everywhere and nowhere.

> Just pull them little strings
> And I'll sing you a song

> Make me do right or make me do wrong
> I'm your puppet.

After she listened to it over and over, she wondered if the Purifys actually felt like puppets, and then she wondered why she cared. It was a song they sang. They didn't write it. Maybe they hated singing it. Maybe they didn't like the melody. Maybe they hated the words. Paige can give you the lyrics, not the tune. Do you know the song and do you hear it when you read the words?

Paige knew a woman, just a girl really, who had memorized practically every song that had ever been written, and she could play and sing beautifully. They met in Berlin, on a summer day, as the Wall came down. The girl had a guitar strapped to her back. Paige swallows hard and remembers Agnes. Agnes is a lump in her throat.

"Agnes was tall—oh Agnes, agony—so tall, she could have played pro basketball if she were a man, and she was built like one, bearing broad shoulders and a heavy jaw. Instead she played the guitar in a militant way typical of those still influenced by Dylan and Odetta. She played when she begged on the street, near the subway at Astor Place, which is where I usually found her, standing not far from a woman in her fifties who did small paintings she sold for a dollar, usually religious themes in a wild style. I bought many, for a dollar, a bargain, and gave them to friends, and some knew they were worth something, that there was a special kind of mind at work in those small paintings, with their vivid blues and muted greens. She might use as background a lime yellow and dot some rose on it, the rose was a rose; or the theme was religious, something like nuns talking on telephones, as if in direct communication with god.

"Agnes ignored the painter. Agnes didn't like art, it didn't seem to her to serve the purpose music and words did, didn't speak to her, and she was deeply involved in speaking. Agnes talked all the time or sang all the time. She tended to shout the later at night it was, the closer it came to the time when she should have gone home if she had had a home, which she didn't. She stayed with me once, but only once, because she wanted to talk all night about music and writing. I wanted to watch *Hill Street Blues* or something soothing: the captain of the precinct and his wife the lawyer end up in bed, to love away their troubles or to discuss stoically their harrowing day, one filled with more catastrophe than anyone else's. Except maybe Agnes'. I like to be in bed when people on television are in bed. But not Agnes, she didn't want to sleep and could talk all night and I don't know when she slept. She could talk endlessly. I think she liked the sound of her own voice.

"Agnes was unattractive. Her lumbering awkwardness seemed to come from her difficulty in just being alive, of her being acutely aware of her bulky frame and plain face. She must have conceived of herself as a burden to behold. She walked with her head down. She stooped over, bending herself to the ground to make her big body less significant or impressive, less noticeable. Tall people stoop over which is why they often have bad backs. I read that in a book I proofed about back pain—I work as a proofreader—I'd never thought about back pain before and after I finished it, having read that it can happen at any time, out of the blue, that you can turn your head, or pick up a cup, and boom, your back goes out and you're in pain for weeks, there was something else to worry about, something else to be anxious about that could happen to you seemingly at random. But can anything that happens in your body be at random? I told Agnes to stand up straight but she wouldn't listen and I'm sure she'll be a stooped old woman if she lives that long. But where is Agnes? Did she go back to Minnesota? Will I hear that voice of hers again?

"Agnes pretends not to suffer. That's her glory. She depresses me but then I'm not able to suffer happily the way she does. Agnes is the most Christian person I know. She doesn't hate anyone and carries her belongings around with her as if nomadism were her chosen lot in life, not simply a sign of her poverty. Most every day I'd see her and sometimes I'd take her for a coffee or a bowl of soup at a diner. She was remarkably presentable and never smelled. I have to admit that if she did I wouldn't have been able to go around with her. It's gotten so I can't walk into some restaurants because of the stench of cockroach spray. It suffocates me. I move away from people who have bad breath. What's happening in their bodies, I wonder. I don't know where Agnes bathed or showered but she kept herself clean. She had her secrets and lived in a secret way. I don't know what's happened to her though, she's not around, and it's so cold out. Will I ever hear her sing again? Her voice cut into the night like a knife."

Cut to: Interior—a studio apartment in Manhattan. It is raining. Paige is sleeping. She awakens and begins to cough. She has no voice. She remembers her dream. In it she is making love with a man. He wants her desperately, the passion is incredible, huge, overpowering, bigger than both of them. But he is impotent. They stop. They start again. He cannot. His flesh is weak. Then he crawls into her arms and lies across her lap. They form the

Pieta. In the dream she says to him, So you would rather be the baby than the penis.

In another dream her father is alive. He speaks to her. Then he dies in front of her, as he always does in her dreams. She comforts her mother, in the dream, by saying, At least I was able to hear his voice again.

"Cut to: A woman at her desk, writing her dreams furiously. She is laughing, she is crying. She tears one sheet of paper out of the typewriter, then another, and another, and after several hours of intense work, she has a pile of papers in front of her. Victoriously she prints the 'End' at the bottom of the last page."

How Paige wishes her life were scripted. how she wishes for inspiration, though she does not find it and doesn't believe in it. Must one believe? How she wishes she did. If wishes were horses…

> Pull another string and I'll kiss your lips
> Snap your fingers and I'll turn you some tricks
> I'm your puppet
> Your every wish is my command
> All you gotta do is wiggle your hand
> I'm your puppet.

If Paige continues and even finishes the Agnes story she might title it *Ordinary Unhappiness*. Though maybe Agnes' was neurotic unhappiness. Maybe it ought to be called Dramatic Pictures. Dramatic Agnes wasn't easy to forget. She lingered in Paige's mind, in the air, as vaporous memory. You might say Agnes was unique. You might say she was pathetic. Wounded certainly, a wounded baby animal. Paige hears Agnes' clear voice as if she were singing in the room, beside her. Then inside her. Agnes' voice quivers in Paige, strikes a knowing chord, hits a funny bone.

Surely you know people like Agnes. Their voices are sheltered in your body. They have become phrases in your body. They are your visitors. Sometimes you push them away, push them out, exhale them heavily. You don't want them inside you. You may want to kill them. I don't want them either. I am too full and too empty. The bombs are falling. People are maimed, dead. I can barely think, let alone speak. What should I do? I must offer you something. I must prove something. I have something to prove. I will prove it to you. Words will be transformed into wishes.

Paige is holding her head in her hands. Noises from the street disturb her, urge her from her chair. She rushes to the open window. The neighbors, Debbie and Ricky are fighting again. They are screaming, their faces ugly, their bodies twisted, distorted by fury and drugs.

"Back home, Jesus says to me, 'Debbie likes to get hit, man, she's sick. Ricky tells her to stop yelling and then slaps her and she goes, More, more, hit me again.' I don't know whether or not to believe Jesus. I don't want to. But I've never known him to lie. He asked me once, 'Are you going to write about my family? It'd make a bestseller, it's a horror story. Everybody'd want to read it. They'd make a movie about it. You'd make millions.'

"Jesus plays basketball with the guys who hang out across the street. Some come from other neighborhoods. Jesus is the only one of his family who's made friends on the block. He's open, gentle. Ricky used to beat him up. Ricky's beat him up since he was a little boy. Now Jesus is bigger than Ricky. Last week he bashed Ricky's head against a wall. He tells me, 'Ricky won't try nothing ever again.' These days Ricky's on crack, not smack, so at least he's not dropping syringes out the window into the backyard, which was upsetting, watching needles fall on the garden.

"I wasn't sure if I were seeing slides or a film of the scene, it all happened so fast before my eyes. First Debbie ran forward and showed me the scars on her arms. That was awful. Then she tells me that her baby Jessica is one year old. She shows me Jessica's picture. Jessica is in Debbie's arms. The image is fuzzy and dark. Debbie's in pink and the child is looking up at her, smiling at her. I think it's a smile. Showing me the picture, Debbie is happy, as if the baby had not been taken away from her."

So many stories. So many voices. All in need. In need of comfort. I am your comfort. I hold you. I let you go. I am true to you. I am a secret. I explain everything. I seduce you. You lose yourself. I am what you have lost. Your elusive past. Your fleeting present. Your irresistible and horrifying future. I am the little things in life. And the big things. I am lyrical. I am logical. I am steady. I am faithless. I am prosaic. I am poetic. I am hard. I am tender. I am the voice of reason. Of sanity. Of history. I will sing you an aria.

"No. I said no. And I said no again, and I said again, No, no, and I whispered No, and I sang No, and I screamed No, and then I said No, again, and again, and then I yelled No, never more, no, and no, and I hissed, No, then called out, No, then I murmured quietly, No, never, not again, no, and then, with more voice, shouted, No. No. No. No. Never. Never."

I find it difficult to separate the beginning from the end, which makes it hard to record stories, to invent them, or erase them. This may be the end for Paige but stories go on and on and on, leading one into another relentlessly. There is no end to stories, they are without mercy. Still, you and I know stories that begin and end, as surely as you and I know that death comes to all things.

"We do not select the stories we write, we do not pick the voices. They take us by surprise and we surrender to them. They write us, they write in us, all over us, all through us. They occupy us. We are, in a sense, puppets—to language, with language."

Not truly, not absolutely, not actually, not completely.

The night draws to a close, but it doesn't draw. The day dawns, but not for Paige. She is asleep, a small creature curled into the corner of her bed. She covers her head with a blanket. She burrows deeper into her dream. She dreams she has something wonderful to say and then she wakes up, and begins her day, first stopping the alarm clock, then making a cup of coffee, then looking for a shirt, then sitting at her desk. To find words. Paige wraps her hand around her neck and rubs her throat. She coughs and coughs.

THRILLED TO DEATH

What makes people insecure is when they feel like they're lost in the fun house.

— President Bill Clinton

Because carnivalistic life is life drawn out of its usual rut, it is to some extent "life turned inside out,...the reverse side of the world." In antiquity parody was inseparably linked to a carnival sense of the world. Parodying is the creation of a decrowning double; it is the same "world turned inside out." For this reason parody is ambivalent.

— Mikhail Bakhtin

It is not only happiness that gives value to life.

— Colette

ONCE UPON A TIME

Rose Hall was riding backward on a train. She was alone. She felt as free as she would ever be. A man across the aisle had fallen asleep, and his head had dropped to the side of his body. His full lips were open and parted, like a fish mouth on a hook. She watched him, drank beer, and looked at the landscape pass by dyslexically. Earlier she had wanted to have many lovers and a large glass of vodka. She wanted everything fast, without problems or fuss. She laughed at her fantasy of no-fuss love, and then she didn't. Even earlier she became furious at an elderly woman who barged in front of her on line. Rose Hall kept silent. She even bit her tongue. She stared out the window and nursed her wounds. It was strange how one thing didn't follow another.

Steve Whitehurst saw a man standing in front of a door. The man was holding a large pot. It appeared to have nothing in it. The street was dark and the man with the pot was in shadow. Steve crossed to the other side. He didn't want to get hit on the head. Protecting his head was weird, he thought, it probably wasn't worth it. He bought a quart of milk and returned home. He intended to take his regular route, if the freak with the pot had disappeared. But he was still standing there, holding the pot. Steve walked several blocks out of his way, past the Italian Boys Social Club. They were hopeful Mafia lieutenants. He was used to them. But the man with the pot set off an alarm. What in hell was he doing? Steve Whitehurst looked around sharply and put his key in the door.

Lily Lee Wallner kicked a stone on the sidewalk and watched it hurtle into the gutter. She had few defenses against flagrant beauty, her own impatience, and the strangeness of daily life. She was impatient with life. She succumbed to pleasure when she could. "I submitted, I gave in," she told a friend. "I was enthralled. I was on thrill." She fed her fantasies as if they were hungry. The sky was a bright plastic blue. Almost transparent. Lily Lee walked into the park, to the dog run. She stood there a long time. The dogs greeted each other or didn't, they sniffed each other or didn't. Small catlike dogs pursued unlikely big dogs. The freedom of dogs was beguiling, and Lily Lee liked to imagine an animal's liberty. She walked away, toward the playground, a fortress encircled by rough-hewn, pale blue walls. Children slid down the slides and screamed with savage pleasure. Worried mothers frowned, and patient fathers and happy mothers smiled. Lily Lee didn't want children. She wanted a dog. Maybe that was a fantasy.

Paige Turner wrote in her notebook: "You've never been a child, or you're always a child. Or there is no childhood, or children are innocent, or they're evil, or children and adults have nothing to do with each other, or they have everything to do with each other, they are each other, or how do you stop being a child—at an event? with a recognition? and when, oh when, does childhood end? and when does being alive stop being only colors, smells, and sounds.

"You're little, you're lying in the dark, and you can barely see but you hear noises, voices. Sounds become words, you put two and two together, two words, two sentences, an explanation, everything's explained to you, you're told about the world, you overhear, you pay attention, drink in, you grow bigger, you make up your own stories, you imagine, things happen to you that you can't control, you make your way or you don't…."

Paige washed her hair. It was long, curly, and red. She'd heard jokes about redheads her whole life. She was sick to death of them, she hated being called "Red." Everyone said her hair was her best feature. Maybe she'd bleach it silver. I have a redhead's temper, she noted wryly to herself. Then she laughed out loud.

It was way past her bedtime. Jeff Brown read *Cinderella* to his four-year-old daughter, Kelly.

"Once upon a time, a wealthy man's wife died suddenly. The stricken man mourned her extravagantly. But luckily he had one daughter he adored. Cinderella was kind, bright, and beautiful, like his dead wife. But he was lonely, and he wanted to make a new home for them. So he remarried. Now his new wife also had children, two daughters from a marriage that ended with death. But theirs had not been a happy union, and years of strife had hardened the woman and her daughters. They were blind to anything but their own needs. One could say that she and her daughters were cut from the same loveless cloth, and loving didn't come easily to them and they weren't easily made happy. In her way, the new wife loved her new husband. But it had been a long time since she'd been loving. She guarded her good feelings jealously, as if they could be stolen from her like her wallet. Right after the marriage, the new wife turned against her stepdaughter. Cinderella didn't like her, either. She was ordered to do menial chores and given no time to read stories, which she loved. Her stepsisters passed their days playing games, doing puzzles, studying, and trying on clothes. Cinderella didn't complain to her father, even though she wanted to. She had a lot of pride, but oddly enough, to her annoyance, her father seemed happy with his new wife...."

Kelly's eyes started to close. Jeff watched her face expectantly. Her eyes opened again, and she pleaded buoyantly, Daddy, read more, Daddy, read.

"So day after day, she did the dirty work, pretending it didn't bother her. Night after night, she sat by the fireplace, in a corner of the hearth, surrounded by ashes. She watched the hot fire burn orange and red, then die. She tried not to feel sorry for herself.

"Her dirty face and hands, and soiled, torn clothes, were a constant shame to her. She felt older than her years. Her stepsisters teased her and called her Cindy, because she sat by the cinders. Cinderella controlled her temper. Her face grew masklike, and she never laughed. But, however she felt about herself, she was pretty in her sisters' eyes, and they saw how their stepfather looked at her. Cinderella hadn't planned to make them suffer by comparison, but they did."

Kelly's eyelids dropped and shut tight, and Jeff, tired, jumped to the end of the tale.

"The shoe fairly flew out of the Prince's hand—or so it is said—onto her foot, making a bond with it. The sisters were astonished. So was the Prince. They were even more astonished when Cinderella pulled from her pocket the second slipper and placed it on her other foot. (She did this with a little satisfaction; she wasn't absolutely selfless or a fool.) With the second shoe on, her godmother appeared. She waved her wand over Cinderella, who was transformed again. This time, even more magnificently. Awestruck, the Prince asked her to marry him.

"Now, this is what everyone still talks about. Though she loved the Prince, and accepted his offer, what pleased Cinderella most was her sisters' change of heart. They were ashamed of their behavior and really sorry they'd been so horrible to her. And Cinderella forgave them and said she would always love them. Then she invited them to live with her in the palace. A few days later, when she and the Prince married, Cinderella introduced her sisters to two eligible bachelors. Immediately they fell in love. This made her stepmother proud, even repentant. And, though everything happened very fast, after many years, they are all still together. And so it may be said that they are living happily ever after."

By the time Jeff recited the words "happily ever after," Kelly was lost to sleep. She looked so vulnerable, he wanted to cry.

In the Brothers Grimm version, the stepsisters' eyes are plucked out by doves. "And so for their wickedness and falseness they were punished with blindness for the rest of their days." He didn't want Kelly to hear that. Jeff Brown and his white wife had recently divorced. The truth was, she left him for another man. Jeff resisted his own ugly feelings and they parted more or less amicably. Jeff was a reasonable man. But ever since the divorce, their daughter Kelly had had bad dreams.

Jeff discussed the Grimm version of *Cinderella* with his law partner, Rose Hall. He told her how bloody and cruel it was. It's wild, Jeff said, no matter what version you read, *Cinderella*'s a divorce story, right from line one. Then, looking out the window, he said, I want to protect Kelly, but in this world you're a fool, living a fantasy.

Frank Green took life as it came. He prided himself on that. But he envied other people their illusions, their delusions, their dreams. He wasn't a dreamer. He wasn't like that. Plain food, plain living, he wasn't going to kid himself. He had his one chance in life, and if he blew it, that was that. He probably had blown it. But he wasn't a crybaby. He didn't care what other people thought about him.

Frank had a dream. He told his girlfriend, Lily Lee: I'm trapped in an apartment. I'm trapped in a kitchen, it's yellow. I hear a noise. Someone has gotten in. Someone wants to kill me.

I see who it is. This person wants me dead, but I can't believe it. I wake up. I have to piss like a racehorse.

A yellow kitchen? Lily Lee repeated, with a wan smile. I'm the kitchen? Frank told her she was being a jerk. "I had to piss, that's all." And then he teased her the way he always did: "You're just half-Chinese."

When it was late at night or early in the morning and the city was silent—like the Tombs, Frank always put it—he opened up to Lily Lee:

"A couple of years ago I felt like, who gives a shit. I hated it, life. Hated myself. I was apathetic. I hated life. Then I wanted to get high all the time. As much of the time as I could. I wanted to feel alive all the time. I drank like a maniac, I went on benders, I caroused with the guys, got stupid, and that started to interfere with the job. I got sloppy. And then I thought about sex all the time. Sex and more sex. I wanted to feel alive. This is before I met you. But the sex was nuts-and-bolts stuff, mechanical. I made up scenes to get myself off. But I had to work at it. I couldn't get off even on my own sexual numbers. It was pathetic. I looked at nuns, I mean, I'm a Catholic, I should be able to, and even schoolgirls, in their uniforms, but it didn't work for me. I couldn't picture it. I can't get excited if I can't picture it. Then I watched porn all the time. But it made me sad. I don't get off on other people's fantasies."

Lily Lee sighed. She said, I know what you mean. Frank Green was a cop. He fascinated her. They'd met at the hospital where she worked as a nightshift nurse. To Lily Lee he was Paul Newman in *Fort Apache, The Bronx*. They turned on the TV.

Lily Lee had a dream: A man's following me. I escape wearing heels but I'm in my nurse's uniform. There's blood on it. On the road outside the house, I start walking and hitch a ride with a man on skis. I close my eyes and don't see how fast or where we're going. Then I realize I'm holding on and we're going uphill climbing the Empire State Building—no, the Eiffel Tower. Then I wake up and there's snow and ice. I hang on to his body, my arms around his waist. At first I'm afraid, then I realize I can ski.

Lily Lee put on her blades and skated around the city. She didn't tell anyone about her nightmare. It disappeared with the day. That afternoon she met Frank, and they went to the carnival. They wanted to see "Bonnie and Clyde's Death Car," but they didn't know if it'd be there. Frank told her that when he was a kid, there were real freaks in carnivals. Now, he complained, the sideshow's on the street. Lily Lee grinned and told him to shut up.

THE OMNIPRESENT TENSE

The scene overpowers Paige. She's excitable. She thinks, I'm such a cheap date, maybe I have a cheap date with fate. The carnival gates are wide open. Everyone's been invited by an imaginary host. There's no one to thank or to be grateful to. The chaotic and tacky splendor is disinterested, like a neutral party. All are welcome. Paige likes that.

The carnival seduces Paige the way it always does, ever since she was a kid. It's a phantasm, a phantasmagoric suite of sights. Anything can happen. A carnival was her first taste of sweet earthly danger. She remembers it like her first real kiss, even though the first carnival was just a bunch of tents and displays, games and food, cotton candy, nothing elaborate. But one day it appeared, out of nowhere, in a vacant parking lot, at the end of the block. Strangers lounged on the sidewalk, men with moustaches and muscles, women with red lips and muscles. The grifters seduced the suckers. The short con artists, small time and hapless, schemed and entrapped. The carney kids seemed to have possibilities she'd never know. They ran wild, her mother said. She was scared of the place and attracted to it. A dark, handsome teenager, years older than her, smiled at Paige, and an unknown thrill curled up her spine.

She's still scared on the rides, thrilled to death.

"And mammoth, now-extinct animals roamed the land, and our ancestors, prehistoric humans, crawled on all fours, on hairy limbs. They didn't have tools or fire. Foliage blanketed the ground. Forests and mountains and lakes and oceans and rivers and valleys were mighty. The hot yellow sun and the cool silver moon and the white nighttime stars generated life, and there was no time. The strange, naturally occurring objects made the world for the creatures below them. They determined the activity of all the incipient or simple humans and the large and small creatures."

Jeff, Rose, and Kelly sit in the darkened theater. The voice-over rolls along as dinosaurs, winged mammals, pterodactyls, and hunched over, crawling, or standing early humans move like ghosts across the 3-D screen. Kelly is a butterfly mounted on her seat. Jeff considers the magnitude of prehistory, first as myth, then as fact. He thinks about evolution, those first human baby steps, the laborious move to stand upright, creatures crawling out of the water onto land and adapting. He wonders if humans are still adapting or if humans are finished, soon to be extinct. He looks at Kelly. She fills him with hope.

Rose has her own hopes. Maybe a life in the country or a life with Jeff, though that might be a bad idea, just a fantasy, and then there's mixing business with pleasure, but none of those rules really matter to her, deep down. Jeff wonders if Rose's in love with him. His wife used to say that, but he thought she was just giving him grief. Rose thinks maybe she loves Jeff. Kelly doesn't like Rose. She wants her mommy and daddy to be together again. Actually, she wants her daddy all to herself.

In the darkened theater, all three discover that wearing 3-D glasses is uncomfortable. Rose is disoriented, agitated. She can't shake an uneasy feeling. Then the show's over and they walk outside. The bright sun hurts Jeff's eyes. Rose squints too. Kelly asks, Daddy, Daddy, go carousel?

Paige wanders through the sprawling carnival, the playground—massive tents, quaint, small buildings, golden facades, enormous terrifying rides, food booths, staged acts, video and computer games, interactive gothic houses of horror. Waves of brilliant color rise and splash over her. A tide of electricity carries her away from shore, from herself. Startling neon signs glare and blink naughtily. Light encases her as if it were a gaudy gown.

Paige strolls slowly up one ramp and then down another, she follows the twists and turns of the road. She's in a labyrinth. She wants to absorb everything. She doesn't want to know where she is. She doesn't want to be herself. Unconsciously she smells perfumes and underarms and hair spray and young and old bodies. The smells of food are memory ridden. Smell is the sense closest to the center of memory in the brain, a psychologist once told her. Even when Paige doesn't remember what is evoked by a scent or aroma, the smell lingers, tantalizingly. Paige believes memory is in every cell of her body.

Steve Whitehurst sees Paige Turner. Her long, curly red hair. He's always had a thing for redheads. Steve notices Paige while standing behind his uncle's shooting gallery; it's one of his uncle's concessions. Steve wonders if she'll come to his booth. He sets his mind to it, to drawing her closer to the theater of rifles. But she walks away, toward the fortune teller. A couple of black kids pick up rifles. Steve tells them, You have to pay first. One says they don't have money. Steve nods, OK, and they go ahead. But just one round, he cautions. Steve hopes his uncle doesn't spot him doing this. Everyone in his family is in the carney business. Steve's not made for the life.

Grotesque advertisements for horror fan Paige's spirits. I have no soul, she whispers to no one. And I don't want one. But I want something. Maybe I'll run away and join the carnival, call myself Dahlia and paint myself purple, I'll think purple thoughts, and be the purple lady in the sideshow. She wonders if, without the idea of a soul, she can think about beauty lasting, or of anything lasting, of goodness living on after death, of anything of her continuing, or of anything at all in her, or anything that might survive the death of her body. She didn't want the thoughts. A friend told her that's why people have children.

Paige is transfixed by the swirl and rage of the raucous action around her. No one has planned it all, it's not plotted, it's not a plot. She can do whatever she wants. But Paige sometimes finds it hard to choose.

The shocking pink-striped facade of the fortune teller-The Cabinet of Dr. Joy—entices Paige. A poster picture of the fortune teller is dramatic. He's an old man with a white beard and wire-rimmed glasses. He looks serious, Paige thinks, as she takes the plunge and parts the heavy curtains. Though Paige doesn't believe in it, she always has her fortune told. Cards, tarot, palm readings, tea leaves, handwriting, crystal balls. The old man doesn't work that way.

Frank and Lily Lee are riding on the Wonder Wheel. It stops. They're stuck at the top. Frank cracks a joke about there being room at the top for the likes of them. He calls himself legal lowlife. Lily Lee tells him to stop ragging on himself. The little carriage shakes back and forth. Frank takes Lily Lee's hand. I have a secret, he says soberly. Lily Lee looks at him hopefully. You can't tell anyone, he goes on. Only my partner knows, and he's a tomb. Lily Lee listens, waits breathlessly. I murdered a guy, Frank says. They're both silent, the little carriage jolts back and forth. In the line of duty? Lily Lee asks. No, he says, not in the line of duty. I was a kid. It was an accident. They are on top of the Wonder Wheel a long time. Frank stares ahead. He's not frightened. Lily Lee is, but Frank's stoicism infects her. Frank asks, Do you think you could marry a man like me? Lily Lee swallows and coughs nervously. Is he serious? Frank goads her, But since you're half inscrutable, I'll never know what the real deal is... Lily Lee bites her tongue. She says, If you keep on this half business. Then she breathes in and out. I know my mother's family will love you, anyway. So that's a yes, Frank says. If we live, Lily Lee answers, looking down, her heart in her mouth.

Paige Turner instantly and inexplicably comes under the spell of the fortune teller. A charming mind reader, she decides. The fortune teller stares calmly at Paige. He takes her into his inner sanctum. He motions that she sit down. He wants to hypnotize her. Does she mind? When he looks at her with his peculiarly intense eyes, she says, No, go ahead. Then she adds, What have I got to lose? Your inhibitions, he answers serenely. But he continues, I don't predict the future. You don't? Paige asks. No, he says, I predict the past. Predict the past? Paige repeats. He dangles a silver object in front of her eyes and speaks in a warm voice and her eyelids grow heavy, as he says they will.

Steve Whitehurst's uncle returns and tells him to take tickets at the sideshow. That's more your line, he adds, to Steve's annoyance. In an uncanny way, his uncle's right. He's more at home in front of the Odditorium than behind a counter where people shoot at targets with ugly brown rifles. The Odditorium is out of date, the name was used a long time ago, but the sideshow business—there's no business like the sideshow business—is having a comeback, he reassures himself. Steve walks over to the ticket booth. He doesn't really like the current freaks who are bringing sideshows back, but at least they don't want the life to disappear. We're up against soap operas and daytime talk shows, his uncle complained all the time, freaking talk shows, freaks for free, but they're just talk, blah blah. People come because they still want the real thing, live stuff, live exhibits.

But not as much as they once did, Steve knows. He smiles at the posters around him, relieves the other guy in the booth, and remembers the redhead nearby. Live exhibits, Steve thinks.

Nothing dies here, everything's alive, vital, the old man chants. You're in a carnival. You're in the funhouse. But it's not a funhouse. It's also a tragic place, a cemetery for things that aren't dead. A home for the hidden, the driven, the obscene, and sometimes something leaps out, but it's not what it seems. What arrives wears a costume, and an event is a mask. It may be something else. It may be light or dark and really be its opposite. But there are no simple opposites.

Paige, you will encounter your contrariness and bare it boldly. Your ambivalence will concoct dreams beyond your wildest wishes. Here, your contradictions may be honeyed and bitter.

Paige tastes bittersweet chocolate in her mouth.

Paige, here you can be anything. Where are you now?

Paige listens to something, maybe it's the fortune teller: Where are you?

I don't know. I can't tell.

Do you see a window?

Yes, I see it.

Go through it. What do you see now?

Ropes, funny china, people in costumes, neon lights, monkeys on trees, crates of fruit, my mother, a stack of orange books, and so many colors, and there are three ways to go, paths....

Take one.

Where am I? Paige asks herself. This is corny. Maybe I'm having a near-death experience.

Where am I? she asks aloud.

You are not yet. You are not I.

I know that. I don't want to choose a path.

Then you'll stand in one place.

I'm at a standstill, Paige thinks. How did the fortune teller know?

Jeff Brown carries Kelly. She's a drowsy bundle in his arms. Rose and Jeff walk to the sideshow. Signs proclaim exhibits and acts—

a bearded lady, a tattooed man, a sword swallower, the largest rat in captivity. I don't want to see a giant rat, Rose announces, disgusted. Her lip curls. Jeff hates that. And as her lip curls, and she says this, an amplified voice blurts: See the incredible rat. Come, look at the largest rat in captivity. Look at the giant rat. They see a poster for a hunger artist. That, I have to see that, Rose says. They pay their money to Steve Whitehurst. Jeff's glad Kelly's asleep.

They enter a room and pass the giant rat in a glass case. Rose ignores it. There's another glass cage with hefty cockroaches and, in its own separate section, a furry tarantula. A man-eating snake rests, coiled, in its box. Then they approach the hunger artist. She is a woman in a large cage sitting on a stool next to an empty refrigerator. A doctor's scale is next to her. A sign I WILL EAT NO FAT hangs behind her head. She is emaciated, so weak she can't stand. Is this a joke? Jeff asks. Rose points to a smaller sign at the hunger artist's bony foot:

> *I have to fast, I can do nothing else... because I could not find the food I like. If I had found it, believe me, I wouldn't have made a fuss but eaten my fill like you and anyone else.*
>
> — Franz Kafka

Paige chooses a path, under protest. Now she doesn't really have words for what's happening, or isn't actually happening, and she can't make it conform to logic. It has its own logic and is indifferent to reality. She's moving and she's not, she's talking and she's not. Nothing dies here, she hears again.

Maybe something's dead in me, Paige says mournfully.

Nothing's dead in you, it's only unavailable. Behind one object lies another, nothing is lost. Life is a veil...

A vale of tears? Paige interrupts.

Life is a veil of self-consciousness, there are many...

Many lives? she asks, hopefully.

You have many possibilities, positions, and poses.

I'm a fake?

There are no disguises. Everything reveals you.

Paige struggles with the riddle and the eccentricity of the riddler. Finally she speaks, but her voice cracks, and she doesn't really have control over it. She thinks it's not hers.

"I want to go where I'm not supposed to go. I want to see what I'm not supposed to see. I want what I'm not supposed to have. I want to have everything, before I die. I want to be everything. I don't want life to end, and I don't want it to be for nothing, at the end. I want something about me to live forever. I want death to lose, I don't want to reach an end. I don't want to come to a conclusion. I want to continue. And I don't want anything in my way."

Steve sells tickets for another freak show, it's hardcore, underground, more expensive. In a back room, people slash and cut themselves with razors and hang weights from their nipples or scrotums or both. There's a bondage and whipping act. Marrieds with children don't usually know about this show. It's word of mouth. Steve wants to have his nipples pierced, but he's afraid of blood and disease. He might do it anyway. Della, the dominatrix in this sideshow, knows how to pierce skin antiseptically and without pain. Yesterday, she told him, "Unless you want pain. My slave did." Steve asked, "How can you stand to watch his pain?" Della the dominatrix fixed her eyes on him and answered sternly, "It's not my pain." Steve was rocked by her frankness, her brutality.

Today he sways with abandon to the beat of the inside-out world he frequents. He doesn't think he wants pain or punishment, but he always feels guilty.

Lily Lee and Frank buy tickets to the back room show. Steve thinks Frank looks familiar. But is he a mark or a narc? Frank figures if Lily Lee can accept him, if he lets her know the worst about him, he can marry her without feeling like the pig he is. Frank's lied all his life and thinks everyone's a liar. Besides he's good at it, and it's an occupational hazard. Lily Lee looks at Frank. She likes his paunch. His excess. Lily Lee wants nothing more than to live dangerously. Frank's her ticket to ride. He's a dark character. But she has secrets she'd never tell Frank. She has more sides to her than he could guess.

Lily Lee's mouth drops open. A guy is pounding a spike through his penis. Frank gapes at a man hanging from the ceiling by his tongue. Surprisingly, Frank is sick to his stomach. Lily Lee remembers, with a pang, that she had another dream. In it she handed a hard-boiled egg to frank. But the yolk wasn't very hard. Maybe she'd tell Frank. He'd probably laugh and say it was a bad dream or bad yolk, that he's a rotten egg. Maybe she does want children.

THE IMPERFECT PRETENSE

Paige isn't sure if she's babbling, in a trance, or daydreaming.

I shouldn't be telling you this, she says aloud.

I may or may not stop you, the old man says. Though you're the one who does that. You may want me to stop you.

No, I don't.

There's no no here.

This is crazy.

You imagine there's something else.

Paige is falling. Like Alice. She refuses to be Alice. She's falling anyway.

She is nowhere she knows. She may lose hope and lose hopelessness, abandon innocence and find her guilt, speak lies and truth, know reason as unreason, discover thoughtful thoughtlessness, and meaning's meaninglessness, be good and bad, and she may uncover things or bury things, forget to forget or forget to remember, and she may deny the dead, embrace hate and love murderousness, she may rage and covet. All her passions are allowed. She may repeat herself, endlessly. She can hold on and hold on, resist nothing, everything, and defend herself constantly.

Paige grips the arms of her chair.

Paige, the old man says, ugliness turns into beauty the way grapes turn into wine, and beauty may be ugly in a bad light.

Grapes aren't ugly, Paige answers, feeling dumb.

Paige is crestfallen, downcast suddenly, and Dr. Joy lifts up her chin. She doesn't know he's doing this. She hears him say: If you don't look for confirmation of your beliefs you'll have an interesting life.

Now Paige imagines he's opened a fortune cookie.

Jeff, Rose, and Kelly emerge from the Odditorium. Rose can't get over the emaciated woman. She's starving herself to death. Kelly awakens and cries out, carousel, I want carousel. Jeff smiles at his demanding little daughter. They follow the signs and walk in the direction of the carousel. Secretly Jeff wishes there'd been a snake woman and a fat man.

The sun is going down, it's cooler, but it's also warm too, balmy, and far above, a mirror to the carnival, the sky is flecked with pink, orange, red, and gold. The sky's on fire. Brilliantly decorated and brightly colored vans and trailers are converging into the center where the carousel acts like a magnet.

Suddenly Jeff and Rose are energetic. The pounding in Jeff's head evaporates, Rose stops worrying about a case she's handling, about the argument she has to make in court the next day, she stops fretting about Jeff.

Paige, wake up, you'll be as awake as you can be. You may remember that you are alone and not alone and that something lives you can never know or grasp fully. This is yours, but it's not yours alone.

Paige wake up.

Paige opens her eyes and senses, weirdly, gravely, that she is awake, that she wasn't completely asleep. She shakes her legs and arms. She imagines she's a dancer and a dance. She knows she's dancing around herself. That's strange, she thinks, I'm not a very good dancer.

Her eyes are wide open.

Paige asks, Am I alone?

Paige, you've come late to your vanity.

What does he mean? she wonders.

I can't see it, she says.

Dr. Joy smiles, then he responds in such a low voice, she can barely hear him. She thinks he says, How can you see all of what's indefinitely, even infinitely, unfinished, with or without you? He pauses and chortles. You and I are easily undone, Paige. And, anyway, seeing isn't believing.

Paige doesn't believe her ears, either.

With Kelly still in his arms, Jeff and Rose keep walking to the carousel. Kelly's beside herself with joy. Streams of people are going their way. Everyone's drinking and eating, giggling and shrieking. Thousands of people are marching in time to organ music. Maybe it's piped in through a public address system coming from the carousel. Jeff isn't sure.

People are wearing silly clothes. People are walking on their hands. People have stockings pulled over their faces as if they're bank robbers. Women are dressed as outrageous men, and men as sensible women, and children are wearing oversized evening gowns and tuxedos. In a sideshow parade, that's what Rose calls it, a carnival king and queen are crowned and then their crowns are stolen from their heads. They're throned and dethroned in a bizarre celebration. Their chairs are pulled out from under them again and again, as they're mocked and they mock each other. People shout, Death to the Dead. Death to the Dead. Death to the Queen. Death to the King.

Rose knows if they yelled Death to the President, they'd all be arrested.

Then, Jeff and Rose buy tickets for the carousel from a woman who claims to be president. President of what? Rose asks the old woman. Had she penetrated Rose's mind? Of these disunited states, the old woman answers. The elderly ticket taker smiles wickedly and turns a cartwheel. I'm eighty, she claims with glee. Jeff guesses the woman's a gypsy and touches his pocket, unconsciously. The old woman watches him do it.

Lily Lee and Frank eat hot dogs and drink beer. When the cotton candy melts in her mouth, she knows she's on earth again. Terra firma, Frank says, nothing like it. Frank has mustard on his lip, and Lily Lee wipes it off with her hand. Maybe she really loves him. It's hard to tell. She's always been romantic, ever since she was a kid and fell for her first movie star and dreamed about him every night. Rock Hudson. Every night she prayed to god that he'd bring her Rock.

Paige is ready to leave. She turns to the old man once more.

"You didn't read my mind," she says. Paige is perplexed.

"Mind reading isn't my field. I told you I predict the past."

"That doesn't make sense," Paige objects.

"It doesn't," the old man agrees. "You were reading your own mind. I was listening."

THE FUTURE OF HISTORY

By now Kelly has climbed out of her father's arms. Rose, Jeff, and Kelly linger at the base of the antique carousel. It's red, blue, silver, and green; the sturdy old wooden horses are white, pink, and black. The carousel goes round and round, round and round, round and round so fast, the whirling structure is a blast and blur as the colors whip into one. But then it slows down, goes slower and slower, and figures appear and shapes become objects, and the colors separate again.

Now the three walk on, Kelly and Jeff choose a pink horse, Rose a black horse. The music starts up and the carousel begins to move, and slowly it gains speed. The sturdy horses ascend their poles and descend, they go up and down, up and down, up and down, in time to the music. Kelly is ecstatic. The carousel turns round and round, faster and faster, the music is loud and familiar, people reach for the gold ring, and Rose is floating above herself, above the world. She's flying. She feels she can do anything. She wishes she were still a kid, but not the one she was when she was a kid.

Suddenly, Rose notices a man with a gun. She always sees things like that, evidence like that. He's packing, she says aloud, and reaches across her horse to touch Jeff's arm.

His act is magic, Paige decides. Aware and unaware, and reluctant, she leaves the fortune teller's pink-striped tent just the way she came. She's not sure it's the same passageway. Does he have a license to do this? Paige wonders. She's a little dizzy, almost nauseated. What's magic? she thinks. Maybe nothing really happened.

Steve Whitehurst asks to be relieved. He wants to leave the booth. He doesn't want to work anymore. He wants to be part of the crowd. Besides, he just saw the redhead leave. He has to find her. He wants to drift with her through the Soul Tunnel of Love.

Steve follows Paige. She's unaware of him, she's still in another world. To Steve she looks blissed out. What if, he thinks, I kissed her, the way the soldier kissed the woman in Times Square? That famous end-of-the-war photograph had impressed Steve when he was a kid. It happened on your birthday, his mother told him proudly. Why not? Steve thinks.

In the distance people scream on the roller coaster. Steve realizes his life has been one long ride on an emotional roller coaster.

Lily Lee and Frank stroll along Lovers' and Others' Lane. She has agreed to marry him. She agreed one time before, but she left the man standing at the altar. The morning of the wedding, she awoke and couldn't move. The doctor called it temporary paralysis. Her mother said, You didn't want to marry him. Lily Lee prays that doesn't happen again.

They walk aimlessly and arrive at the carousel. Lily Lee wants to grab a ride. Frank reluctantly nods yes. To him it's silly. They buy tickets from the woman who claims to be president. Now her clothes are on, inside out.

So many people are around, more and more of them. It's working my nerves, Frank tells Lily Lee. He hates crowds, crowds worry him, the possibility of danger and disaster. Frank touches the gun under his belt, the bulge on his right hip. His gun never leaves his side.

Just then a huge float passes by. It's painted red, draped with shiny red satin, and lit by Chinese lanterns adorned with crystal spangles. On the side of it is a sign: HELL. Frank nudges Lily Lee, See, baby, now we can go to hell together.

Paige drifts and weaves through the crowd. Steve is near her, following her, but he's also caught up in the makeshift parade. Some acrobats join the throng and turn cartwheels. Dancers in pink tights and toe shoes stand on their toes. Everyone glides along to the canny rhythm of the organ music. The red float named Hell passes Paige too. Comic red devils leap up and down on the top of the float. They stick their tongues out and cry Death to the Father. Paige touches her red hair. Nothing ever dies, she remembers. The devils point at each other ironically and shout: Death to You. Death to You.

Steve gathers up his courage. He moves closer to Paige and introduces himself, and no, he doesn't kiss her, he simply says, Isn't this weird? Paige nods.

Then she sees Dr. Joy. She thinks it's him, anyway. He's dressed as a clown, with a fright wig, red lipstick dotted on his cheeks and an enormous, painted-green mouth. Dr. Joy spots her, signals, and stands on his head. Everything's upside down, Paige exclaims to Steve. Steve puts his arm around her, as if to steady her, but really he's steadying himself. He wants her.

Rose, Jeff, Kelly, Frank, and Lily Lee are going round and round on the carousel, round and round and up and down. Turning and turning, even frank is subdued, nearly content. Things seem possible and unpredictable. Kelly grabs a ring, Jeff kisses Rose, Frank starts to get emotional, and Lily Lee cries for no reason. There seems to be no need for restraint.

Then, suddenly, there's a noise, a huge roar, an explosion, and the float named Hell goes up in flames. The fire rises and burns wildly, grandly, it's out of control, it's not being controlled, and the red satin cloth, the Chinese lanterns, everything is immolated in its glorious blaze. No one's afraid. People cheer, joke, dance, and laugh, as if tomorrow will never come.

Paige is ready for anything. Craziness has erupted, and she's carrying weird, anarchic instructions. Don't look for confirmation, you can't see, you're undone...

Steve's almost naked with his longing and lust stains his blue eyes. Paige wants him to want her. His desire is a delicacy on her plate for her. The heat in his eyes turns them liquid and silky, empty of everything. He has an illusion of her, of what she could be. She sees that. He might be disappointed. There's always disappointment and regret, and Paige wants regret less than she wants to want anything. His heart beats under his shirt. Paige likes that.

Later, when Steve and Paige ride through the Soul Tunnel of Love, she relishes the anonymity of being a stranger, the fantasy of being strange with a stranger.

Eventually, though the fire still burns and the shouts and laughter continue, Frank becomes aware of the man with the gun. It pulls him from one world into another. The man touches his gun so Frank draws his. He shouts: Police officer. The man fires, and they exchange shots. Rose is hit in the shoulder by the round of bullets. She isn't seriously hurt, but the dramatic event will change the course of her life. Kelly's in shock, startled by the sight of blood, the sound of gunfire, the confusion around her. She howls. For hours she's inconsolable.

In what seems only a few breathless seconds, Rose is rushed to the hospital, and Jeff, with Kelly crying in his arms, accompanies her in the ambulance. Frank and Lily Lee are escorted by two cops, who know Frank, to the nearest police station. The unknown man, the assailant with the gun, gets away. He loses himself in the carnival crowd. The cops pick him up later. His gun's registered to his brother.

Lily Lee didn't leave Frank at the altar. One night, though, shortly after their marriage, Frank went berserk and threatened to kill himself. Lily Lee insisted he get counseling or she'd divorce him. They never had children. She wanted a dog and finally bought one.

Rose dissolved her partnership with Jeff, gave up law, and moved to New Mexico. She fell in love with a dancer named Gwen and, one day, opened a storefront law office. She couldn't stay away from it.

Jeff reunited with his wife for a while, then they separated again for good. He became an expert in DNA, and in his spare time read about extinct forms of life. For years he worried about Kelly's future.

Kelly wanted to be a musician and played in a few groups around town. For a couple of years she had a drug problem. Jeff thought it was the result of the divorce, even the trauma of the gunfire at the carnival. Kelly thought it was about being the child of a mixed marriage in a racist country. She overcame her drug problem and studied art history. Kelly focused on color, its meanings and interpretations, aesthetic and cultural, in contemporary theory and history.

Paige and Steve had a torrid and occasionally torporific relationship. They played in ways she and he had never before tried or done. To both of them their involvement was extreme, exhausting, but it was an accomplishment, achieved against overwhelming odds.

Out of the blue, Paige broke up with Steve. By way of explaining, she wrote him a letter:

"I liked your following me. Ordinarily I wouldn't have, I don't think. That carnival deranged me, rearranged me maybe. It was a good and a bad start for us. You don't know where you're standing when you're with me, you said. I didn't know where you stood in my scheme of things. I know I shouldn't have a scheme of things, but I do. Dr. Joy was a joke, you said, but he wasn't funny. I couldn't take it all in, and I couldn't take in you and your scene, and my decisions along the way made it hard for me to deal with yours. There's no way to apprehend or appreciate everything about anyone else. I'm selfish or just limited like everyone else, or both. I didn't see the end coming, I couldn't. Then one day I didn't feel for you. I'm giving you my version. I don't want to defend myself, and I know I am. It was chance. I'm just what you met that day. This is what I made of things. You kidded me about how it was bigger than both of us. It was. You and I nearly believed and then I stopped believing. I want to believe in what can't be seen in the moments I'm not there. But I don't have confidence. Maybe we were just hanging out. And in the end there was my ambivalence, my mixed feelings, as you used to say, always there, and where we started from and what I brought with me...."

Paige never finished the letter. In her mind she addressed it to Steve, but it wasn't really for him. What she had told him, the last time they met, was: It was a fantasy, and now it's not anymore. I don't know what it is. I'm sorry.

The next day Steve had his nipples pierced and for about a year was one of Della's slaves. Then he lost interest in Della, quit the carnival, and wistfully thought about becoming a priest and taking a vow of celibacy. But he didn't. Instead Steve learned the computer software business. To his good friends

Frank and Lily Lee—they'd met at an s&m party—Steve cracked inside jokes about hardware and software, of the hard and soft wear and tear on his life.

ONCE UPON A TIME AGAIN

Forever after, Paige Turner pondered the wonderful and disquieting events of the strange day and night at the carnival. It became a turning point for her, one she never completely understood. She couldn't explain it to herself or anyone else. She often dwelled on the sensations of losing herself, and not losing herself, or being herself and not caring who she was, of having been in a trance or hypnotized, of standing in a place out of place, of not seeing and seeing, of being frightened and calm, and all this was familiar and mysterious. She never forgave herself for the way she broke up with Steve and worried, long after his face was a dead letter, whether she'd used him.

Over the years Paige discovered she'd memorized the day and night at the carnival. The details were kept in her mind, like precious objects in a box. She mentioned the day more and more, at odd moments too. Occasionally she embellished it, and sometimes she chose new words to describe it. Sometimes she said it was indescribable and indefinable, but she never believed that. And sometimes a detail imposed itself, one that she hadn't remembered the last time. The telling of the tale came to have the character of a fable or myth, whose truth or falsehood was hers to cherish.

And much, much later, when years had passed, many years, and she was very old, and her red hair was white, and not long before she died, when the events of every day and every night merged together, when every thought was liminal, and every conversation the remnant of a hypnagogic dream, Paige strained to live the day and night again fully, even to read her mind. Her mind wandered. It might never have happened. Not that way, not that way, that way, yes, that way, I believe, yes, yes, I think it must have been that way, it might have, yes, like that, yes.

And so, to the end, Paige held the thrill close, like an old friend.

THREE

THE TRANSLATION ARTIST AND OTHER STORIES

DRAWING FROM A TRANSLATION ARTIST

1

In recent years I have been characterized as a translation artist, grouped with others who have similar concerns, tendencies, or affinities. I'm slippery categorically, the way words are, since they are my medium, my art; but I can accept, after a fashion, my association with the group (some call it a movement; I don't), because I believe every thing, object or person, is a translation from something or someone else. I consider how history ranges and settles, seamlessly or roughly, in the present; how writing can be accurate even with the inherent obliquities of words, and how naming is usually re-naming. Basically, all my written transmissions are, in these senses, translations. Nothing is denied by me as an effect or influence. (Uninvited memories spring up; forgetfulness occupies its own omniscient realm.)

Things get lost, turn up, go missing again, but in an intimate way an object isn't lost if it was never known to exist: Imagine, as I might, a day in the 3rd century for a man in the Far East who might have been a relation. I see him in a loose brown robe, in a field, wearing a wide-brimmed straw hat against the sun. (Is my consciousness anything like his?) Yet about the day and the man,

I feel no sense of loss. But I lose my favorite jacket—maybe it was stolen. I only know it's gone because I once had it and now want to wear it. I need it, search for it, nervously tossing clothes out of the closet. Head bursting, I retrace my steps, mentally or actually. If I hadn't noticed or needed it, it wouldn't be lost to me. (Someone else has found it.) A lost tree in a lost forest. (Entire histories get lost.) This is similar to the diminution of a friend's or lover's affections, which lack is not immediately noticeable; but when love is needed, it's not available. "I can't see you, haven't you noticed, you lost me, I'm gone."

Disappointments and private disasters can provoke self-persecutions or re-enactments of scenes meant to ascertain the exact moment when a mistake occurred or a bad turn was taken. I avoid such endeavors; yet, as a translation artist, I am not of the "what's done is done" variety. I am, rather, of the "done, undone, redone, done over, done more differently" breed. (I may be a neo-classicist.)

The days and nights of the 1960s or 1980s are images now—words and pictures—and schoolchildren may skip over the assassinations of JFK and Malcolm, or the Iran-Contra scandal, like cracks in a sidewalk. A translation artist might want to reclaim the cracks or ruptures those sinister events caused and acquaint viewers with their stealthy after-effects and after-images—enigmatic historical figures or periods as regenerations, not memories. (Steven Spielberg's *Jaws* is the work of a translation artist: the killer shark is a remake of *Moby Dick*, a presentiment of American disease and fear, which is why Spielberg's translation can be viewed again and again and still evoke horror.)

World or national tragedies differ in scale from intimate or personal loss, though they translate into it too. Also, the need to retrieve history's artifacts and narratives veers off from the need to remember them. For recovery or retrieval from the past, another want, curiosity or engagement is required. A translation artist draws on and from previous conditions and renditions—a painting, news photo, snapshot, text; the actual event existed primarily in representation.

The often painful act of recuperation is performed typically to produce jolts to the system, neurological, aesthetic, cultural, political. (I may intend to activate my translated object like a bomb or, less hyperbolically, software.) There's a kind of skeptical idealism involved. On the one hand, the past can't be recaptured or relived; on the other, as a translation artist, one doesn't expect to capture the past but to interfere with settled notions about it, which is in some sense idealistic.

In 1985 the lost *Titanic* was found, the result of a secret CIA mission to find two missing nuclear submarines. The *Titanic* and its sunken treasure lay at the bottom of the deep blue sea. Pieces eerily intact were brought to the surface, but they have not been translated into the present. They only haunt it as specters of a tragedy in history, because the remnants of the *Titanic* have not been recuperated (I doubt they ever will be). The tragic-historical aura of the porcelain and crystal glass is shatterproof.

2

I accept change in forward, backward, and neutral gears. Art offers me a meta-place where idiosyncratic gestures and odd alignments get tested. Ideas about form, scale, discipline, practice (studio; no studio) are shattered regularly, and the resultant mess on the floor, or foundation, can be swept away or utilized in a piece. Let's say that I, a writer who translates from realities and unrealities onto the page or into cyberspace, find it insufficient to evoke objects for memorialization only—no monuments to mark disasters or fallen heroes or innocent victims. No. (Physics insists that matter returns, that it doesn't die. I might claim matter as a zombie. Others wouldn't.)

As a translation artist, I resist sentimentality and nostalgia. Looking back, for me, must be a cool operation; so I remain detached, whatever my first attachment was. I hold some occasions close, some people, dates, like John Lennon's death, and who told me he'd been shot. (Those few with "superior autobiographical memory" remember every single day of their lives.) One can be overwhelmed with the ennui of time passing, the "where did it all go-ness." But people can't know where things have gone or how the past will be stacked in memory or what will return later when thinking or in revery, awake or asleep.

When I turned thirty, I thought, not atypically, I'm an adult, there's no going back (though in some ways I have and do), assume your responsibilities; at forty, I thought, I'm a middle aged man, "in the middle of my life"—a difficult realization, especially since maturing forces involuntary translations (caring for sick parents; uninvited deaths; hair loss) and is often incomplete. Time keeps slanting my perceptions and shaping my interpretations. I wonder, as I write a story and draw portraits in it, or claim recollections of a dead day, what is beyond recognition. (Are there ideas and times that can't be brought forward?) Artists for re-creation monitor present-day comprehension through new iterations. Things don't mean the same thing forever. Most things disappear.

3

Some things don't disappear. Kafka writes in my fictional life, where his hunger artist invests in translation art-making and vice versa. And, if I write the words, "In recent years," as I did, I hear the echo of his first sentence from *A Hunger Artist.* "In recent years...." The words recur in translation, since I don't read German.

There's a play by Eugene Ionesco called *The Lesson.* I saw it when I was a teenager. The play rotated my thinking 180, and eventually turned me toward translation art. In his play, a teenaged student wants to learn Spanish. The teacher tells her to say, The pen is on the table, in Spanish. She protests that she can't, she doesn't know Spanish. He says she can, she knows it. Just say it, he says. He insists. Haltingly, she speaks, in English: The....pen...is...on...the...table. There, he says, that's right. That's Spanish. It's the same thing.

There's the story, "Pierre Menard, the Author of Don Quixote," in which Jorge Luis Borges tells the tale of Pierre Menard. To understand Cervantes' great novel, Menard immersed himself in it and rewrote it in 17th century Spanish. Since he wrote it again, but in the present context, Menard contends, it was a better work than the original. Crudely, one might believe Menard is copying Cervantes, but Borges' assertion, through Menard, is a radical concept, at the heart of postmodernism, upsetting dearly held beliefs and truths about creativity, originality, and authorship. For one thing, making and remaking can't be separated, like writing, rewriting, revising can't be, and also, which came first is not the right question. (The original may be an atavism.) In any case, Cervantes never left Borges for long, and vice versa.

4

Gertrude Stein drew inspiration from Cubism, especially from Picasso's and Braque's paintings, a kind of borrowing occurred, because through them she found delight and an object to translate into writing. The object wasn't simple: a broken picture plane. How could she break syntax as they did a flat, painted surface. So, Stein unmoored words and created uneasy repetitions to write prose like a Cubist work. Also a painting could be apprehended in the present, which fanned Stein's desire for reading and writing in the present tense. Whether her language experiments succeed or fail, they are never futile. Stein can never fail a translation artist.

I (and you) start somewhere, lean on or draw from art and life, draw meaning from others' lives and work. Where a story takes off is invariably *in medias res* and enmeshed in other stories. Inspiration may be a reprobate, but I have to get myself going, that's all. I might ask you: Tell me a story. I listen. I hear where and how it begins. But It was hard for you to begin it. You said, Let's see, let's see, where should I begin. I say, Begin anywhere. I read Virginia Woolf's diaries and swoon and fall into her great mind. *Bartleby the Scrivener* goes to work with me. I look at a map drawn of America that marks the towns and cities where soldiers who died in war once lived, people I had no idea about.

I can draw something from all of this, I think. It takes time. Drawing, writing, eat up time, it can be slow work, often it's meticulous work. (All things can be done fast, too.) I imagine artists drawing with their heads down, bent in concentration (a hoary image). I see a hand moving on paper, erasing a line, doing it again. It's so human. Maybe it's intimacy, the sense of a presence, and willfulness or agency that confront and content me. In the second decade of the 21st century, I want to assert, slowness is fine, though I like my fast Lenovo, wirelessness, tiny, light things that make big sounds and carry masses of information. (Still, objects, like people, can crowd me.)

At the beginning of the 20th century, speed and machines were everything.

Walter Benjamin wrote in his seminal essay, "The Work of Art in the Age of Mechanical Reproduction:"

> For the first time in the process of pictorial reproduction, photography freed the hand of the most important artistic functions which henceforth devolved only upon the eye looking into a lens. Since the eye perceives more swiftly than the hand can draw, the process of pictorial reproduction was accelerated so enormously that it could keep pace with speech.

Benjamin, before Borges, assaulted the primacy of the original and proclaimed photography, its reproducibility essential, the century's most salient art form, one that would in its course eliminate or supersede others. It would also rid art-making of the hand.

I like the shapes of hands, watching hands pick up a fork, and noting which hand is used, or scratching a head, an arm, or caressing a cheek. On a cloudy day not long ago, I pondered the many negative associations to the hand—like manual labor. Being a grimy worker, with filthy nails. Hands instantly show your station in life. (Probably why there are so many nail salons in New York City.) In art, the hand became a fetish—the artist's hand, even its griminess, was artful. But the hand raised craft over idea. And it wasn't a machine of the future, it wasn't modern, or modernist, it didn't break with the past. It couldn't. It was attached to the human body, and necessarily to human development and history.

The camera, Benjamin hoped, could make art democratic, because anyone's hand could press a button. Also, everyone has eyes which operate anatomically in the same way. Yet the eye isn't neutral, my eye is not like yours, yours not like your sister's. Seeing is a craft too, since it can be taught. And, subjectivity prejudices how and what we see, so vision isn't divorced from undemocratic causes.

Less abstractly, the hand that ties people to their animal bodies doesn't allow for the distance technology offers as a demonstration of progress, which, in the 20th century, was a matter of belief in Europe and America—society was absolutely moving forward, getting better.

Now the fast thumb is a marvel, the 21st century digit, speed in the hand.

5

There's no way around beginnings, middles, and ends, which ghoulishly stroll the streets like zombies.

I'm visiting a cathedral in Santiago de Compostela, in northern Spain, that was consecrated in 1211, and breathing its musty, incense-scented air. The capacious stone cathedral draws thousands to it every year, Christian pilgrims following the same trails as ancient pilgrims and feeling tethered to those first travelers. They are inspired to walk the true path with them. The pilgrims end their walk at this ancient site where St. James once preached the gospel. Arriving, entering the church, they experience transformation, perhaps, or bliss. (I can't know this.) They all stand in line at a column, and when they reach the front of the line, they bend forward and place a hand on the column, where St. James's hand once was, and by now so many centuries of hands have touched the column, a hand print is grooved into it. Outside bagpipers play and welcome more pilgrims.

The Celts invaded Galicia about 450 BC and stayed until the Roman Conquest. Incongruously, the bagpipe took hold and is the region's national instrument.

Cervantes must have heard bagpipe music when he visited the ancient town, if he did, and looked with curiosity at the pilgrims. Maybe the author, who centuries later led Borges, like a pilgrim, to make authorship mysterious, noticed a pilgrim there, a picaresque creature leaning on a gnarled cane, who, having once caught Cervantes' eye, one day returned in his imagination. The pilgrim was transformed into a character he named Don Quixote.

SEVEN TIMES, TIMES SEVEN

For Barbara Probst

I

Tall and short buildings cleave the urban sky. Some people, housed in a suite of offices or a loft, ignore their neighbors, others are nosy and pry. Blinds and shades, doors, locks, and keys offer privacy, and walls restrict sight, and limit sound, sometimes; but walls also entice curiosity, so the voracious hide cameras in bedrooms and bathrooms. Spaces, designed by and for people, usually contain the same objects, with rooms that designate their placement: a computer goes there, TV and bed there, desk here. Table, chairs, couch. Set pieces, really, and spaces for clutter.

Outside, sidewalks, streets, and roads.

People leave their homes and offices to go somewhere, do something. There's a goal, a motive, since humans also design their days, writing lists, making plans. Some have nothing to do, and plan on spontaneity to see them through. They often feel tremulous.

Universal signs punctuate the syntax of space, and let the restless saunter along sidewalks, reading messages, or loiter at corners, even blindly cross roads, without harm.

Walk on the right, the left.
One way.
Dead end.
White lines, black streets.
Yellow CAUTION.
Green GO.
Red STOP.

II

A red light changes, a pedestrian steps into the crosswalk, a car swerves to avoid her, tires skid, she's down. A scream, another scream, cell phones out, a crowd gathers and gawks. "What happened? Did you see it?" a man yells. "I'm calling 911," a girl shouts. Horns blare in unison. Traffic creeps, because of all the rubbernecking.

Emily is spaced-out, aimless in the living room. She once slid across its shiny floor, a kid screaming with happiness. Now she is pacing the length of it.

Emily hears a crash and horns, and rushes to the picture window. She can't tell where the noise came from, and looks toward the park. A horse and carriage, ferrying overheated tourists, clip-clops on a broad path. To Emily, a dark, silent blur.

Maurice approaches his building, and there's a loud screech. He looks at the blue sky. A hawk, he thinks; a few have nests in the nearby park. He's a tall man, Emily's father, with a long nose, dead straight from one angle, wickedly crooked from another.

Emily looks down and then up, across the street to a majestic building where her best friend, Grace, once lived.

In the park, Grace has just scooted out of the path of a horse and carriage, and is hating tourists. She lifts her head high, angling her neck, and sees the building where she once lived, tiny in the distance. A brilliant bluebird lands near her, when Grace hears a terrifying crash.

Maurice quickly glances up, at his apartment on the sixth floor. The windows reflect the glare of the afternoon sun. He can't see anything.

The sun is shining bright yellow against the blue sky, heading in its path toward the west where it will drop. On the roof, Emily's mother, Jane, in dark glasses and a forest green shirt, has been watching a teenaged girl dancing on a nearby rooftop.

Jane hears an ominous cry, and clamor. Since 9/11, she has expected another disaster. Now she looks down at the sidewalk, where she see her husband, Maurice.

Maurice is still as a statue, praying it's the hawks.

Stunned, Grace sees the alarmed bluebird fly away. Grace doesn't move.

Emily falls to the floor, just in case.

III

Divisions between people aren't neat, not anywhere. Sidewalks don't have places for hiding, and, outdoors, corridors for walking and driving are invisibly drawn, so collisions can be physical and metaphorical. Each character has a point of view, reasons and emotions; each can assume a position. People walk into and out of the frame, onto pavements, into alleys, into doorways, they disappear and appear again.

It's a pleasure to grab the last seat on a park bench.

"You can't be everywhere at the same time," a woman tells her friend.

"I wish I had eyes behind my head," the friend answers.

"You're so paranoid," the captious woman says. "You'd look totally weird."

IV

People fascinate each other and invent stories about them, they capture them in movies and novels. To want to know energizes human ingenuity. People buy and make objects; and they are objects to each other, also. Face-reading gets a lot of play, mind reading, too, but mis-recognitions and projections guide conversations, confounding both tellers and listeners. Luckily, people forget way more than they remember.

V.

"No Trespassing" stirs transgression.

Fantasies spool out like thread.

Memories shake loose.

Wishes get buried.

Thoughts go homeless.

The lost can't be found.

Torrents of experience, multiplicities inside multitudes, overwhelm omniscience.

VI

Ludwig Wittgenstein wrote: "Only describe, don't explain." Imagine simultaneity.

VII

Time passes like a stranger walking down the street.

CINDY SHERMAN

I

Nothing changes from generation to generation except the thing seen and that makes a composition.

— Gertrude Stein, "Composition as Explanation"

Cindy Sherman keeps changing the way the world looks, and how it looks at itself. Her photographs have, since the 1970s, fused with the "natural" scenery, the environment, and seem now to have been here forever.

Sherman was born in Glen Ridge, New Jersey, in 1954, and grew up in Huntington, Long Island, New York, a child of the suburbs when suburbia was burgeoning. This is usually where the story of the American 1950s starts: after the Second World War, the United States became a world power. It was a time of optimism, expansiveness, and growing prosperity: TVs in every house, two cars in every garage, and the reign of Detroit and IBM. Meanwhile, Hollywood movies invented America not only for Americans but also for the world.

This version of history ignores another America: discontent, poor, but also aroused after the war. Black American men who had fought against racism abroad, in a segregated army, returned to Jim Crow America. Women who had worked in factories were displaced when the soldiers returned. Frustration and unrest were also byproducts of the war, along with the Cold War, the nuclear arms race, and a manufactured paranoia about domestic communism.

In 1963, when John F. Kennedy was assassinated, Sherman was nine; she was a teenager when Martin Luther King Jr., Malcolm X, and Robert Kennedy were murdered. Figuratively, she grew up with the Vietnam War, the civil rights movement, the second wave of feminism, the gay liberation movement, and with Warhol, hippies, and rock and roll. The 1960s ended and the 1970s began with America's loss in the Vietnam War, Watergate, and President Nixon's resignation. By then, American optimism had been shredded.

Sherman came of age in the mid-1970s. She attended the State University of New York College at Buffalo, switching from painting to photography, which wasn't unusual: Artmaking was changing almost seismically, with artists' reevaluating image-making, the relationship between art and politics, between text and image. All of culture was under scrutiny, like T. S. Eliot's "patient etherized upon a table." Humanism was interrogated by feminist theory, psychoanalysis, and deconstruction. Identity politics, postcolonialist theories, and issues of representation, to name a few, challenged artists indirectly or directly. In any case, different things were happening in their studios.

My mercilessly partial gloss on living history serves as a background or a small picture of Time. Maybe it's a historical prop against which to foreground Sherman's life and work. Were this partial history a board game, I'd suggest: Cindy Sherman starts HERE, during an extraordinarily charged intellectual, political, and aesthetic period.

II

Composition is not there, it is going to be there and we are here.
— Gertrude Stein, "Composition as Explanation"

Sherman started with portraiture and depicted solitary girls and women dressed up, made up, performing womanliness as convention and disguise. She acted the parts, concocted the poses, subtly transforming the girl next door into vamp and superstar. Soon she pictured her characters in situations for which she built the props and sets: her studio became her own movie house, where she mounted photo-dramas. Her characters—abject, frightened, complacent, bewildered, sexy—and their states of mind, economic position, or sexual feelings might be gleaned from their enigmatic expressions and surroundings.

Sherman mined images of femininity and masculinity from Hollywood, fashion, and advertisements. Through her mind's eye, anyone could appropriate or become any image. Images were available, everywhere. Appropriation, in Sherman's world, began at home, a fact of life as well as a new artistic strategy: being an original was highly unlikely, and no longer urgent. Uniqueness and the "original" were, for postmodernists, dubious requirements and values for art.

Sherman concocted ever more elaborate environments and stranger backgrounds: faces obscured under gooey muck, prosthetic body parts hung in space. She emphasized distortion and disturbance. She made things very hard to look at. Grotesque-looking beings appeared to be survivors of terrible wars. Worldly women existed unhappily or stoically in exaggerated displays of wealth, or as muses, with warts, in art history.

Sherman knew how to achieve a look, *the* look. A knowing artfulness and determined vision enabled her to represent the photographic illusion—of glamorous, confused, desperate, or whimsical women—then destroy it. She achieved "realness," entirely through artifice. By the late 1980s, she had contributed toward making Aretha Franklin's 1960s anthem "A Natural Woman" a curious assertion.

III

> *It is understood by this time that everything is the same except composition and time, composition and the time of the composition and the time in the composition.*
>
> — Gertrude Stein, "Composition as Explanation"

After Andy Warhol, Marshall McLuhan, and the advent of post-modernism, surface was no longer superficial—face value had value. The surface signified, because people existed in, and as, images to themselves and to each other. People had images, which made meanings and produced consequences: pretending and posing could be true, but not Truth, not an essential Truth. That didn't exist. And, just as there are no lies on an analyst's couch, because an analysand's misrepresentations are revealing, Sherman's art attested that people's hopes of being someone else are also a reality. Fantasies do become realities.

Sherman's decision to dissolve "human-being-ness," to create degraded, horrifying figures, confronted human pride and disrupted the facade of socialization people believe separates them from other animals. Her bald moves built even more space for a viewer's unconscious activity, which might account for the experience of feeling struck dumb in front of her work.

Her representations showed disorder, nonhierarchical chaos; her explorations of human adaptability pictured endemic discontinuities. In her art, the state of being human suggests endless, terrifying possibility: anything might happen in Sherman's work, as well as in life, and it does.

The human species skates on thin ice if it imagines that identity is stable, that chance and randomness don't play their parts, daily. What Sherman's characters wear—for instance, haute couture—can only cover their naked bodies, never protect them from harm. Her work undermines and frustrates the great wish for security, and also for continuity, an illusion our hapless species needs to believe. Her fragmented, mutating faces and bodies rip at the fabric of identity, relationships, institutions, and treasured traditions in art.

IV

Photographs don't tell more than they show; they don't explain or speak. They are entities, objects. What they show is perceived by viewers, in part, as projections and through identification. Photographs do ineluctably display something, but that thing is a matter of interpretation.

Sherman's work foregrounds the picture itself as a template on which viewers can seek themselves, deny recognition, or recognize others. She doesn't create windows to see through or beyond; her impenetrable surfaces resist that type of entry. Instead, Sherman figures into her compositions the reality and position of a viewer: the viewer becomes an intrinsic element in the photographs. The pictures intimate a person standing there, looking at them. It will be said that all pictures need a viewer to complete them. But not all pictures incorporate the viewer the way Sherman's do. She constructs a photographic entanglement by the method with which she manufactures the images.

Playing all the roles—camera, subject, object—she is also initially a viewer, the picture's very first viewer. She performs inside and outside of the frame, as seen and seer, even seeker. Her several positions conceive a "subjective" and "objective" framing. When Sherman stands outside of the frame, she can experience it as a viewer might, and can physically register as a viewer, to imbricate, imaginatively, a viewer inside the frame. She creates a dynamic object relationship among the elements. If Sherman were a novelist, I'd propose: she has incorporated the reader into every text, by allowing for a subjective space for the reader/viewer.

It's often written that, because Sherman plays parts before the camera, her photographs are about her identity. They are not. If they were, the work would not be as generative as it has proven to be. It would sit in frames, not doing very much, and would not be so influential, or "great." By great, I mean expansive, effective, with depth, intimacy, and immediacy.

Her photographs are not about her. They are about us. Human beings want to look at themselves, and the ubiquity of the camera and its photographic products demonstrates that obsession. People construct ways to look at themselves and others. It is an incessant desire, impossible to satisfy, which creates more pictures. Humans stare at each other longingly, or with disgust, anxiety, curiosity. People watch people, as if everyone might live in a zoo or be a zookeeper. People police themselves: species survival might require knowledge of every kind of condition that could be endured or character and behavior that might be encountered. Sherman's art registers the relentlessness of people to see who they are, or who they might be or become. And what will happen to them.

V

> *Seen thus in her sacramental black silk, a wisp of lace turned over the collar and fastened by a mosaic brooch, and her face smoothed into harmony with her apparel, Ann Eliza looked ten years younger than behind the counter, in the heat and burden of the day. It would have been as difficult to guess her approximate age as that of the black silk, for she had the same worn and glossy aspect as her dress; but a faint tinge of pink still lingered on her cheek-bones, like the reflection of sunset which sometimes colours the west long after the day is over.*
>
> — Edith Wharton, *The Bunner Sisters*

Edith Wharton created fictional figures with words. Cindy Sherman creates visual fictions. In hers, figure and ground might collapse or contradict the other, and disturb the eye with disjunctive objects. In her photograph *Untitled #512*, 2010–2011, there's an unlikely pairing, of character and terrain. A tall, dark-haired woman stands on a rocky plain: she is isolated; the place appears barren. No plants or trees, just boulders, earth, and a person. The woman, in her thirties or forties, wears a long, elegant cloak that, like her hairstyle, indicates she might be a flapper. Somewhere, it could be the Roaring Twenties.

Her cloak is a pale, pinky beige, satin or silk, trimmed with white feathers. Her feathery collar nearly covers her chin. One shoulder is drawn up, suggesting reticence or secrets. She wears white leather, strapped shoes, her legs positioned as if she were modeling her outfit. Her facial expression is impassive, but sharp and deliberate as she stares at the camera, the viewer. Like her cloak, the ground is a subtle tan, with brown. There's a crevice not far from her, with fluffy white material in it. Like clouds or cotton, the white stuff is as decorative as the feathers on the woman's coat. The tonality of the picture encourages a rapid and fluid movement of the eye, from figure to ground, which join formally. But the woman clashes, an out-of-place figure looking out. A misfit in a misbegotten place. Even a hallucinatory figure in a dreamscape. A flapper who creates a flap.

The longer I look at the image, or project and identify, the more I think of the persistence of gender and gendered relations. To what extent does gender shape what I see and order the visual imagination, and more, the world? The space itself is gendered: it's the Wild West, an uninhabited frontier to be conquered, etc. She isn't the Marlboro Woman, though she certainly might be commenting on the Marlboro Man.

VI

So far then the progress of my conceptions was the natural progress entirely in accordance with my epoch as I am sure is to be quite easily realised if you think over the scene that was before us all

> *from year to year.... There is the long history of how every one has ever acted or has felt and that nothing inside in them in all of them makes it connectedly different.*
>
> — Gertrude Stein, "Composition as Explanation"

From what Sherman has seen, learned, and experienced, she has made "a new composition." She has drawn on Stein's "the thing seen" imaginatively, and, with her own particular consciousness and extraordinary visual sense, she has forged a singularly distinctive, unforgettable, and distinguished art. I only wish I could see how people will react to it a long time from now.

STILL MOVING

...I am
bound more to my sentences
the more you batter at me
to follow you.
— William Carlos Williams, "January"

A new train set changed the living room into her playground. Just a little engine and two cars, red and green, going around the metal track, but the little girl imagined more, because the trains followed the curves, stayed on the track, and kept circling and going, going. Her father sat beside her on the floor, like her, beaming.

A very long line of freight trains took a long time to pass. She knew it would come to an end, and was patient at the railroad crossing. The cars of many colors—yellow, red, green—lumbered by, boxes on wheels, while the train's lonesome whistle kept calling, Here I come, here I am, here I go.

Freight trains, at all times of day and night, wailed through hundreds of small towns, just a gas station, a luncheonette, maybe a beauty parlor, towns undone by human failure and natural disaster, flood, drought, towns with no product but the wind blowing.

Her toy train rounded an old track.

Estranged mountains bulged under the sky, the big sky, the endless sky. Anyway, no one could see an end to it, which reassured her, since so much seemed to be coming to an end. It felt that way.

But it seemed impossible—the universe dropping off, ending, there would be an end, and then there would be nothing, a no more, a vacuum of no more. Her imagination couldn't let her go there.

A jumble of metal and tires, grease stains, goop, the shop looked a big mess. The guts of cars, tools, scattered all over the floor, but he knew where everything was. He'd say to his wife, "I know where it all is, just don't touch anything." His place was like the back of his hand, and he was just as attached to it.

Folks brought in their cars and trucks for fixing. Dented, broken down, crashed. The fixer-uppers. The "keep 'em going until I get some money" cars. Junkers. The shit that happened to their rides, to them, these people, their cars, some he knew all his life, accidents waiting to happen.

Some guys were satisfied, he saw them in cities, at peace with themselves. Businessmen and their pricey briefcases, proud papas, with IRAs, their babies pressed to their narrow chests. Cocks of the park. Their young women expected everything. His friend told him, years ago, "Oh, she's not for you, buddy. She's too good for you." He didn't believe it, then.

Big Joe gave her a ride when she found herself stranded in town. He just appeared, and she figured he had time on his hands. His hands, arms, were covered in tats that disappeared into his skin, darker than hers. She'd arrived from the city, and, after a time, not surprisingly, discovered they were the only black people around. It happened often enough that the anomaly was really normal.

He'd lived around here all his life, Big Joe told her, except for the time he went to 'Nam. He lived near town, not in it, camping out. "I like it. I don't pay rent. I don't have responsibilities. Except to people I like." Big Joe smiled at her. She said she was glad.

He'd been around, and played pretty good guitar, good enough to work the bar circuit. Maybe he was really lonely, but wouldn't admit it. She was, and she wasn't. She was used to being alone. She couldn't do her work any other way.

He was way too old for her, and they had hardly anything in common. But what's common, she thought. He isn't. She had never met anyone like him. Still, after a while, she knew they'd run out of talk.

Big Joe took her for long drives in landscapes completely new to her, and their growing silences worried her.

"No, she's a girl," her mother would say. Or, "I'm a girl," she'd say. Her straggly hair, or that she was lean and tall for her age—just turned eight. "She looks like a boy," they'd say. Well, she wasn't. They seemed disappointed, some of them. She'd be a pretty boy, or maybe she was less pretty for a girl. For a girl. It didn't make any difference to her.

She and her mother camped in fields where trees without names sheltered them from the sun, and a sky of dazzling stars lit up their nights. She did her homework, and then ran around until she fell down, breathing like a racehorse.

They met strangers everywhere, some on their own, or they got to know other families. Some people were friendly, but most kept to themselves.

"A boy or a girl," they'd ask.

In the distance, a freight train roared at the foot of white mountains. A young boy, no more than ten, turned to watch it. Where was this one headed, what was it carrying. One time a train had stopped, and he'd run closer to it. He waved at the conductor, who wore a stiff gray hat, and had a scarf around his neck. The boy wondered what that job would be like, riding all across the country, he knew one day he'd need a job. The conductor waved back, so that was nice. The boy watched the train until he couldn't see it anymore.

His mother would call his name soon, for lunch, or maybe she'd want him to go into town with her, or maybe they'd decide to pull up stakes, which is how one man in the camp put it. Pulling up stakes. Which people actually did.

His friends at home were jealous, because he did exciting things. He met people who had horses, two or three of them, and they let him ride them. That was a big deal.

He watched his mother write in a book. She kept notes about everything. He knew she had thoughts she didn't tell him. Troubles, too. She explained that she tried to observe what was around her. She told him it was important to remember, and he said he'd remember everything.

But he might forget that woman and her dog, Blackie, in the last place they stayed. Or, the train today in the distance, the shape of the white mountains, how the sun hit them, or that conductor, and how he waved at him.

His mother called his name, and he ran to her.

Bobby's nails and hands were covered in grease, gas and oil embedded in the lines of his palms. He was easy reading for a palmist, his future simple: just a lot more dirt.

Bobby hurled a knife at his kitchen wall, and the pink ceramic vase his mother loved, with tiny yellow flowers, crashed onto the floor, smashed into smithereens.

When she was alive, his mother went for manicures every week, had her hair curled in a place not far from town, and, when he was little, she took him with her. Bobby liked watching his mother get her nails filed, cleaned, fingers dipped into little bowls of warm water, and then painted a color. Red, sometimes pink, one time orange.

She sat under a bonnet to dry her hair, which was wound around little rollers, while Bobby colored animals in his book—red and pink. Sometimes his mother worried that her hair came out too yellow or orange, brassy. The women told her no, they all liked it, and told stories about their lives, and one of them always knew something that the others didn't. He couldn't remember her name, but his mother told him she had a beehive on her head. He didn't understand that.

The beauty parlor was warm in winter, hot in summer, a whirr in the air, the space bonnets blowing heat, and the women's voices rose high, unless they were whispering. Sometimes they'd laugh and scream. His mother laughed, too, and he'd laugh along, but he didn't know what was funny.

When his mother was ready to leave, all of the women would give him a kiss goodbye. He'd protest a little. In the car, he'd tell his mother her hair looked beautiful. "Do you really like it?" she'd ask Bobby. "Oh yes, Mama, I do."

"Any of that shit," his father yelled at his mother, "any of that shit comes off on him, it's on you."

STORIES TELL STORIES

Early in the 20th century, simultaneous with new approaches in linguistics, Soviet filmmaker Lev Kuleshov explored how meanings in film occur, through sequencing and editing. The Kuleshov Effect shows that viewers gain more meaning from the juxtaposition of two shots in sequence than from one isolated shot.

It's entirely familiar that words mean as they do only in relationship to other words, and also that, by setting an adjective beside a noun, adverb beside a verb, words qualify each other. Sequencing in film changes meaning radically. The brain causes it, but in each viewer the effect joins with overdetermined processes, which include individual psychology, environment, history, culture. This concatenation of elements, and others, results in, let's say, a person's version of reality, and a viewpoint, from which people construe or "make up" different stories to tell themselves and others. People don't see the same movie—or experience the same reality, for that matter.

Berlin Road Movie (1971) relies on the Kuleshov Effect, using unsettling jump cuts and shots augmented by duration, repetition, and looping. The film is in black-and-white, and color, about nine and one-half minutes long. Shot from a vehicle, likely a car, out the front window, it positions the viewer as another passenger riding in a car along a country road, trees and fields on both sides. A pickup truck is in the distance. Gradually, the car/camera gains on the truck, until the viewer can see a figure in the driver's seat.

After 39 seconds, there's a jump cut. Now the film is in saturated color, of the face of an elderly woman, a bright pink scarf on her head tied under her chin, and she's in a burnt-yellow sweater. The woman wears large-framed glasses, her skin is weathered, wrinkled, her mouth set downward, and from the way her lips curl in, and cheeks sink, she appears to have few front teeth. The woman is looking away from the camera, toward something out of frame. The shot—a moving portrait—lasts several seconds.

The film returns to the road.

The camera/car has passed the pickup truck; then another car speeds past it. The car is heading toward a vanishing point at the end of the road. It takes about 40 seconds to arrive there—as if the car were going through a tunnel, there's light at the end of it—when the film cuts back to the woman's face. She is looking down, and smiling. Then, the road again. Three minutes and 12 seconds later, more or less, a cut to her face. She isn't looking at the camera, but her head is lifted up, and the camera stays longer on her face. She glances, very briefly, at the camera, then quickly looks away. The film cuts back to the road, as the car/camera goes through a village, where there is some slight traffic, two cars, a bike. Three minutes and 44 seconds into the film, the woman appears again, in profile, drinking a glass of wine, it's a tight shot, her sharp chin at the bottom of the frame.

The road again, the village again, two cars with headlights on, it may be raining, a bike, a motorcycle. At four minutes and 25 seconds, there's a cut, again, to the woman's face: she rubs her nose. Her eyes stare into faraway space.

Then, surprisingly, the film loops back, repeating the long opening shot. But now the first cut to the elderly woman shows her looking directly at the camera, and then looking away, smiling and drinking wine. This episode is followed by the car/camera riding toward the horizon, through the same tunnel of trees, into the light. Repetitions continue, the order changes, some shots last longer. Those shots of the woman the viewer has already seen combine with other already-seen shots, but differently.

Watching the film the first time, without stopping it, the way it was intended to be viewed, I found myself riding in the car, moving forward, toward some place. I recalled that I had once been driven along that same road, through East Germany to West Germany. There was only one road, the scene was pastoral, and the journey seemed like a visit to the Old World: I had those thoughts as I watched Jonas's film.

When the elderly woman entered the picture, literally, my thoughts changed: She represented East Germany, a person Jonas most likely met on the film-journey at one of the rest stops provided by the East German government. She lived nearby. She manifested, even in her face, even inscrutably, East Germany's history. She knew the War. I read into her. The set of her mouth, at first, grim, bespoke almost instantly an attitude I held about life in the East before the Wall came down. Grim.

The film moved on.

When the elderly woman appeared again, smiling or drinking wine, I interpreted the story differently, mildly rebuking myself for my first associations. Her smile, the red wine, and the pink scarf composed a very different image. Now smiling, her image countermanded my prejudice, preconceived idea, or stereotype. Now, on the screen: a woman, the image of a woman, who was enjoying herself, drinking a glass of wine, at lunch or at the end of the day—after work? Like anyone in East or West Germany, I thought, she had her good days and bad ones. Ultimately, I didn't know what I was seeing or what story to tell myself. I couldn't make up a story. The film stymied that. For one thing, there existed no third term, no other object—person or thing—to help build that story.

From images or words, meanings run rampant; human beings are like interpreting machines. Whether one wants to be against interpretation or for it, meanings occur, haphazard, benign or malignant, often unconsciously: only consciousness of one's responses affords any freedom from them. Joan Jonas's work, her version of storytelling, has its own methods that abjure easy summary.

The structure of *Berlin Road Movie*, relative to Jonas's more mature work, is simple: A portrait and a road contrasted, big movements and small ones, short and long. Later videos and films—and performance and gallery installations—play with more complex structures and elements. Building a coherent story from any of them is an effort of will: interpretations don't come easily. At least not to me.

Jonas sometimes borrows from myth, fairy- or folk tales: in performances or in videos, the actors or Jonas herself might be costumed in ways reminiscent of figures from them. But Vladimir Propp's *Morphology of the Folktale* (1928) delineates how far from them Jonas's work actually is. Like Kuleshov,

Propp played a key role in the early twentieth century, and his semiotic work underlies the field of narratology. Propp considered fairy tales as "tales of magic" and "wondertales." About folk tales, he theorized that all "are constructed on the basis of one single string of actions or events called 'functions.'" His structural model insisted that "function, and not theme, motif, character, plot, or motivation is the fundamental unit of analysis," and that "functions are independent of how and by whom they are fulfilled; from the standpoint of structural analysis....the deed itself matters"...."the number of functions available to fairytale-tellers is thirty-one."

Propp's rigorous, important analysis is a heuristic device for understanding how narrative sometimes functions. It doesn't apply to Jonas's oeuvre, because of her refusal of logical or causal structures. She concocts visual events, gestures, and movements, and sets them in collision. Jonas attends to ineffability, to fast-moving impressions, to the unremarkable remarkable, to looking and not knowing one is looking—upon realization, always a curious sensation. As in an action painting—she began as a painter—Jonas applies colors, strokes various objects into a scene, or masks them, against a background that changes. She lets things happen in the foreground that don't determine other happenings, say, in a video or on a stage.

The completed piece may defy reason or explanation, and the result can't be told or narrated easily. This is the inenarrable, which is her narrative territory: what can't be narrated. Her stories don't necessarily add up, the way a life doesn't, though meanings will be inferred by viewers, and they may reside in the text, not simply or definitively, most likely as a panoply of possibility.

Flannery O'Connor wrote, "Mystery is the great embarrassment to the modern mind." Joan Jonas risks everything in her work: She looks at human mystery, the murky stuff of life, not for the love of obscurity or ambiguity. Her art also doesn't demystify. In that unpredictable wilderness, gnarly feelings can separate from motives or goals, people come and go, strange things happen without beginnings, and events don't have discernible endings. There are no absolutes or inevitable conclusions. More important, there may be no need of them. Jonas's great project says, in so many ways and approaches: There is no embarrassment in not knowing.

HEAD AND HEART

I'm almost certain Kiki Smith introduced me to David Wojnarowicz. I knew about him, his Rimbaud pictures were pasted on walls and stenciled on sidewalks in the East Village. In my mind's eye, we're on a sidewalk, maybe on Houston Street; it's windy, late fall or early winter, and Wojnarowicz is standing behind Kiki.

Consciousness superimposes scenes from the present onto the past, or mixes one distant moment with another; memory has forever been Photo-shopped. The technology replicates a natural, involuntary default position in the brain, or a human inclination to fuse events. Photo-shopping can deliberately distort or corrupt historical events; human memory is distorted, first, by subjectivity or point of view, then by the passage of time. Was it a dream, a photograph, did I hear the story, did it actually happen?

The clock marks seconds, minutes, hours; the calendar, days, months, and years—these human productions divide now from then, and from the future. The unconscious doesn't obey time, which also confuses memory, and can make days feel endless or too short. Maybe that's why people invented what Shakespeare, in *Richard II*, called time's "numb'ring clock."

I picture Wojnarowicz with his head down; he was tall, I'm short, which would influence how I saw him, and he me. He might have been looking sideways, and appeared shy or elusive. He had a long face, uneven features, and a smoker's raspy voice. Other adjectives pop up: gangly, rawboned, intense, weirdly funny, restless, sad, sensitive, vulnerable. But this isn't a portrait of the artist as a young man. Wojnarowicz's portrait was, in a profound sense, shot by his time.

Wojnarowicz knew he was homosexual before the word *gay* took its place; he came of age with Stonewall and the movement it incited—gay liberation. Then, an individual's "coming out" was a revolution of great and intimate proportions, a public and private declaration of startling consequence. Wojnarowicz's art and writing were born and nurtured before, but fomented in and exploded during, the AIDS crisis.

Artists and writers are often very different from their work. They work with and against their education, fear, anxiety, hope, angst, values, to build characters, find words or concepts, build structures or images that defeat or deny these things their power, or sometimes to venerate them. The gap between person and artist can be inexplicable, but people, including artists, often conflate the two. Art historians and critics might merge them, judging the work by the person or the person by the work. But history judges what history also produces.

What is now called "history" was Wojnarowicz's lifetime, his present, which insidiously produced what mattered to him. His best talents were made furious use of during the 1980s until his death in 1992. His impassioned writing became a powerful voice of the AIDS epidemic, his blunt-force-trauma art a singular and passionate face. Wojnarowicz's work, I believe, even without the exigent circumstances, or influence, of AIDS, would have been knife-sharp and arresting. Without the consequences of AIDS, though, there would have been time for him to mature as a person and an artist, to have a future.

Consequence and influence share territory. They can't be predicted or entirely comprehended, since the two radiate from a myriad of sources and will settle without foreknowledge and, usually, without acknowledgment. Mostly, people don't get to choose an influence, unless they're conscious adults, and by then the wish to be influenced—to absorb—means that a person has been, in a sense, prepared. The preparation for influence develops independently of consciousness, while simultaneously creating it.

In the 1980s, being infected by HIV and developing AIDS was an unchosen, horrific fate, fatal. People were very frightened, and felt hopeless. Not every artist or writer responded as Wojnarowicz did. His responses were unique, thoroughly felt, and driven by an urgent necessity. In his time, his work was extraordinarily moving—it stunned. It will never be experienced again as it was then, in that very dark moment.

Contemporary artists sympathetic to Wojnarowicz's work, who say his work influenced them, find meanings in it that have been profoundly useful to them. They are a diverse group, their work dissimilar in appearance from his, and from each other's. Some of the artists might say: "His work gave me courage." Or "Wojnarowicz was a courageous artist." Courage in an artist or writer is different from the courage of firefighters, who rescue people and risk their own lives. Artistic courage might be conceptualized as an internal drama about overcoming rules or inhibitions, dicta of all kinds, the art a manifestation or result of a multitude of processes.

Art won't save people from burning buildings, but not all risks are the same or equal, and shouldn't be measured by one ruler. During his time, Wojnarowicz's work might have sprung from rage, fear, and compassion or been inspired by them, his approach or sense of form enabled by and called to address them. An abiding necessity to save himself and others arose.

A cruel disease had suddenly and quickly made helpless victims of an already stigmatized group. The tragic waste of the disease, and also the injustice of stigma, probably urged Wojnarowicz toward a kind of overcoming. To have his life be meaningful, he would keep living by doing his work. He would rage on.

Artists are not mythical beings or romantic heroes. In their chosen fields and in a certain time, they make aesthetic, intellectual, conceptual decisions; they may react variously to social and political questions and to concerns central to their mediums and practices. As artists, they evolve from and are influenced by not just other artists, but also their own psychology, religion, race, economic background, and more. Influence is everywhere, and they take chances, too. Everyone who lives sometimes does, everyone sometimes has to. That curious notion of character also comes into play: existentially, artists and writers become who they are, and make what they do, in the moment they act.

Sometimes an artist's work opens up a space. I'll call it a "mental space," a space for themselves and others, where random thoughts, images, ideas germinate and occur—these might have consequence. When that happens, when an artist's choices do that, an artist might be called courageous. Something that was broken got metaphorically fixed; something that was blocked breaks through. A solution arrives to a problem no one ever mentioned. Some will notice that in the work, and it helps them.

Shannon Ebner, Wade Guyton, Henrik Olesen, Adam Putnam, Emily Roysdon, Zoe Strauss, and Wolfgang Tillmans, among many other artists who mention Wojnarowicz's influence on them, probably recognized, reacted to, or internalized something they gleaned in his work; usually they mediate it so thoroughly, a viewer wouldn't spy it. Or, because it was an idea for them, an idea, say, without materiality, it never materializes in their work.

Harold Bloom theorized that influence produced anxiety and troubled poets who turned to writing poetry after reading other poets. Bloom studied the Romantics, but wrote *The Anxiety of Influence* (1973) under the sign of Modernism. Ezra Pound's call was "make it new" (though Dante shaped his poetics). Influence from that purview was a staining or tainting, an inhibiting or retarding, of an artist's originality.

To rejig the concept of influence as an actor-agent in the work of artists and writers, to make influence newer, the computer must be restarted with another program. Influence occurs, in this register, because an artist perceives in another's work a space, or opening. Maybe it's whimsical, wishful, a fragment of a fragment. Rarely a direct taking, more like the flow of information. Rarely "stealing," as Picasso said great artists do rather than borrowing. Instead, something is shown; intimated; associated, or noticed; and, it feels true or right or necessary. A diffusion is transmitted and received. Influence re-conceived would be a heuristic device, an emboldening or an encouragement.

One artist can and often does encourage another. One artist's courage in making, or what another perceives as such, becomes another's space to take up. *Courage* and *encourage* have a similar root: in Latin, cor means heart. To have a heart is to give heart. To give heart is to embrace and charge others with a kind of love.

Afterword by Andrew Durbin

WHAT IS COLLECTED: MADAME REALISM

For the first time, all of Lynne Tillman's Madame Realism stories have been collected in a single volume, complete with the Paige Turner novellas. There are six other pieces, including Tillman's critical appraisal of the artist David Wojnarowicz. For many readers, these stories, whether you first encountered them in serial form in *Art in America* in the late 1980s or in an earlier version of this book, *The Madame Realism Complex*, changed—and continue to change—what fiction looks like, what it can do. Criticism as fiction, fiction as criticism: Tillman inverts the two or rather erases their differences, cobbles together a new genre, or a *complex* of genres, a new way of looking at art and at the world, her world, your world.

"It's often said that position is everything in life," Tillman writes. Like many, I've always taken hers for mine. It is an elastic, translational position that has remained current for the twenty-five or so years that these stories have been appearing in print, a quick-footed approach to thinking that nimbly steps between histories, cultures, artists, friends, lovers, situations, whatever they may be. Usually they are now, even when they might have been written twenty years ago.

Her now is our now. With this new book, Madame Realism, Paige Turner, the Translation Artist have arrived at their moment. "May I begin?" Paige Turner asks us in "To Find Words," squarely in the middle of Lynne Tillman's *The Complete Madame Realism and Other Stories*. Yes, please.

For this new book, Tillman expanded *Madame Realism* because she knows, as her character knows, that the world changes—and as the world goes, we go. Big and clunky as it is, "the world" is often Lynne Tillman's revolving subject. In these stories, her characters, like Madame Realism, follow the plot to where it leads (it invents them, really), to paintings and museums and people, funny people, uncommon people, and the bygone eras that have given way and given shape to ours, to our oceanic feelings, our "contemporary events." Of course Madame Realism distrusts the notion of contemporaneity: history and the present are far too complexly arranged to suggest that one simply follows the other. Rather, she is interested in our words and the words behind our words, our images and the images behind our images. Crucially, she sees these words and images in a constant flux as history cherry-picks them (Tillman is obsessed with the controlling narratives of bias, especially class bias), those it keeps and discards in its fickle moods.

Us and them, as Madame Realism sees it, you and the past that lets you call yourself you: balanced on a timeline tightrope she steps nimbly across, Madame Realism walks histories and refuses certain temporal distinctions, collapsing *them* into *us*, their body into our body. This is the phenomenology of the present, the things that happen and that make us happen, too. At a dinner party she observes, "We are like current events to each other." Madame Realism trades in on this currency.

I've always seen Madame Realism as a kind of lens, or a system of lenses, a portable Phoropter Tillman generously made available to those of us who like to think on our feet. I often meet her and try on her glasses when I go for a walk. Since meeting her, I've had what I call "Madame Realism moments": events, parties, or visits to exhibitions that raise me up into a dense, multi-layered fiction of realities, threaded with rich social, political, and art histories, that heightens experience, composes it into a mesh of recognizable differences that form a plot, a plot to follow. They are moments in thinking where I use my "I," mostly because Tillman licenses its use in her own critical appraisal of museums and history, individuals and cities. In her steady, hard prose, Tillman fashions her character into a set of glasses that we put on in order to see things as she sees them: objects and individuals drifting in history's lazy river, bumping up against one another, occasionally locking arms to float together, break apart, lean in for a kiss. In a word, no straight lines—just the jumble.

This book jumbles. You learn to jumble with it.

An example: Once in a summer in Kassel, Germany, on a hill overlooking the vast, wind turbine-dotted countryside of the state of Hesse, in the Museum für Sepulkralkultur. I was on an assignment not so different from some of Madame Realism's and had arrived the previous day from Frankfurt to visit the Fridericianum, the world's first public museum, where I was invited to write an essay on posthumanism, something I knew nothing meaningful about. Built in 1779 by a French Huguenot, it is a stately and imposing building that occupies a large open courtyard. It is best known for hosting the art quinquennial dOCUMENTA since 1955, when the museum reopened after post-war repairs to the building were completed. (The Allies had flattened it in 1943.) Feeling quite post- after a day in the Fridericianum, or, as Madame Realism once put it, needing "a break, an epistemological break," I broke with my museum-planned schedule for an afternoon walk through the city's outskirts near my hotel. Small, but pretty, Kassel is mostly parks and recreation, trees and vistas that look out to the hilly countryside. An astonishing ninety-percent of the city was destroyed in the war. There is no old city. What was the old city had served as administrative center for the Nazi army and as a sub-camp to Dachau and it has since kept itself small, humbled into a breezy quaintness.

Aimless, I went down a narrow street, past a hospital and a few construction sites promising something new, until I came by surprise upon a manor joined to a large concrete cube through a glass entryway: the sepulchral culture museum (the museum's brochure is insistent that it isn't about death, but the history of our response to death). What was this? No one had told me about it. Inside, a stairwell led past a small office with some information and postcards of the world's famous crypts and sepulchers. The cheerful attendant at the front desk, a local university student, told me that the museum was free and "totally unique." It is "one of seven museums like it in the world," he said, sliding over a brochure. Like what? Around the corner from the office and down a small, slate-gray staircase, Walt Disney's *Skeleton Dance* (1929) played on a monitor in a little cubicle to itself—the opening salvo in the permanent exhibit on what we do when the people we know die.

Mostly, the museum draws from pre-twentieth century German death culture despite the Disney film, from pendants and prayer books to coffins and gravestones—a skeleton dance of artifacts, the kind of thing Madame Realism would have liked, I thought, these human symbols of the great, permanent dreamland. Hand-carved effigies to lost priests and dead girls, boys who'd been bayonetted in foreign wars; missing, of course, was Germany's most famous contribution to the culture of death: any reference to the Holocaust, the event that prompted the destruction of the museum's city. I thought about what Lynne Tillman would do in a museum of coffins with this absence, which grew wider and wider as I crept further in. She would turn to Freud, as she did in the story "Madame Realism In Freud's Dreamland," where she observes an exhibition of Freud's collection at SUNY Binghampton:

> Substitutes for the dead, she thought. In his essay "Fetishism," Freud defined the fetish as "a substitute for the woman's (mother's) phallus which the little boy believed in and doesn't want to forgo." He theorized that "horror of castration sets up a sort of permanent memorial to itself by creating this substitute... It remains a token of triumph over the threat of castration and a safeguard against it."
>
> Is this collection, or any collection, necessarily fetishistic? Collections of tokens and memorials... Collecting always points to what is missing and has not been collected, or can't be found. Collection, Madame Realism considered, must always represent the absence of something and the impossibility of entirely fulfilling one's desires. It would be impossible to make a collection that would hold all of everything within a particular taxonomy. One could collect something that was limited in number, but would that ever be truly satisfying to a collector, who most likely desires to continue looking for substitutes or tokens?

I considered what I could not find in the Museum für Sepulkralkultur. Not much of the twentieth century, or at least its definitive moment, the Holocaust or the Allied destruction of the Germany cities, including Kassel. This repression felt like an astonishing act of self-censorship, "a means of obscuring a world," as W.G. Sebald once wrote in an essay on German memory of its own destruction, "that could no longer be presented in comprehensible terms." The museum became incomprehensible to me, confused in its memorial program. Lynne Tillman, following Walter Benjamin, calls this incomprehensibility the "chaos of memories," which prompts the mind to order what cannot be ordered. Freud began his own collection after the traumatic death of his father. The Museum's collection more or less ceases before the Second World War (upstairs there is an exhibition of contemporary, but foreign, burial practices), reversing the impetus from reaction to repression of the death such that I felt, surrounded by so many coffins, that all of this was created less to memorialize German sepulchral culture than it was to erase the century and its horrors that led to Kassel's annihilation in the first place. Or is that unfair? The dead rose up.

Why remember the culture of death if not all of its disparate, horrifying parts? "So many stories and interpretations were congealed in a single object" in Freud's collection, Tillman observes. I could not help feel that it is the objects outside the collection that sets the narrative terms of what *is* collected. As Tillman does, I considered what was missing—much of the story, the blanks she often tries to fill in. It is a riddle, like the riddle of the Sphinx she considers when she observes a little replica of the mythical creature in Freud's collection.

> Madame Realism studied the Sphinx closely. Its composite body was like pieces of a puzzle that fit together but in an odd way—joined and disjointed, cohering but lacking coherence. It seemed appropriate that the Sphinx was sometimes female, sometimes male, and part animal or bird. Or both. Madame Realism realized its strange parts, though meshed, subtly forced a recognition of difference. In this peculiar creature or monster, there could only be an illusion of unity, since the Sphinx itself suggested the differences that are usually obscured. The sum of its parts is not a whole, Madame Realism thought. Even the question the Sphinx put to Oedipus was in parts, and so, Madame Realism speculated, the content of its question was like the Sphinx's body. And probably the answer—"Man"—must also be conceived of not as a unity but as representing parts: "Man"—fragmented, composed of differences, a collection. Is "Man" an answer or a question?

It seems that man is neither. Rather, "man"—as answer, as question, as Oedipus—is a plot, one that begins, as in the case of Sophocles, as soon as the word is spoken. The protagonist can move forward, as does the plot of *Oedipus the King*. Madame Realism knows this, that man is an arrangement of narratives, counter-narratives, lies, cover-ups, absences, tricks, questions, and answers. Her project is this excavation of this plot, its facts and its conspiracies. It's your project, too. Turn the page. I left the museum.

I've gone astray. But isn't that where Madame Realism is, astray, off the path, not quite lost since being lost would suggest she hadn't meant to go there, wherever there is, new territory, some other country, the borders—and politics—of which she is still trying to understand. Or get to know. Blanks she seeks to fill. Searching for "necessary irrelevancies," as Tillman writes. In "Madame Realism's Torch Song," she sits with a man named Wiley at a fire. They talk about MTV, what Marilyn Manson said about Lionel Ritchie. They talk about drama, delusions. Fire. A torch song is a song of love, usually unrequited love. Who does Madame Realism love? "Beauty's a ghost that haunts us," Wiley observes. They stare into the fire together. "What ghost are you?" Wiley asks Madame Realism. "Everyone dead I ever loved," she responds. I love Madame Realism, to put it very simply, and I often light my torch for her. It sees me through the dark.

Sources

"Madame Realism," in *Madame Realism*, artists' book with drawings by Kiki Smith (New York: LINE grant, 1984). "Madame Realism Asks: What's Natural About Painting," in *Art in America* 74, no. 3 (March 1986). "Dynasty Reruns," in *Art in America* 74, no. 6 (June 1986). "Madame Realism's Imitation of Life," in *Fake: A Meditation on Authenticity*, exhibition catalog (New York: New Museum, 1987). "On the Road with Madame Realism," in *Art in America* 76, no. 5 (May 1988). "Madame Realism: A Fairy Tale," in *Silvia Kolbowski: XI Projects* (New York: Border Editions, 1988). "Madame Realism in Freud's Dreamland," in *Art in America* 79, no. 1 (January 1991). "The Museum of Hyphenated Americans," in *Art in America* 79, no. 9 (September 1991). "Madame Realism's '1999,'" in *Leonardo* (March 1992). "Lust for Loss," in *Back to the Front: Tourisms of War*, ed. Diller + Scofidio (Lower Normandy: F.R.A.C. Basse-Normandie, 1994). "Madame Realism Looks for Relief," in *Haim Steinbach*, exhibition catalog (Milan: Edizioni Charta, 1995). "Madame Realism Faces It," in *Art in America* 87, no. 2 (February 1999). "Madame Realism Lies Here," in *Here Lies*, ed. Karl Roeseler and David Gilbert (San Francisco: Trip Street Press, 2001). "Madame Realism's Torch Song," in *Marco Breuer SMTWTFS* (New York: Roth Horowitz, LLC, 2002). "Madame Realism's Conscience," in *Mr. President*, exhibition catalog (Albany: University Art Museum, 2007). "Love Sentence," in *Conjunctions*, no. 22 (Spring 1994). "To Find Words," in *Serious Hysterics*, ed. Alison Fell (London: Serpent's Tail, 1992). "Thrilled to Death," in *Jessica Stockholder: Your Skin in this Weather Bourne Eye-Threads & Swollen Perfume*, exhibition catalog (New York: DIA, 1996). "Drawing from a Translation Artist," in "Drawn from Photography," *Drawing Papers*, no. 96, exhibition catalog (New York: Drawing Center, 2011). "Seven Times, Times Seven," in *Barbara Probst*, exhibition catalog (Berlin: Hatje Cantz, 2013). "Cindy Sherman," in *Cindy Sherman: Imitation of Life*, exhibition catalog (London: Prestel, 2016). "Still Moving," in *Highway Kind: Photographs by Justine Kurland* (New York: Aperture, 2016). "Stories Tell Stories," in *Joan Jonas Is On Our Mind* (San Francisco: Wattis Institute, 2016). "Head and Heart," in *Brush Fires in the Social Landscape* (New York: Aperature, 2015).